DARKED
MIRROR

DARKED
MIRROR

The life you choose to live results in the life you live. Caught up and can't see your own reflection nothing but a Dark Mirror.

AUTUMN AURORA

Rev. date: 08/18/2017

To order additional copies of this book, contact:
Xlibris
1-888-795-4274
www.Xlibris.com
Orders@Xlibris.com
758985

ABOUT THE AUTHOR

Autumn Aurora is a mother of two. She is a new author from Inner Harbor East, Baltimore. She is a talented writer as she grips the attention of her readers. She's a very outgoing and driven person and is currently one of the traveling hands massage services in her city. She meditates to calm her mind as she would be working on too many things to bear. She's seen a lot at a young age and would like you to know all about it. She is currently trying to turn the book into a movie while writing part two. Hold on to your seats as Ms. Aurora take you on an exciting journey.

CONTENTS

CHAPTER 1

It Was Just Head

Anaya

I WOKE UP to the sound of the annoying alarm clock and the house phone ringing continuously. That only meant one thing—today was Monday, and I overslept again for school. My grandmother went to work, but she knew the alarm clock alone just not gone cut it.

I didn't know why I had issues getting up in the morning. School was not the problem; I could probably tell the teachers how to be better at their jobs. I also have something new to wear every day along with a candle apple red 4Runner to drive for several days of the week—why wouldn't I be excited for school? I guess I was just not a morning girl. As my grandmother always say, "It could be a fire, and I would burn in it." She was right—I wouldn't wake up to the smell of smoke and definitely not the sound of the smoke detector.

I sat here, daydreaming and staring at the wall like I'm not already late enough. I jumped in the tub, adding skin so soft always did my body good. No lotion was needed. I slid on my matching white thong set, redid my ponytail, and sprayed a mist of my Versace Blonde. I hurried and slipped into my blue flowy skirt and my white halter.

I didn't have much time, but I couldn't help but stop and admire myself—slim, five-foot-one, caramel complexion, and with a rear end they like to call a camel hump. My thick long black hair pulled up with just a few strands scattered lightly, touching my back; and my long black lashes and thick eyebrows that I had to keep trimmed so I wouldn't form a unibrow. I have curves in all the right places, and on top of that, I'm an A/B student. *I am the perfect package*, I thought to myself as I grabbed a v8 from the fridge and ran out the door. As I unlocked the door to the truck. I see my "main apple scrapple," Tonya, walking toward me. We both jumped in the truck, let all the windows down, and hit the play button on the CD player. I instantly got chill bumps as Patti LaBelle's beautiful voice came through the speakers.

I walked in homeroom soon as the bell rang. I was always running late, but always on time. The day was going by rather quickly. I ate the rest of my prime pizza at lunch before I got ready to ace the last period like I did with all the others. While I was walking down the hall way, there were girls who posted up like they didn't need their education but education needed them. They were staring, pointing, and whispering. I could care less about what they were saying because they could only be saying two things—"There goes that bitch. She think she's cute" or "I love her shoes they are to die for." I mean really, my crew and I are the most popular girls in school, and I'm the flyest. Running late again, I ran down the hallway as my long ponytail rubbed my back and swung side to side.

"Anaya," I heard a male voice call my name. I looked back, but I didn't see anyone until Stanley jumped out.

"Boy!" I screamed. "You scared me!"

He put his hands around my waist and spun me around.

"Put me down," I said. "I'm already late for class."

"It's the last period," he said. "You have a good GPA. It won't hurt you to miss class today. Besides, I have something important I wanna talk to you about."

Oh boy, not again, I thought to myself. Stanley had asked me to be his girlfriend once before, but I told him that I only wanted for us to be friends. Last I heard, he use to date the girl named Mia, but he left her to ask me out on a date—so I heard—which explained why she said smart remarks whenever we're at our basketball games.

"Well, why can't you tell me on my way to class?" I asked.

Damn, he smelled good. Don't get it twisted; Stanley was definitely eye candy. He was six foot three with sun-kissed skin and beautiful hazel brown eyes that would mesmerize you if you looked at them long enough. He was bowlegged, and I heard he had a great meat package.

He was raised in a good home with both parents, got good grades, worked, and was a senior of the varsity football team.

So what was my problem? I liked bad boys, hustlers, and drug dealers—those were easy money. He was too clingy; he wouldn't let me come up for air. I felt suffocated at one point- he was there everywhere I turned.

"Okay, Stanley. We can talk for a minute," I said as I followed him down the staircase and into the basement. It was only one flight down, since we were already on the first floor.

"You look so damn sexy in that blue skirt, Anaya. You already know I really like you, and I haven't dealt with anyone in almost a year now. Look, I want you to be mine. I hate hearing all those guys saying how beautiful you look and how good you smell when you walk by because they know you are not my girl."

I couldn't resist him. He was talking, but I couldn't hear anything. Every time he licked his lips, it turned me on.

I pulled him toward me and shoved my tongue down his throat. I swore I felt his tonsils. He grabbed me with his hands as our tongues made love. I felt his hardness on my leg. I then stuck my hands down his pants and played with his manhood. I put his hand up my shirt so he could squeeze my breasts. He turned me around with one hand and grabbed my ponytail with the other, smashing my breasts against the wall.

As his wet lips tickled across my earlobe, he softly whispered, "I just wanna taste you Anaya." He strongly bit the back of my neck which had me wanting more. He then slipped to his knees, pushed my legs open from behind, put his head up my skirt and slid his tongue underneath my panties. We had no worries of being caught. He sucked my clitoris as if he was sucking on a peach. I couldn't believe how good it felt. I don't know if he was simply the best pussy-eater ever or if I was turned on from the spontaneous adventure we just encountered. Either way, I was intrigued.

I hurried up, took a feminine wipe out my purse, and wiped off. The bell was about to ring in three minutes, and I didn't want to get caught coming out of the basement stairwell with Stanley. I told him I would call him after I went home; then, I came out from the basement. *Saved by the bell*, I thought as I walked off to the hallway, blending in but standing out in the crowd.

I caught up with my girls. We would always meet up at the same spot in front of the school before leaving.

"Hey, Mona," I greeted. Mona and I had been close since ninth grade. She was a redbone and a five foot seven cutie. She was overweight and had a huge top and bottom and a nice waist. She had a baby face, and her breast set right underneath it. She always wore stretched tight jeans and a high-top Reeboks to school. I guess she was content with her wardrobe. She wasn't really quiet; she was more on the sneaky side. She lived in the county but had family down the hill near Broadway, so even though she rarely came outside, she knew a lot of people.)

"I haven't seen you all day in school," Mona said.

"I was looking for you during the last period. I knew you were here because several people said they saw you. They were talking about your shoes and that you were walking down the hall with Stanley."

"Yeah, I bumped into him running late, and of course he stopped me because he wanted to talk."

"Oh goodness! Is he still talking the same be-his-girlfriend mess?"

"Girl . . . yes."

"Anaya! He find as all out doors damn!"

"Yup, he is that, but he's just a little too much on the soft side for me. That doesn't make me feel safe and protected. I like those street niggas," I said as I twisted my lips.

"What are you doing today? Chilling in the dark listening to your music while you talk to your mystery lover on the phone?" Mona started laughing. "You think you know me, don't you, Anaya?"

"I do."

"What will you do after you take the truck home?"

"Imma ride with my uncle to pick my grandmother up if he hasn't left yet. I'm supposed to go meet this dude named Pop who live on Greenmount that DJ wanted me to meet. He's a friend of a friend. He's supposed to be this big-time hustler up there near Barclay. My uncles would literally kill me if they knew I was anywhere near there, but I'm going to wait and see if this dude pages me. If so, I'll get Tonya to go down with me in a cab."

"Hey, ladies." Jessica said as she appeared. Jessica was part of our group, but she had been missing in action lately. She's pretty with her smooth chocolate skin. We were the two short and sexy ones in the crew. She had deep dimples and pretty long black hair. She was small-chested, but she had a nice ass. She became an exotic dancer—or in other words, "stripper"—down Eldorado's after her father left her mother for another woman and moved to Atlanta. It must be working for her because she almost dress as good as I do. She recently started dating some dude she doesn't want to tell anyone about, so we call him the *mystery man* for now. He's probably an old white man.

"Hey, Jessica."

"Where's Tonya?" Jessica asked.

"Girl, you already know how Tonya is. She has to stop and talk to everybody she passes, trying to sell that chronic. I can hear her now— *DJ let me old sompen*," I said, imitating Tonya.

"Girl, you're funny. You said it just like her!" Jessica said. All girls busted out, laughing.

"Ouch!" I screamed as Tonya came up and pulled my hair.

"Tonya, you play too much. What took you so long?"

"You know I had to make a couple sales then I ran into DJ. I got him to give me half of that blunt he had left," Tonya said as the girls started laughing again. "What's so funny?"

"Nothing," we all said at the same time.

"Come on, y'all. Let's go. You know I like to have the truck back at a reasonable time. After I drop you monkeys off, except you Mona, I'll call you later and tell you how the blind date went," I said as I made a ugly face.

We all hopped in the truck. Patti LaBelle "burning" was still on my music player from the morning ride. I got chill bumps all over again as I played back from the beginning. I drove through school traffic with the truck's windows down, getting all the attention.

"What you doing after you drop the truck off?" Tonya asked.

"Oh, I forgot. I want you to catch a cab with me somewhere later, but I'm riding with my uncle to pick up my grandmother from work first."

"So where is it that you want me to go?"

"Girl, DJ wants to introduce me to this guy named Pop. He said we would be perfect for each other. You heard of him, up there off Greenmount?"

"Are you talking about Bobby's brother?"

"Oh really? Didn't know he had a brother."

"Yeah, that's why he stay fly. That's who he works for."

"Oh, I learn something new every day. I heard his brother was getting that paper. Is he cute?"

"I've never seen him before."

"Well, DJ gave him my number. Once he pages me, I'll call you. We can catch a cab from your house."

"Okay," Tonya agreed as she hopped out the truck.

"You said you going to your aunt house right, Jess?" I turned to Jessica and asked.

"Yeah, I have to grab a couple of things then I'll get picked up later. Call me, and let me know how everything went. Maybe, y'all can come down the club this weekend. I can sneak y'all in through the back this Friday at seven. It's going to be real crowded, so they won't be paying attention. There are a lot of cute guys with money at Eldorado's on Fridays too."

"Okay. I'll let you know. You know I'd rather watch a woman teach me some moves too then watching a sweaty ass cheesy dude, so okay, maybe I'll call you if it's not too late," I told Jessica as she jumped down from the truck.

"Hold it, hold it, hold it," I kept repeating. Why is it that the closer you get to your front door, the more you have to use the bathroom? I'm just glad the front door was open. Thank god my cousin gets out of school before me. I ran upstairs and shut the damn door.

I banged. "Hurry up, Nathan! I'm about to pee on myself."

My cousin, Nathan, and I are more like brothers. The little turd gets on my nerves, but I love him. He comes out looking all serious as usual.

"Go head," he said.

I run in and shut the door behind me. "Hey, has uncle Will been here? He didn't leave yet to go get grandma, did he?"

"Yeah he left like ten minutes before you got here."

"Really? He knew I wanted to go. Why would he leave so soon? He normally waits for me to get back when I have one of the cars," I replied; then I thought, *I am a tidbit late fooling around with slow poke Tonya.*

"He said something about grandma having a doctor's appointment. Your mother went too."

"What?" I wonder what's that about my mother. She never picked up grandma. "Come to think of it, how many doctor appointments has grandma gone to? She just went two weeks ago."

"Oh, I don't know, Nathan said as if I was actually asking him. "You know they're secretive, and they won't tell us nothing."

"Is that my pager I hear beeping?"

"Yeah."

"Okay, I'll check it after I take a bath and change. It's too hot out there, I feel sweaty." I was also thinking that I needed to wash Stanley's tongue off me too. My nipples got hard just thinking about that intense, spontaneous moment.

I changed my clothes and put on a tan high waist jean shorts, a black t-shirt that had the quote *I'm too pretty for you* in red letters, and my red pumpkin seed sneakers. After I sprayed on some Versace Blonde, I went downstairs to see who I had waiting on my pager. I think it's the number DJ mentioned. I dialed it, and it rang once before a guy answered.

"Did somebody call Anaya from this number?" I asked.

"Hold on. Yo, Pop!" he yelled as I waited.

"Hi, Anaya. How are you doing? This is Pop."

"Well, what makes you think this is Anaya?"

"Because you're the only person I've been waiting for to call me. I heard quite a bit about you even from my brother. Can you catch a cab and come down and see me? I'll pay for everything."

"Wow! You don't waste no time," I said. I knew he would act this way since DJ told him about me. He always complimenting me on how beautiful I am, and so does Pop's brother. "Well, okay. I have to take care of a few things then I'll catch a cab right down. I'll be bringing my home girl down with me." That's cool right?

"yeaNo problem, I'm off Greenmount and Twenty-Fourth right across the street from the store. You can't miss it."

"Okay," I said playing the game before it actually started. Never jump when a man wants you too. Always make him wait. I called Tonya and told her I was on my way around.

"Nathan, I'm going around Tonya's. Let uncle Will know that his keys are on the table in the kitchen, and I hope you're not worrying about Grandma. I'm sure she's just getting a follow up after having her breast removed from that damn cancer, but it's been over a year and the cancer has been removed, so she's fine."

"Okay, I wasn't worrying," he said, always with the nonchalant attitude.

"Cool, tuff cookie. See you later."

Oh, forgot my watch, which one should I wear? I'm thinking Gucci, even though I'm carrying a Kate spade bag. This nigga needs to know who he's about to fall in love with and what I already have even without fucking with niggas like him. Shit, guys try and talk to me all the time with fat rides and money. What will he do any different to make him special?

Gucci it is. Now I'm ready to walk these streets of Baltimore, and I must say that I walk them well. This is my last year of high school to decide what college I want to apply too; nothing can stop me. I walked up Tonya's steps, hoping her mother was asleep upstairs. That woman can't stand me for no apparent reason. Every time I call or knock on the door, if she answers, the first thing she says is *Tonya is not here!* Knowing damn well she lying, I went to the door and knocked. *Shit!* I thought. *Here she comes.*

"Hi, Anaya. Tonya is not here. She left," she said. What I tell you.

"Okay, Ms. Brown," I said as she shut both doors. *The Bitch*, I thought. I sat on the step. Five minutes later, Tonya opened the door.

"I was wondering what was taking you so long to walk around here," Tonya said.

"Girl, I knocked on the door. Your evil mother told me you weren't home as usual."

"My mother don't make no sense. She saw me come out of the bathroom, and I asked her if anyone was at the door. She told me no. You know my mother is jealous of you. You're the only person she acts that way with."

"Remember the time you told me that you were finished cleaning up and asked me to come around? And as you came out, she asked if you were done, and you said 'yes'? She said 'no, you're not bring your butt back in here and Clean the walls and ceilings.'" We both started laughing. "Well, don't shut the door. You have to call a cab for us. Let's walk. I want to smoke this blunt. We can flag a cab down on Harford Road."

We rode down Twenty-Fourth Street, which was packed with people. This was a part of the east side which I didn't visit often. People stood around like zombies. Crack heads is what they call them. We pulled up to the address I was given and saw people sitting on the steps. We got out of the cab, but I didn't see the person that would fit Pop's description—at least not from the way DJ described him.

A random guy came over and gave me a $50 bill for the cab. I paid, got the change, and tried to give it back, but he told me to keep it. *Okay, if you say so*, I thought as we walked toward the steps to ask for Pop. DJ came from around the corner while Pop's brother followed. I felt much better now that I saw familiar faces.

"Was'sup, y'all. Where's the mystery guy? How was he able to ask me to catch a cab down here, but I'm seeing everybody but him?" I asked. *He was probably peeping, ensuring that I didn't look like a donkey*, I thought.

"He had to run somewhere real quick. He rode pass us and told both of us to come around and meet you. He'll be back in like five minutes," DJ said.

I sat on the vacant steps next door while Tonya was talking to DJ until a black Mercedes with tinted windows pulled up. I assumed it was Pop who stepped out the passenger seat because he fit the description— five foot seven, light skin, and with cat eyes like Stanley's, but his was more greenish. He had a totally different approach. What is up with all these light skin dudes I keep on encountering? He was pretty cute. He wore jean shorts, a green polo shirt, and a pair of fresh Diodores. It was like he was just chilling. I always look at a man's feet.

"Anaya?" he asked.

"Yes, that would be me."

Damn, they weren't lying. Wow! He's making me blush already.

"I like your dimples," he said.

"I like yours too."

Normally when guys compliment me, they all sound the same; but for some reason, the same words coming out of his mouth sound more sincere.

We sat outside, talked, and listened to his brother crack jokes until a crack head came over looking for Pop.

"Pop," she said, not even knowing who Pop was.

Pop's brother jumped up and threw soda in her face. "Bitch, don't ever bring your junky ass in front of my door. Get the fuck away before I kick you up your ass!"

He was my "rode dog" in school, but he was a little off- he didn't take shit from anybody. She was lucky that she left because he would've kicked his foot up her ass.

"Pop, our cab is here. We'll have to do this again one day."

"What about tomorrow? We can go get something to eat."

I was a little nervous about dating him even though I liked older guys. He seemed like he might be too old for me. My uncles would kill me first than ask questions later if he knew I was hanging on Twenty-Fourth and Greenmount with a drug dealer that's too old for me.

"How old are you, Pop?" I asked.

"Twenty-two."

Well shit, that's not that bad. There's something about him that I liked. I was curious and wanted to find out more. "Okay, I'll be catching a cab down here on Friday around six. Don't have everyone catering to my needs except you next time."

"Okay, that's cool," he said. I smiled as I walked toward the cab to get in, but he stopped me. "Anaya, hold up. I would like to apologize for having you waiting. Here, please take this, and buy something nice for our date this weekend."

"Are you trying to buy me Pop?" I asked seriously.

"No! Not at all."

"Do you not like what I have on?"

"Yes!" he said, sounding embarrassed. "I was just say—"

"I'm just teasing," I said as I cut him off. "Thank you that was very thoughtful. I'll do just that."

As we were riding home in the cab, I couldn't help but hear my grandmother's voice in my ear—*nothing is free.*

"How much did he give you?" Tonya asked.

"Three hundred dollars," I told Tonya.

"How do you do it?"

"I'm like poison from Batman and Robin. It's my scent," I said as I giggled.

"I'm starting to believe that too. Shit, I gotta bend over legs up just for a hundred dollars. A damn shame!" Tonya said.

We both laughed. I got out of the cab around Tonya's, so I wouldn't have to answer the whats, wheres, and whos. As I walked toward the house, my grandmother sat in her usual spot, adding and subtracting numbers for her lottery and smoking her favorite cigarettes with no filter. I heard her nasty cough before I saw her. I didn't know why she wouldn't just quit. I couldn't stand the smell of those things.

Grandma, won't you smoke on this joint? It's only herbs rolled in top paper instead of puffing on those cancer sticks—wake up and stop dreami ng, I had to tell myself. No way would or could I tell my grandmother that I occasionally puff on the "magic dragon" or else I would never see another Gucci watch, Dooney and Bourke bag, or Chanel sunglasses again. Shit, I would never see outside to wear them anyway. In another life time . . . maybe.

"Hey, Grandma how was work today?"

"What did you say, Anaya?"

"I was asking you how was your day today? I wanted to come along for the ride, but uncle Will left early. Where is my mother? Nathan said y'all went to the doctors. Why did you go to the doctors this time?"

"Just had to get a yearly check-up after the mastectomy."

"Oh, that's what I told Nathan."

"And your mother went down the street."

"Okay, I'll see her if she comes back down. I'm in for the night. There's a murder mystery coming on at nine o' clock. Wanna watch it with me?"

"As soon as I'm done with my lottery."

"Okay. I'm about to take a bath. Hurry up, Grandma."

I lived for the movie night that made me feel like a little girl inside, curled up in her bed.

CHAPTER 2

Boys will be Boys

THIS WEEK WENT fast. It was supposed to be a hot today, and black people liked to act a fool in the heat. There must be something in the humidity; and of all days, I was not driving. I was glad that I had these fresh pair of concords under my bed, so I'd be rocking these today.

I had a much better day when I woke up on time. I slipped on my red DKNY tennis skirt set and my mother-of-pearl bangle to soften the look. I looked pretty good, only if I could get rid of this big ole donkey ass. I knew guys liked it, but I didn't! Unfortunately I couldn't hide it. Ugh! I twisted my ponytail into a knot. *I'll get my hair done after school,* I thought.

Tonya's door was open. I knew I could open the screen and yell for her because her mother was at work. After she went out, we were off to school. School was dragging for some reason today, but thank god the bell rang for lunch. My girls and I had different lunch periods, but Tonya and Jessica would join me from time to time.

"Don't you two belong in class?"

"Yes, but have you heard what people are saying?" Tonya said.

"No, what?"

"Girl, Stanley told Mia he was in love with you, and he didn't even wanna be seen walking with her because he didn't want you to think he was still dealing with her."

"What? Now that's cold. He already knows I could care less about who he walks, talks, or sits with for that matter . . . we are just friends!"

"Really, well what type of friend knows that your pussy taste like strawberries!" Jessica said. I was speechless. My eyes got bigger than they already were. I didn't even tell my friends about that hallway action because I knew they would say "stop playing with his emotions; he really does like you." *Not that I'm a slut because I let him taste me in the hallway . . . or did they know where it took place?* I thought to myself with a dumb you-are-busted look on my face.

"Don't think of a lie. Give us all the details later," said Jessica.

"As for now, Stanley's ex is telling people that their crew are banking you after school, and we all know that's not gonna happen," Tonya yelled out as if they were somewhere listening.

"I am not thinking about Mia or her wannabe crew. Anyway, I'm not a fighter . . . I'm a lady." I smiled and continued to eat my salad.

"You're always so nonchalant about everything," said Jessica.

"Yeah . . . until a bitch gets in her face. I know you. I've seen her in action. Don't forget 'Miss Queen B.'"

"I didn't say I wouldn't put my hands on a bitch. I'm just saying I don't like fighting. Now y'all two better hurry up back to class with your bathroom passes before the bell ring and y'all get detention, then I will get my ass banked!

"All right, girl. We'll see you after school in the same spot?"

"Yeah, and don't be late today, Tonya. I'm trying to get home. I have a hair appointment and a date."

The bell rang. It was Friday, and it was hot outside. As I walked to our usual meeting spot, Stanley ran behind me and lifted me in the air.

"Put me down!" I said as I pushed him away. "I am so mad at you that I don't even know where to start! Was my pussy so good that you had to tell everyone that you ate it? And you need to control your little friend. She should be worried about kicking your ass, but instead she's out for me. I don't have time for these ghetto drama moments!" *Hoes need to know the difference between being somebody girl and being fucked!* I thought. "And now your girl's ready to bring out the cat paws."

"Guess I should've expected this sooner or later. The way she used to throw slurs when I came to the games when I was in middle school."

"She must've been mad because she was the one trying to get your attention, but you were trying to get mine."

"What can I say . . . when I'm hot, I'm hot!" Whatever Stanley said made both of us start laughing.

Tonya came yelling, "Get away from her! You started enough chaos!"

"Who me? I didn't start anything. I stopped dealing with that girl a long time ago. She's been wanting a reason to mess with Anaya since she came to this school. She knew Anaya always had my attention, and if Anaya would've let me—she would've been my girl instead of Mia."

"Can't get the real deal. You settle for sloppy seconds."

"Okay, okay. I get it." I said as Tonya and I both started laughing.

"Okay, y'all got me. Come on, y'all. Let's go. I have a hair appointment."

Seven of us walked: Me, Tonya, Jessica, Stanley, his brother, and two of his homeboys.

"She really gone be pissed now when she see me with her man and his entourage."

We waited for the light to turn red so we could cross from St. Lo Drive to the Alameda and Harford Road. I saw her and her two followers, standing on the corner and looking right at us. We ran across the street, laughed, joking, and acting silly as usual as if we heard nothing about a fight; but clearly everyone else did. People stood around everywhere way more than usual.

I told you, when it got hot black folks, they don't know how to act; when they hear that one of the schools most popular girls was getting her ass whipped, this is the type of crowd you get. I gave Stanley my united colors of Benetton back pack while crossing the street.

"Don't go over there, trying to fight that crazy girl. I'm here, so you don't fight. I'm not—"

"Just wanna be prepared in case her crazy ass tries to swing."

As soon as I put my foot on the curb, she came charging at me with a lock in her hand. If Tonya wouldn't have clipped her, she would've done some damage. I jumped on that bitch so bad, she had Jordan print on the side of her face. There was blood everywhere. It was caused partly by me, stomping a mud hole in her head; but it was mainly by her, landing on the lock, causing her tooth to get knocked out. Of course, her girls tried to jump in, but so did mine. We were out here fighting like a bunch of voyagers until Stanley picked me up in midair. Everyone started running because they heard police sirens. I would rather hear the sirens instead of my grandmother's or uncle's voice, telling me how disappointed they would be if they saw me acting like an animal instead of the young lady they raised me to be. I knew I had some explaining to do once I got home, but once I explained it wasn't my fault, they would understand. Our motto is "if someone hits you, hit their ass back," but damn, we just acted like a pack of wolves.

I walked in the house, went upstairs, and took a bath. I turned the radio on as I sat on the edge of my bed and began thinking of how this day started and how it would end. As I thought about the fight, I realized how females could be so stupid and naive when it came to men. She went through all that trouble worrying about me whether I wanted him or not. He didn't want her, and now she had to get a tooth replacement. Well, all I had to say was, I hope she have a dental plan.

As I sat on the end of the bed, pampering my body, I turned the volume of the radio up. "Ow! That's my jam!" I said as I sang, "You can cha-cha-cha to this Mardis Gras / I'm the dopest female that you've heard thus far." I love Mc Lyte.

I checked myself in the mirror. I had on my blue leather pumps on from Cazin's in Mondawmin, a long blue plaid skirt, and a wife beater with a blue bow that I stitched in the middle. I can wear a tank every day. I loved how they hugged my body with no bra on and how it layed against my stomach. *I had a nice shape only if this ass wasn't so big*, I thought with a heavy sigh. Well, god gave me this ass. All I can do was to keep it looking and smelling good.

My hair didn't look so bad either; I loved pulling my hair up in a ponytail. I could get a wash and curl real quick since it was only 4:30, and my date was not until 6:00. My grandmother was downstairs. I explained everything, and that was that. As long as it didn't happen in school on school grounds and it didn't affect my grades, I was good. After the talk, I left to go get my hair done.

CHAPTER 3

Too Much Chemistry

Pop

WHEN MY HAIR got finished, it was 6:00 on the dot. I could be late since it was only dinner. Besides, I doubt if he made reservations, so I guess I would go over, sit with Tonya, and get her to call me a cab. My hair did feel good as it blew in the wind; it was long, thick, and shiny, bouncing with every step. When I approached Tonya's house, I saw her and her brother, Edward, sitting on the steps down the street, fussing some dude out as usual.

"What's up, T?" I asked.

"Nothing. Just chilling," she replied.

"Where's your phone so I can call a cab?"

"Where you going?"

"On a dinner date with Pop, remember?"

"Oh, that's right," she said as she handed me the cordless phone.

While waiting for the cab, my dirty mind couldn't help but wonder. "What do you think about Pop?" I asked.

"He doesn't seem like your type. He's cute, but I just see you with a tall, sexy, motherfucker!"

"But I did here. He was getting that paper, and he just brought a key. We both know he's not stingy."

"He seems pretty nice. I haven't heard anything negative about him, and I can tell he has the hots for you already."

"What makes you say that?" I said, wanting to hear more.

"The way he was smiling like he just won the lottery—and DJ said he has been asking him questions like if he saw you in school the other day and what you had on."

"Wow! Well, time will reveal. Girl, I can't help thinking about having sex with him. His dick looks big and thick—damn. I have to make him wait. I want long term fun with him! Shit, by the time I finish teasing him, he'll be dying to rip these sexy thongs off my ass."

"If you have on any?" Tonya said

"I know right!"

"Don't give him any, Anaya. I don't know what it is that you do, but guys flock to your ass. What makes it worse is after you decide to give them some, you start acting like a nigga then they end up knocking on my door asking me where you are. How did they find out where I live? Shit! To be honest, I don't know how you do it. If I'm turned on by someone, we fucking!

"Girl, it's called self-control. The ones I want I save my goodies, give them everything, but make them lust. The ones I wanna have fun with, I fuck them whenever I want then leave when I want. They're the few you're talking about. You know I get bored easily. I swear. Sometimes I think I should've been a man. My thoughts and actions say nothing, but 'fuck them then leave them,' is how I feel. I know its nasty for a woman to run through men like a man does. Therefore, it's not cool to be a hoe, but shit ain't wrong with being a freak!" We both busted out laughing.

"Now see, that's why I love you. You're honest and outspoken to the core. That's why guys fall for you so damn hard! You keep it sexy and classy in these streets, but you are a damn freak by nature, and no one would ever expect it."

"I love you too, Tonya." We hugged and kissed. The cab came down the street. Before it got the chance to blow the horn, I walked toward it.

"Have fun. Call me if you need me."

Tonya and her brother Edward always had my back.

We were driving over to Twenty-Fourth when my pager went off. Pop asked me if 6:00 was a good time, and I said yes; but I had to get my hair done, and its only 6:40. I was never on time for anything anyway; he'd get used to it. Plus, it's good to keep a man waiting and wondering.

As the cab pulled up to the house we were at yesterday, I noticed a lot of fellas posted up in front again. I knew summer was near, and it was hot outside—but damn! To be safe, I asked and made sure it was not a stash house, and he didn't have a girlfriend at the real house the way these niggas play games. When I thought about it, he wasn't here when I arrived the other day.

I stepped out the cab, and he came running from across the street. First impressions meant a lot to me. This was the second time he didn't greet me, open the door, and pay the cab man before I got out. All these guys out here—poor man, he probably thought he was going to get jacked.

"What's up Anaya? You're late."

"I was just coming from paging you on the phone booth across the street next to Sammy's store."

"Yeah, I saw it. I knew that was you."

"I was on my way here. Sorry, I'm late. I was getting my hair done. You didn't make reservations anywhere, did you?"

"I did. I wanted to make sure we have a table, but I was able to change it to 7:30. Is that good for you?"

"Yes, that's fine," I replied, wondering where was his car located. I knew that after dinner, he would be calling me a cab to go straight home once we got back to his place. That's my self control plus I can be on his mind all night. I'll let him know on our way from dinner.

"I've been meaning to ask you . . . Is this a stash house?"

He looked at me like I was crazy; then, he started laughing. "No, I stay here with my mother and my brother. Why'd you ask me that?"

Did he really have to ask that question? I thought. "I am dumbfounded with all the people that were sitting around and running in and out the house."

"Oh, they're just homeboys. Mainly my brother's friends. There's nothing to be worried about. You're safe as long as you're with me."

I didn't know what it was, but there was something about his big, hard, manly-looking hands that looked like he would beat a nigga's ass if they even looked at me the wrong way. I felt weak at the knees. There was something about bad boys, drug dealers, and gunslingers, the wannabe Tony Montanas. He got that look like 'Imma go and beat this nigga's ass real quick and come back and fuck the shit out you later.' As if he knew what I thought, he stared at me with his piercing light cat eyes as if they were talking to my pussy because I was almost certain she was talking back!

I snapped out of it and controlled myself. I couldn't let him think that he would get the goods that easily. His homeboy with the S500 pulled up, asking Pop if he was ready. I wondered if he even had a car of his own. Was it parked somewhere because of the business he conducted? Did he pay this guy to be his chauffeur? I knew he had money—but damn!

"There's something about that color green that made me like you when I first laid my eyes on you," I told him.

"What this green right here?" he said as he opened the door for me with one hand and pulled a huge knot of money out with the other.

"The green shirt you had on, Pop. You're funny," I said as I blushed.

"Of course that don't hurt either. I know it don't. I hear about you.

"What, what do you hear?"

"That you like the finer things in life. All good things, don't worry."

"Okay, that's cool," I said as I got in.

If I wasn't mistaken, the driver hadn't taken his eyes off me since I climbed my ass in the car. He pulled off after Pop gave him the information prior to his arrival, taking one last glance in his rear view mirror. He was looking all like chocolate with his fine ass, like a dark-skin version of LL Cool J, with his Adidas Kango on. Don't get me wrong—I was single; I could look and slide my number to whom I please. I just met Pop as far as I know. He could have a girlfriend, but I wasn't about to do that; it was not my type of party. Not wanting to give him eye contact, I looked over at Pop to try and figure out why he didn't notice his driver undressing me with his eyes—it was because Pop was doing the same thing.

Okay, I was getting nervous. I didn't know much about these dudes. They could be plotting to rape me and leave me somewhere dead—a seventeen-year-old getting in a car with two older men. All I could hear was Biz Markie's voice, singing through the speakers, "you, you got what I need but you say he's just a friend." It was not a good song right now, so I grabbed Pop's face and took him out of the trance he was in.

"Hey, Pop."

"Hey, Anaya."

"What's the matter?"

"What do you mean?"

"Why are you staring at me like that?"

"I'm just admiring you. I think you're extremely beautiful. Don't take this the wrong way, but your body is amazing. Everybody can't do hairy legs, but the way your hair lay down on your brown skin makes me wanna pull all that hair on your head and bring you closer to me. I know this is our first date, but I'm gonna make you my girl."

I had a ball stuck in my throat because nothing came out. Did I hear him right? I knew he didn't just say what I thought he said. I didn't know if I was stuck on the girlfriend part or if my legs were shaking from the grab-my-hair situation. He was still talking, but I froze. By the time I looked up, we were in front of Mos restaurant. He got out to open the door for me. I didn't even get a chance to ask him questions because I was shocked the duration of the ride.

We walked into Mos, and as usual, guys stared at me like they had never seen a female before. This was the type of attention I had been getting all my life so I was use to it. It was just something Pop had to get use to. I needed a secure and confident man, and if that was what he was, he wouldn't have a problem with it. As we sat, talked, and waited for our food to come, a girl came over and said 'hi' to Pop. I could tell that she must've been an old girlfriend of some kind because he had an awkward look on his face like *oh shit, this bitch gonna be trouble!*

First of all, it was rude for this trick to come to our table while we talked. It showed no class, but since I was classy and respectful, I would like to hear what was so important that it couldn't wait.

She was cute, a little tall, kinda skinny, but nothing that stood out—just the average chick. She started off by saying, "So this is the new girl—"

Pop cut her off before she finished. O so "she's less of an old girlfriend and more like a recent." He stood up and said, "Don't come over here with that disrespectful shit."

"Yeah, he gone whip her ass too," she said as she turned and walked away.

"I apologize for that. Here comes our server with our food. I'll explain that situation to you tonight."

Tonight . . . I'm going home. I thought to myself. Instead, I simply said, "Okay, we can talk about it, but I know boys will be boys, and men will be men. We just met, and you have current situations—I get that—but you need to tie your loose ends before trying to start something else. That's all I'm saying. I don't expect that I'll have to go through anything like that again?"

"No, of course not," he said, but deep inside, I knew I should've made sure this was our last date.

The speech he gave in the car wasn't hard to believe, except for the *girlfriend* part. What he didn't know about me was I had more male hormones than female, and I grew up around men. A man would say anything to get in these panties, but what got my attention was the way he said, "I just wanna pull all that hair and bring you close to me." He might have more drama later, but I'd wait and see because I'm not calling it quits until I have some of him.

"Okay, let's eat," he said.

I swore that the way he licked his tongue out and the way his big wet lips curled over his lobster made me eat mine in slow motion. I felt like I was having sex at the table. My kitty was throbbing down there like it had its own heartbeat. I felt my nipples getting harder and harder through my white tank, and of course, I had no bra on. Finally, we finished eating, and he paid the bill.

The S500 waited like clockwork. We got in the car and headed back to his house. There was no need to drop me off; I'd let him call a cab when we get there. I didn't want either one of them knowing where I lived. My family would kill me twice, knowing that I jumped out an S500 with a drug dealer who was five years older.

Pop started to talk to his buddy who was driving. "Man, you wouldn't believe who came rushing to my table on the same old tired shit."

"Denise?"

"You know it."

"Damn! Yo, that chick is crazy. I don't know what you gone do with her."

"So who is she exactly?" I asked.

"An ex, ex, ex! Sorry, Anaya, this is Steve. Steve, this is Anaya."

"Hello, Steve. Thanks for the introduction after the second ride," I said.

"Nice to meet you Anaya. She's not just an ex. She's a crazy ex!" said Steve. "They broke up over two months ago, but she keeps coming around, trying to talk to Pop. Now, Pop is finally in a relationship."

"Ho—ho—hold up. Pop and I are just friends. We just met this week. Tell him, Pop." They both started laughing. "What's so funny?"

"Anaya—that's your name right?"

"Yes."

"Pop really likes you. In all my years of knowing him, he's never talked about a female the way he's been talking about you . . . in only four days of meeting you—and I see why. You're gorgeous with your nice thick eyebrows and—"

"Okay, okay . . . Steve you're getting a little carried away, man."

"My bad, Pop. Treat her good, homie, or Steve gonna take her," he said as he laughed. I could tell that they were close enough to joke around like that. "When Pop wanted something as bad as he wanted you, he'll do anything to get you, and you won't be able to resist. He's a pretty charming guy."

"Well what do you have to say about that, Pop? Your homie is doing all the talking for you, Mr. Slick."

"Nothing slick about me. I say, just wait and see." We pulled up to the house. "Are you coming in for a little while to talk, or are you ready to call it a night? It's only 9:00, but it's up to you."

I knew it was early, but I also knew I should carry my ass home the way I felt down below. This would take more than self-control; it was going to take some suffering. "Okay, I'll come in for a few, then you can call a cab."

"Good night, Ms. Anaya. It was nice meeting you. Hope I get the chance to see more of you."

"Thank you, Steve. Good night."

I walked inside the house. It appeared to be neat and clean but old and outdated. If he was getting so much money as everyone says, why wouldn't he get a place of his own?

"Come on, let's go upstairs."

We walked down a long hallway to the back room which was locked. We went inside. It was pretty big. He had a king-sized bed with Ralph Lauren comforter and four huge pillows to match, an expensive-looking cream antique dresser with a flat-looking TV, and a CD player on the wall. He waved his hand across it, and it opened. He had a remote to the ceiling fan and an air conditioner in the window. There were sneaker boxes which made me feel like I was in footlocker.

"You can sit down. Make yourself comfortable. Which do you prefer fan or air?"

"Air."

"Here's the remote. Put it how you like while I go to the bathroom."

I thought he walked over to a closet, but I came to find out that he had a bathroom in his room. I was impressed, considering the location. Downstairs smelled like old plastic due to all the covered furniture, but that only meant one thing: *he ain't leaving his momma.*

I went into the bathroom once he came out to freshen up a little. There were Ralph Lauren everywhere—towels, mats, and seat covers—a gold tissue box, tooth brush holder, and gold soap dish. Now, this was some real gangsta shit . I know quality shit when I see it; his shower room was screaming it out loud. He had the rounded stand-up shower with the jets on the walk, aiming at different parts of the body. I wanted to take my clothes off and jump in. Damn—God, please help me be a good girl and stick to my rules. I heard Jodeci's voice singing under the bathroom door, "And all my life I've prayed for someone like you / and I thank God that I, that I finally found you."

I was in trouble now. It wouldn't have been so bad if I had had sex in the near future, but I hadn't. Its been over five months. The fact that I had already been dreaming about fucking him was not good. I went out the bathroom as he came back into the room, putting a cordless phone on the charger.

"Oh, I didn't think you had a house phone," I said.

"Oh, nah, I keep it locked up in my room. I have a different number than the rest of the house. Someone is always on that one. I didn't feel like coming upstairs to use mine so I just called from the phone booth. Plus, I handle a lot of transactions so I'm always standing somewhere near. By the way, I wanna give you the numbers to both lines, and I'll get you a key made in case you might need some money, and I'm not here to give it to you. The front door is always open."

This dude was serious.

"What about a key to an apt and not your mommas house?" Sometimes my mouth just says what my mind thinks.

"I have no need to get that right now, so I stay here and pay all the bills. But whenever you ready to make that move, just let me know."

That made me smile.

Lying across the bed on my stomach, I clicked my heels together out of nervousness. Okay, what was up with him? Did he have a little dick and couldn't fuck?

"Would you like me to take your shoes off so you can get comfortable?"

Bitch, no. I'm ready to walk down those steps and get in a damn cab, I thought, but instead I said, "Sure." He sat on the bed while I lied across it. We talked. He couldn't keep his hands out of my hair.

"Do you have a car?"

"No. I don't need one right now. I do a lot for Steve. I even got him that car, so it's not a problem. He's on call whenever I need him. He's like my friend chauffeur." We both started laughing. "Come here, Anaya sit on my lap for a minute. I wanna look you in your eyes when I say this."

I got up and did what he asked.

"I never did this or said this to any other woman before. I saw you in my dreams, and I've been looking for you. I actually gave DJ a reward for introducing us. You don't have to respond right now. I know I'm moving kinda fast."

Kinda, I thought.

"But when you know what you want . . . why wait? Starting right now, I'll be honest with you about everything."

I was thinking that he wanted to be honest about everything, except the shit he didn't want me to know—like hoes and baby mommas. I hadn't gotten the chance to ask him about that."

"I know you already know what I do. I have people outside working for me. I'm outside to keep my eyes on them as well as the other eyes I have watching. I don't sell anything myself unless its weight such as quarters, wholes, and halves."

I didn't understand why he thought I would understand the words that were coming out of his mouth, but I did.

"See, Tonya's brother, Edward, moves a lot of those numbers. Since he was feeling like Mr. Honest man, I was listening to whatever he had to say." He opened a drawer of that beautiful dresser where he had all his nicely folded Ralph Lauren underwear and tank tops. Some still with tags.

He rolled the underwear back and asked me to look at what appeared to be the bottom of the drawer. He popped it up, and underneath was a key of dope lying on top of layers of money. My legs started to tremble; my pussy throbbed. He felt my legs trembling and said, "Come here. I'm sorry. I didn't mean to scare you. I shouldn't have showed you that."

If he only knew, it wasn't that kind of tremble.

Let's rewind., we had a buddy named Tori that Tonya had a little crush on. They never talked, and he had a crush on me. One time he asked me to ride up to New York with him to 152nd Street on the train to keep his company while he get a half key. He would pay me $450. We would do a little shopping, catch the bus back, and he would be with me the entire time. The package would be in the shopping bag. I already put my life at risk just by going, but this nigga went, got a whole key, wanted me to put it in my purse, but didn't wanna pay me extra money. That's a lot of weight, so I went to the bathroom, broke a chunk off for myself, then wrapped it back up the way it was. Of course he later found out, but because he liked me, he never mentioned it. I came to find out that I had a little over an ounce. Tonya thought I was crazy. I had no idea what to do with it so I had her brother working for me for a min . . .

"Come here. Let me hold you," Pop said.

I climbed on his lap, wrapping my legs around his waist. I laid my head on his chest, going along with the fact that he thought I shook from all the drugs and not turned on by all the white and the green. His big lips kissed my forehead. He grabbed a chunk of my hair and pulled my head back. He was getting turned on, thinking he was comforting this young seventeen-year-old beauty, and bit the front of my neck then kissed me like I was never kissed before. I wrapped my long fingers around the back of his head, pulling him as close as I could get and stuck my tongue so far down his throat, he probably thought I was a doctor.

As I squeezed my thick legs around his waist, I felt his dick growing harder and harder, pressed up against my already wet pussy. A green light went off in my head, and all I saw were dollar signs.

"Oh, Poppy, I can't! I have to go. It's getting too late. Besides, I have school tomorrow."

"Tomorrow is Saturday," he said. *Oh, shit,* I thought. "Stay the night with me. I'll make sure you get home first thing in the morning."

"I can't. My grandmother is expecting me." My grandmother always say: "Ain't nothing open after twelve but legs because you are too young to get in clubs." I started laughing nervously because I knew that *that* was about to be open if I stayed. "And I don't stay the night with strangers I just met," I said as I smiled because he knew I wanted him just as bad as he wanted me. "But I can come over Monday after school. Maybe we can see a movie or something.

"What about tomorrow?" he asked as he dialed for the cab.

"I have plans for the weekend. I'm sorry." I was smart not stupid. I knew that if I wanted what was in that drawer, I had to stick to my own rules. Never give the pussy too soon, and never be anxious to call or see him again. No matter what he showed you. As far as I know, that could be someone else's money even though I didn't think so. And I was always told: "Put that phone down!" You're not supposed to chase boys. Boys are supposed to chase you!" I wasn't even calling a boy that time, but it didn't matter. I still learned from it.

"Okay, I don't want to run you away before you're mine, so have fun this weekend. I hope you'll get time afterward to call me."

I heard a horn blowing.

"Yeah, me too."

"It must be your cab."

He gave me a hug and walked me to the door. As I was walking down the steps, he said, "Anaya, wait right there."

The last time he told me to wait, he gave me three hundred dollars. "I forgot to give you the money for the cab, and . . . I like that Gucci watch you're wearing. I like your style and the way you carry yourself. I can tell that you appreciate the finer things in life, so I'll give you some pocket money. I hope you think of only me while you're out on your plans this weekend. Call me, and let me know if you made it home safely."

"Okay, I will. Good night . . . and thank you."

As I was riding home in the cab, he had no idea how much I thought about him already. I knew he thought my plans were with another man this weekend, that's why he gave me some so-called pocket money. I started counting; there were all Ulysses S. Grants and Benjamin Franklins—$350, $600, $800, $820, and the $20 must be for the cab. Okay, this is scary crazy. He gave me a total of $1100, not including dinner. He paid for the pussy already. I could've easily gave him some, but I knew this was a small thing to a giant. He got a key of dope—not coke—sitting in his drawer that haven't even been touched yet. I mean,

I'm not trying to use him. I was digging him before he showed me the goods. I was just making sure it was more for me where this came from.

Once I get a man tucked in my pocket, I didn't care whose big ass or tits he saw. The only ass he'll be thinking about was *this one*. I knew one thing—he seemed to be giving and showing too much too soon. It was some triflen females out here that will set his ass up to get robbed; if not, killed real quick. He was lucky he picked the right one.

I got out the cab around the corner. My block was filled with old nosey people. My grandmother would find out I got out a cab by myself before I got in the house. This way, I could say I was around Tonya's house, but as long as I was in on time, she won't say anything. I guess it was my guilty conscience, knowing I was just with a twenty-two-year-old drug dealer. I messed with one before when I was fifteen. He was a year older, and my uncle drove around looking for him with a shot gun in his trunk. I could only imagine what would happen to Pop.

Finally, I was home, and I could kick off these heels. I could hear my grandmother's TV, which means she was asleep. I went upstairs, gave her a kiss, and turned her TV off.

It was 11:00 p.m. My uncle must be gone out for the night. I was glad he left before I got in or else he would make a conversation.

Asking where I was – and the last thing I wanted to do was lie.

CHAPTER 4

Sex and more sex

"SHUT UP, BITCH! Get your pathetic ass down here. You can go back to sleep after you do what I tell you to do! Now, pull me a glass of orange juice, then come back upstairs. I need you to braid my hair for work in the morning. Hurry up! It's already 2:00 a.m.!" My father yelled. My mother did everything he asked to keep him calm so he wouldn't wake me, but I was already awake. He awakened me every time he came in after hanging outside with who-knows-who and doing who-knows-what. I just wanted him to hurry up and fall asleep like he always did so my mother could get back in the bed with me. She always slept in my bed on the nights she knew he would come home drunk. She slept with our patio stick like she protected me from somebody or something, but I had no clue what. All I did know was she rarely let my father in my room without her.

I woke up sweating, and the phone was ringing. As I answered, I heard my grandmother yelling through the receiver for me to get up for school.

"Okay, grandma," I said. "I'm up." I overslept again. Every time I had those dreams about when I was younger, living with my mom and dad, I overslept.

The week had went by fast., and I was excited to have some fun this weekend. Tonya and I was going down the Baltimore Arena to the Eazy-E concert. Jessica still wanted us to come down the strip club, even though I really didn't wanna go. Maybe we could talk and find out what's up with her. She was dying for us to check out her expertise anyway. I needed to figure out how I would pull all that off. The concert was late as it was already, and I was not about to get punished over a strip club maybe next week.

I thought about staying over Pop's one of these Saturday nights. I'd ask Tonya; she was good at figuring out that type of stuff. I couldn't wait to tell Mona about my date. I was too tired to call when I got in last night, and for the most part, I only see her in school, and she went on a family vacation for a week but I'll probably call her later or see her if I go over my uncle's house. She lived three doors down with her mother off Belair Road and Putty Hill Avenue. She didn't really hang out that often, and even though she preferred to chill home in her room, she always kept some side dick. Her mother didn't mind her having company. I guess she was like "don't fuck with me and mines, and I won't fuck with you and yours." It was crazy, but that's my girl, and I loved her. I couldn't wait to tell her about the huge dick that I didn't get yet.

Decisions, decisions—what should I wear today? I needed to hurry up. Thanks to Avon Skin So Soft in my water, there was no need for lotion. I cut the tags off my panty set, a basket full of nothing but panties and bras I rarely wear. If I wasn't buying them, my aunt was. She always found the cutest things. My first pair of thongs at fourteen had a butterfly right in the center that covered my hair perfectly. She also told me to spray IsoPlus Oil Sheen after trimming or rub a little Kemi Oyl down there. It made it smell nice and sweet, they couldn't help but eat it. She didn't say all that, but what else would be the reason? I didn't know then, but I knew now. I slid on my white sweat pants and T-shirt I got from Simon Harris down Gay Street with my name going diagonal across my back with my blue patent leather dotted Nike. I'd have gold fever today, wearing my gold rope with my crush diamond heart pendant, my herringbone, and my gold stud earrings. I drove the 4Runner again to school today, and I was so thankful because if not, I would be late.

I blew the horn. "Tonya hurry up!" I screamed. "We have less than ten minutes to get to school before the bell rings."

"I'm coming," she said as she ran down her front porch steps.

"Oh, wow! Sneakers again? Twice—that's a world record," Tonya said.

"Girl, since last Friday, the animals were released from the Baltimore Zoo and marched to the corner of the Alameda and Saint Lo Drive. I thought I would be on the safe side today. That hoe must've tapped me with that lock some type of way. She was pretty fast, but my adrenaline was too high to feel anything."

"Well, she wanted your ass," said Tonya.

"Well, she almost had me. She must've thought I was about to sit there and serve myself to her."

"Wasn't happening. I hear that shit with your short ass."

"Shut up, Tonya. Oh, look, is that a parking space?"

"I think so," said Tonya.

"Yup, sure is. We are in there like swimwear," I said. "Okay let's go get these hours over with."

"Look who else is running late."

"We just have to run into him this morning, don't we?" I said. "Tonya, please don't talk to him right now, I'll never get to class."

"Anaya, I really like Stanley with his sexy ass."

"I do too, just not like that—"

"What's up Tonya, 'sup Naya?"

"Nothing."

"You okay from last week?"

"Oh yeah, I'm fine. Thanks for asking."

"Anaya, can I talk to you on our way to class?"

"Stanley, the last time you wanted to talk, others knew that my vagina tasted like strawberries."

"Anaya, stop. That shit tasted so good. I had to tell somebody, but I only told my brother," he said.

"Right, and who would he tell it to? But seriously, I'm not mad, I just really have to go."

"Okay, Anaya. Will I see y'all in gym?"

"Yup."

The smell of his cologne and the way he walked with those bowlegs—damn. He was the epitome of sexy. Only if he knew that I was trying to help him out before I'd be fucking him this weekend instead of going to see Pop. He acted out because his mouth got a taste. Poor boy, he'd be going crazy if his dick got some. When we all got together, we had fun. The way me and Stanley be all over one another, one would think we messed around, but it was only for fun. I didn't wanna use or hurt him because once I got bored, it was over. Besides, I didn't like to shit where I play. Since I had to see him in school every day, I kept my distance. Especially now that I was horny, I would definitely give in to him this go round.

Sitting in French class, I prayed for the bell to ring. I knew just enough to get my last credit for foreign language. I could never understand with Ms. Pat, speaking only in French, was talking about. All I could picture was a bird with glasses because that's what she looks like. After lunch was gym then science. I had to love my science teacher, Mr. Collin. He was the funniest teacher ever.

There went the bell; it was music to my ears. The cafeteria was busy and loud as usual. I stood in line to order a prime time pizza and butter crunch cookies. Tonya and Jessica were always here on Friday, even though Jessica left early and Tonya's lunch was next period.

We all got together and sat in the gym most Fridays. We loved our gym teacher. He knew we didn't all belong when we all came together, but he never said anything. We always got our spot underneath the bleachers. We talked, laughed, smoked a joint, ate our cookies, and drank our juice. This was our time.

Stanley's brother, Bobby, and his crew were already there waiting for us, but Stanley hadn't got there yet. Bobby was tall and cute, slightly bowlegged, but he didn't look like Stanley. They had a younger brother that was hella fine too. Bobby and Tonya used to joke around, and even though Tonya liked him, they never dealt with each other like that.

Bobby asked us to come over his house after school and said he invited a few friends over to come down and trip. We used to walk down there sometimes. They lived by Mervo. Plus, their mother was the coolest.

"All right, we'll come down," Tonya said.

"I thought we were going down the arena to see Eazy-E tonight?" I asked.

"Girl, that's not for another two weeks."

"Oh, I could've sworn it was this week."

"Nope, so you wanna go?" she asked.

"I don't care."

As soon as I said that, Stanley came. He was a senior, so he had half day classes. He came in and said "what's up" to everybody and sat down beside me. Considering he said he wanted to talk to me earlier, he didn't say much. After a few minutes, the bell rang.

"I'll call you after school, Anaya," said Stanley.

Before I got a chance to say "okay," big-mouthed Tonya said, "Don't worry about it. We're coming down your house later."

"Oh, for real? Are you coming, Anaya?" Stanley asked.

I smiled and shook my head. "Yeah."

Finally, there were fifteen minutes left in science. If people didn't learn what they needed to know by now, they could just forget it. Mr. Collin turned into a crack head. If you gave him two dollars, you could play hooky in his class. Now that the end of the school year was approaching, his class stayed crowded. I was surprised he still had a job especially as a science teacher. I was sure he was doing more "experimenting" in the lab than anything else, but he was nice. Everyone liked him, and he knew what he was talking about. Finally, the bell rang. I thought this should be a pretty interesting weekend.

As I turn on to my block, I forgot it was carwash Friday. My uncles had a total of five cars, and every weekend, they would come and wash their cars out front. Both were married with their own homes, but we all loved grandma so much that we just didn't want to leave her. I pulled the 4Runner behind the Mercedes, hoping he would leave it here for me to drive later, even though I knew he wouldn't.

"Are you picking grandma up today, Uncle Ron?"

"No, she said she wanted to catch the bus," he said.

My grandmother was very independent, but she was never interested in getting her license and learning how to drive. I went in the house; took off my hot sweats; took a quick bath; and put on my tennis skirt, shirt, and peach and blue Huarache sneakers to match. I went downstairs and called Mona on the phone.

"Hey, girl. Where have you been? I haven't talked to you all week," I asked.

"I've been too hot to come to school, and I put in my transfer for Parkville next year. I can't stand the people of Lake," she said.

"I would just ignore what they say about you and not let them run me out of my school. You can dress how you want," I said.

"But, oh well, Parkville is closer." I thought ub were out of town somewhere.

"Girl, do remember last Friday when I told you I was going on a blind date to meet this guy from Greenmount?"

"Speaking of last Friday, I heard y'all stomped the mess out of Mia," said Mona.

"That girl came charging at me with a lock. She really had it in for me to go through all that. She nipped me with it a little bit, but once Tonya clipped her, she landed on it knocking her own tooth out. How dumb—but that's over, I'm not thinking about that girl," I said. "Anyway, the guy I met was Pop. Have you heard of him?

"Just . . . he was supposed to be getting a lot of money down Greenmount," she said.

"Damn! Was I the only one who didn't know? Well, he is sexy, very generous, and has a big you know what!"

"What? How do you know? Oh Lord. You gave him some, didn't you? You're gonna take his money and drive that boy crazy," said Mona.

"No, I gave him none. We were kissing, and I was on his lap with my legs wrapped around him. It was big and hard, pressed up against me. Girl, I ended the session real quick. Before all that he was like . . . 'I want you to be my girl whenever you ready.'"

"What? I know you said no."

"I don't even know him. I didn't say anything. Tonya and I are going down to Stanley's later."

"Anaya, you need to stay away from that boy. I'm waiting for him to run up to you, crying in one knee in the hallway, asking you to be his wife," Mona said.

"Girl, stop. That'll be the day I'd transfer right along with you." We both started laughing.

"All right, girl. I'll call you later about to go sit out front with Tonya and watch my uncle wash these cars."

"Yeah, I was talking to your uncle Will yesterday. He said that he left the truck over your grandmother's so you could drive it to school today," said Mona.

"Yeah, you know he likes to have it here for his late night creeps."

"Do you think his wife knows?" Mona asked.

"Girl, I don't know. I stay out of it. He does what he does."

"Knowing his wife, she's probably doing the same. She's never in the house," said Mona. "I think he's bored. He's always asking what I'm doing every time he sees me outside."

"Mona, my uncle is a ladies' man. He's far from bored. If I didn't know any better . . . Never mind." *Glad we're friends, and there are boundaries that friends won't cross*, I thought.

"When are you going back down Greenmount to see Pop?"

"He wanted me to come today, but I'm going down on Monday instead. That way I can cry about the time because I have school in the morning. You know, he gave me over $1100 already."

"What? Oh, I know you're gonna give him some."

"Girl, you would think as horny as I am, I shouldn't be going down Stanley's with Tonya."

"Oh, please! Don't Give that boy none."

"I know right! But with Pop, see he gives and gives to get what he want. To make sure he stays wanting more from me, I'll make him wait. Besides, I'm not hard up for money. I get money like that all the time, and I don't have to lay up in no bed to get it!"

"Your spoiled ass," Mona said.

"I know. I'll call you later." I heard Tonya outside, talking with my uncle. We hung up. I pulled another bowl of cereal and sat outside with Tonya.

As I sat down, my uncle said, "I was asking Tonya what were your plans for today. She said y'all going to visit your boyfriends."

"I didn't say that," Tonya said, laughing.

My uncle always tried to get information out of people. We catching a cab and go hang out in Towson mall.

"Oh yeah? Do a couple things for me, and I'll give you thirty dollars." My uncle does this every weekend. I guess he felt as though if he gave it to me, I wouldn't have to be out here, begging from none of these knuckle heads, and he was right. *I didn't fall victim to none of these clowns out here. I had good grades, and no baby daddies, had plans to attend a local four-year college for fashion design. I could not imagine not being able to come home and visit often. I also couldn't imagine working a job while trying to focus on my education, so I still needed these weekend carwash sessions*, I thought.

"Thirty dollars . . . " I started laughing because he knew I couldn't do anything with that. "Now I have money to go shopping, but I don't need them asking where I got money from when I come home with bags."

"I need you to go upstairs, iron the shirt and pants that's on my bed, wait till I get out the tub, and wash the tub out for me."

"Shoot! I'll do it!" said Tonya.

"I bet you will" I said.

Tonya witnessed this just about every weekend, so she knew I was about to drop nothing but hundreds at the mall.

"Okay," I told my uncle.

I ironed his clothes; they looked like they came from the cleaners. After I was done, I went outside and walked to the corner. It was 5:00, and my grandmother should be walking down from the thirty-sixth bus stop by now. I didn't see her, but I saw my uncle Jim, coming down the street. Maybe he saw her walking down and picked her up. He turned the corner with his black Seven Series BMW.

She was in the car, and she looked tired. It was awfully hot today. He parked in front of the Mercedes that was being washed. I went over and opened the door for grandma to get out.

"Too hot out here for you, grandma, or did the patients get on your last nerve today?" I asked.

"It's a bit hot outside, but I'm fine."

I knew my grandmother. She was always energetic, and she loved walking. It was not often she'd allow my uncles to pick her up, and today she looked drained.

"I'll be fine once I get in the house and sit down," she says.

Yeah, it's probably the heat, I thought. On top of that, she was not getting any younger. She just needed to take a nice, warm bath and relax. I went back outside, waited for my uncle to finish washing his car, and took a bath so Tonya and I could leave for the mall. Uncle Jim called me over to his car. Now I felt different, thinking *oh boy, what have I done or what have somebody saw me do?*

Praying he knew nothing about me being in a black Benz last week, I said, "Hey, what's up?"

"I want you to take a ride with me. We'll only be gone for twenty minutes. Tell Tonya that you'll be right back," he said.

I did what he asked, then I hopped in the passenger seat. Twenty minutes is a long time if you have a guilty conscience. He began by asking me how was my day going, what Tonya and I had planned for today . . . the usual. My uncles were more like my brothers—very loving, caring, fun, and concerned brothers. The difference in the two was uncle Ron was fun, loving, giving, flamboyant, and exciting—he's a show off. Uncle Jim was funny, humorous, laid back, and stern.

Whatever he do for you would be earned. There was a lecture that came along with every dollar and every outing. He was a family man that thought everyone should work hard for what they get, except his wife. He can be pretty intimidating at times.

We pulled up at the back of a supermarket on Belair Road, and he parked the car. My heart was beating fast. He started off by saying, "You're growing into a nice, young lady. You know, Ron and I would do anything for you as long as you're doing what you're supposed to be doing for yourself. Respect yourself, and never let a man disrespect you. Read, learn—all that you can. Be the best at whatever it is that you're doing. I don't care if you have to start out somewhere—sweeping floors—just be good at it. It builds character. Make your momma proud of you. Momma is not gonna be around forever."

He always had these one-on-ones with me. I was just glad it wasn't about the Mercedes. He continued by saying, "Don't be a follower; be a leader. If you do something wrong—because none of us are perfect— just make sure no one else told you to do it. Believe in your heart that you can be and do whatever you want. There are no limits. You're special, Anaya. You have gifts, but you have to know that."

I was quiet, listening as I always did, taking it all in. It was best to be a listener and not a talker at times. Even though he knew I was ready to get out the car, he also knew that eventually these conversations would stick one day. He finished by saying, "Life can be hard and confusing at times. Don't let it get the best of you. You have to learn how to adapt to change and keep moving forward. When the time is right, we'll talk more."

His conversations were always different yet the same. He always made sure I understood and asked if there was anything I wanted to talk about, but me being the fast ass I was, couldn't wait to enjoy my weekend. I simply said, "Yes, I understand; and no, I have nothing I want to talk about."

On the ride back home, I wanted to ask him why grandma had been so tired lately. But I thought my own thoughts were foolish, and I was just being an opinionated, mouthy, young lady. I simply asked myself, *How would he know? She just needed a stress-free weekend of relaxation out of the heat.*

We pulled up to the house. Tonya was gone, and my uncle must be finished washing the car. As my foot hit the first step, I could smell the

Pall Mall cigarettes and hear my grandmother's nasty cough. I always made her mad by talking about those funky cigarettes, so all I said was, "Grandma, where is uncle Ron?"

"I think he just got out the tub," she said.

It was almost 6:00. I know Tonya went home, so I called her and told her I'd be around in a few. I walked upstairs and started washing the tub. As soon as I was done, my uncle came out of the room. I understood why he was getting dressed here and not at home. He was married, but he had mad bitches, its just what he did. *Handsome fly and bitches*, I thought. He came out the room, smelling like Lagerfeld with the crisp white button up shirt on that I ironed nicely. He wore plaid shorts and a pair of blue leather Docksides.

"Dag, uncle, you're looking funky, fresh-dressed to impress."

"Ready to party, money in your pocket, dying to move your body y'all—and those songs,"

"Shoot, that's Mc Lyte!" I said as I continued singing.

"Did you wash the tub?" he asked.

"Yup. I just finished. I'm about to go around Tonya's now."

"Okay, have fun."

Now he knew that I didn't wash out the tub just because I liked to. Of course, I wasn't going to ask for any money. I proceeded down the stairs to leave.

"Anaya," said uncle Ron, "here, girl, he handed me $350."

"Thank you," I said.

I loved my uncle, and he always knew how to put a smile on my face. I asked my grandmother if she needed anything before I left, she said no, so I told her I was going around Tonya's .

I turned to the corner and saw Tonya sitting on the steps, talking with her brother and a few other people. Once she saw me, she stood up.

"Are you ready?" asked Tonya.

"Yup, we're going to Towson right?" I asked. "If we go all the way to Towson, we won't have much time to be at Stanley's. Do you wanna go to Burlington in Northwood shopping center? Edward said he'll drop us off, and we can walk to their house from there," she said.

"I needed a bathing suit. I wanted to get it from the bathing suit store, Water Water. I guess we can see what they have. You're not driving around dirty, are you?" I asked Edward. Edward was cool and would split a nigga wig in a second when it came to us, but he always had a dark side that cared about nothing—not even his own life—which is what scared me about him the most.

"You know I would not have you and my baby sis riding around in a car with drugs in it," he said. We got to the shopping center, and he asked if we needed him to wait. We told him no, and that we were walking over some friend's house later.

"Well, page me if you need me, Tonya. I'm going down Eldorado's later," he said. Edward stayed at the strip clubs. It was a wonder he never mentioned seeing Jessica at all.

After walking around in Burlington for about a half an hour, I realized that I didn't see anything in this store, but key chains—as if I didn't have enough already. We accumulated so many key chains, we could knock a person out with our keys. We grabbed a few. Tonya was mad because I could always find my middle name, Lauren. We grabbed some hearts. I found one that quoted "Can't nobody love me better than me."

We always put a few in our pockets. "Klepto" was what my aunt called me. I didn't know why I stole when I always had a pocket full of money. We walked over and looked at some swim suits. Tonya was on the other side, stealing who-knows-what. I grabbed a bikini and put it in my purse. We got in line and paid for a keychain or two.

As we were leaving the store, a gentlemen grabbed my arm. "Excuse me, miss. Come with me."

All I was thinking was my dumb ass got over a stack in this mom bag. Now, I was going to jail and would be punished for the rest of the summer for stealing two-dollar key chains and a thirty-dollar bikini. I was so embarrassed. We went into this little room with a desk, two chairs, TV monitors, and a two-way mirror. The man went in saying, "I'm store security. I saw you put the swim wear in your purse. Can you take it out please?"

Hoping he knew nothing about the key chain, I took the navy blue and gold bikini from my purse. He placed it in a basket with other items that must've been confiscated from previous thieves. He then asked me to turn around and look at the camera. "I am going to take your picture. Since the theft was under one hundred dollars, I will not call the police, but your picture will be placed on the store board for thieves who are not allowed to enter this store for two years."

All I could say to myself was "Thank you, Jesus! Amen! Hallelujah!" I didn't have to come back. I was glad that he didn't ask me to take my sun glasses off. The picture was a little dark. Hopefully no one will notice it was me. Shit, I didn't even notice they had a board on the wall for thieves. I ran out that store and around the corner so fast, I didn't even see Tonya behind the wall peeping.

"Anaya, what happened? Did you escape?" said Tonya.

"No, dummy! He took the swim suit, took my picture, and let me go because the theft was under one hundred dollars. Now, give me your swim suit for making me come here instead of Towson."

"All that ass can't fit in mine, and you pay two hundred dollars for swimsuits. I don't know why you didn't just pay thirty dollars for that one," she said.

"I know better Next time, let's get away from here before they realize some key chains are missing too."

After walking and talking about the two-way mirror and how stores have cameras hiding inside the mannequins' eyes, we finally arrived at Stanley's. His brother was sitting at the back of the house on the curb with everyone, drinking coolers and smoking weed.

"What's up, everybody?" I said. "Where's Stanley?"

"Oh, he went inside the house to make a sandwich."

As I was walked around the corner to go say hi to their mother, I couldn't believe whom I saw coming my way from their house—Stanley's ex, Mia. Now, don't get me wrong If he dealt with her—so be it. Just let me know what's going on so I didn't have to stand there with my back against the wall. I didn't know if I should keep walking classy or charge this bitch and act trashy. She was with one other girl.

Ouch! The look she gave me cut like a knife. I didn't think about that girl as long as she stayed out of my way. I tapped on the screen door. Stanley's mother saw it was me and gestured to come inside.

"I was just coming in to say hi. The last time I came down, you said not to hang outside your house and not to come inside to speak, so I didn't wanna be rude. How are you doing today?" I asked.

"I'm doing fine, Anaya. I just finished telling Mia that I don't want you two fighting and carrying on out there. You're two beautiful young ladies; you need to act like it."

"I didn't have a problem with her, but I understand," I said.

"I told Mia to stop worrying about my son. You can't make a man want you," she said.

"Where is that big head boy anyway?" I asked.

"He went just went out the back."

"Okay, well, let me go outside. I'll come say goodbye before I leave."

"Okay, baby, make sure you do."

She was the sweetest. I was sure Stanley told her he had a crush on me, but knowing him, he told her not to say anything to me about it.

I got back around the corner, and everyone sat on the curb, laughing and joking. Stanley stood, telling another one of his crazy stories. Their homeboy passed me a watermelon cooler. I sat down beside Tonya and joined the party. Tonya was flirting with Stanley's brother, but he acted as if he didn't know.

I couldn't take my eyes off Stanley, standing up there, looking sexy as ever with his bowlegged self. I couldn't help but notice how the sun bounced of his shiny, wavy brown hair and made his eyes look lighter. Throughout his conversation, he would lick his juicy big lips. All I could think about was where those lips should be right now.

Why was it so hot, and why was I bothered lately? It had been almost a year—out of sight, out of mind. The last guy I was somewhat dating was so in love with me. It broke my heart when I didn't want to be with him. We had never seen a guy act like that before. We really thought he was going to harm himself. His father hated me. He refused to get a haircut—I thought he turned Islamic for a minute. Thanks to Stanley's stunt, he pulled in the hall way and got all my sexual desires doing jumping jacks. As I sat there deep in thought, Stanley grabbed me, pulling me to my feet. It was a little after seven, and the sun started to go down. It didn't get dark till slightly after eight. Everyone was laughing and tripping, not paying attention to Stanley and me. He pulled a jay from behind his ear, lit it, took a few puffs, then passed it to me. I didn't smoke that often like Tonya, but when I did, it had to be in top paper; Stanley's the same way.

After we finished smoking, I was about to sit back down.

"Anaya, can I talk to you for a second?" Stanley said.

Awe, boy. Here we go. He is begging for it, I thought. The few puffs I took had me floating. I didn't know where they get their weed from, but it was always nice and smooth. "What do you want to talk about, Stanley?"

"Anaya, I don't bite unless you want me too." He puts his arm around my neck in a buddy kind of way. We went inside the house through the back door. "Come upstairs with me. There's something I want to give you."

"Stanley, what are you doing? Go get it, and bring it down," I said. He kissed me dead in my mouth.

"Shut up, girl, and stop being stubborn," he said playfully. "Now, come on."

Whenever we kissed, I get weak in the knees. But that shit right there—that we smoked—is enticing it. He grabbed my hand, and I followed. He had a cozy athlete's kinda room; a queen size bed; and a blue, yellow, and red Nautica spread. There were football posters on the wall, but what caught my attention was the Einstein poster on his wall that reads: "Try not to become a man of success, but rather try to become a man of value."

This boy was deep, and I got turned on. He shut his bedroom door and pressed play on his stereo. All I heard was, "And who can love you like me (nobody) / Who can sex you like me (nobody) / Who can lay your body down (nobody) / Nobody, baby."

I told him how much I loved Keith Sweat, but I was hoping he didn't bring me upstairs to hear a song I had already heard. He went into his closet and pulled out this gigantic basket.

"Here you go," he said. "I got you every fragrance in Bath and Body Works because you always smell so good. I got you all the CDs of the singers you told me you liked, except Patti LaBelle because you said you just got a new one since the old one was scratched."

He didn't say 'this basket was filled with money because green was your favorite color,' but I have to admit that this was not only sweet, but it was also extremely thoughtful. He actually had me blushing. When he said every lotion, spray, and body wash, he meant it. If there was anything missing, it didn't matter; there was so much there. It had Lauryn Hill, Keith Sweat, D'Angelo, Madonna, Michael Jackson, Stacy Lattisaw, Brian McKnight, and several others.

I was impressed. I couldn't help but kiss him to say 'thank you.' But once our lips locked, it was like fireworks. He slowly leaned in, forcing my body to fall on the bed with his body pressed against mine. We rolled around on the bed, taking turns on top, kissing with so much passion. He started kissing, biting, and sucking harder on my neck.

"Stop! I don't want any marks on my neck," I said, but I had no self-control. He took off my top and started sucking my erect, hard nipples.

He asked, "Can you do me a favor? I want to tie your hands to my headboard."

I was nervous to say *yes*, but too hot and turned on to say *no*. I loved it when a man dominated me.

"Yes," I whispered.

He tied my wrist to his bed. He started kissing my navel while taking my skirt off. "I've been waiting for this for so long, Anaya," he mumbled as he kissed my inner thighs, licking behind my knees. Once my skirt was off, I was completely naked. He came up to me, kissed me deeply again while placing his wet lips on my ear. He whispered, "I want you to relax, okay? Because now, I want to taste your cum."

I didn't think I'd ever been this wet before. He continued to kiss around me, biting and kissing my inner thighs until he finally gave me one nice lick. *This was completely different from the one in the school hallway,* I thought. My eyes were shut, and I saw stars. He licked, sucked, blew, and nibbled until I had multiple orgasms. I wanted to push him away, but my hands were tied. I squeezed my thick legs around his head, but that didn't stop him.

"Oh my gosh. It's about to happen again," I told him, but he stopped and untied me before I could. I laid there, looking lifeless and confused as I watched him walk over to his dresser and open his drawer. He pulled out a black and gold condom wrapper.

"Do you want to cum again?" he said. I shook my head yes.

"I can't hear you," he said.

Getting turned on all over again, I opened my mouth and said, "Yes."

He took his shirt off. *Wow, what a body!* I wanted to wrap my arms around him and rub my hands up and down his muscular back badly. He took his shorts and boxers off; my eyes were amazed. I couldn't believe it.

He said, "Keep calm. You're about to feel something really long, thick, and hard."

I bit my lip and moaned nervously. He kneeled on top of my body, kissing me while rubbing his finger up and down and around my extremely wet vagina. He finally pushed himself inside me. They were nice, long, deep, and thrustful strokes. I bit on his bottom lip to keep me from screaming. It felt so good. I never wanted it to end.

Then, he stopped. I thought, *no, don't stop!* I looked at the clock. It had been almost twenty minutes. He must've came and didn't want to say anything. I hoped not because once I start, I'm like a vampire—I'll drain you of all your semen.

He slipped his shorts back on and left the room without saying anything. I lied there, clueless, thinking if I needed to wash up so I could get dressed. He came back with a tall glass of ice water.

"Here, drink some," he said. He must've read my mind. I had my mouth open from all that pleasure that it became so dry like I had no saliva left. I drank some water; then, he sat the glass on the night stand. He kissed me and said, "Oh, you're gonna be mine" right before thrashing his manhood back inside. He was making more noise than I was. I wanted all the control, but he wouldn't let me get on top, so I moved my pelvis around in a circular motion. He bit my neck so hard, I could've thought he drew blood. He cuffed my body nice and tight followed by *I love you*. It felt like he released all of what he had. He laid on top of me, still squeezing my body tight.

I hated to interrupt this love connection, but I tapped his shoulder and cleared my throat. He had no response. I knew my pussy was addictive, but deadly, no.

"Stanley!" I said a little louder than usual.

"Yeah," he finally answered as if he was in the middle of a good night sleep.

"Roll over."

"Why, where you going?" he asked as he rolled over.

"I needed to use the bathroom, wash up, and get dressed."

It was 9:00, and I was surprised Tonya or anyone hadn't come looking for us. They liked the idea of Stanley and I being together—I guess, the way we played around and joked so much. They were probably thinking—*it was about time*. I slipped my clothes on. He never took my tennis off. It was kinda sexy being naked, looking at my huaraches while he had my legs in the air.

After leaving the bathroom from washing, I went back in the room to slide on my panties and get my purse from where he had placed the condom on a paper towel. It had been a while for him. He dosed off, so I let him stay asleep. As I walked to open the bedroom door, Stanley grabbed me from behind and started biting my neck and caressing my breasts. He turned me around and stuck his tongue in my mouth before

I got to say anything, kissing me while he walked backward toward his bed. He was rock hard, and this nigga already had a condom on.

He planned this, I thought. He turned me over as if I weighed eighty pounds, positioning me on my knees. He flipped my skirt up and moved my string of my thongs to the side. He stuck his big dick so far in me that it felt like it was in my stomach. He gave long, deep, and quick strokes.

"You were trying to leave this dick. I didn't say we were finished!" he said.

It felt so good that I couldn't say a word. All I could do was bite my own arm while my eyes rolled back in my head. Every time I would get wet from too many orgasms, he would go down, lick me clean, shove it right back in. By the time we were finished, his alarm clock said it was already 9:45.

We both lied there for a while. A little after 10:00, I got up to look for my panties, which were laying on the floor. As I put them back on, he asked if I was ready. I shook my head. He gestured that I get back to bed. I looked with a shocked look on my face, thought he was asking if I was ready to go. I liked the fact of knowing that he could go as long as I could, but it was getting late.

"If I said yes, I'll be here fooling with you all night."

"But you were amazing."

"I do need to wash up. I can't go home smelling like sex."

"Would you like to take a shower?" he asked.

"Where are your parents?" I said.

"They went to their friend's house and played cards at seven thirty."

"Oh, okay."

He grabbed me a towel and started the water. I grabbed a body wash out of the basket, took my clothes off, and hopped in the shower. While washing, I heard a knock on the door.

"Can I come in Anaya?" Stanley asked.

"Sure."

He opened the door, wearing nothing but a big dick and a condom. I pinched myself because I had to be dreaming.

"Can I get in the shower, Anaya?" he said.

I couldn't believe this, but I said yes. He had me climbing up the bathroom wall as he tasted me. He then lifted my right leg up and squatted low so he could enter me. Some of my hair got wet, but I didn't care. It felt so good in the shower. Now, I didn't wanna leave. Afterward, I called home, said that I sat outside with friends, and asked if it was okay for me to stay a while longer.

"Okay, Anaya. You're getting older. Just don't go too far," my mother said.

"Can you call grandma, and let her know I'm staying at your house? I don't wanna worry her. She's been tired, and I know she'll be falling asleep soon."

"Okay," said my mother.

After we were done, I applied lotion and slipped on a pair of Stanley's shorts.

"All these years, you finally gave me some," he said.

"I had fun," I said.

"Did you?"

"I did."

"So when are you coming back so we can have another night like this?"

"Not sure. Haven't you had enough of me for one night Stanley?" I asked, smiling inside because I already knew the answer to that.

"Anaya, I could have sex with you every day. I haven't ran into a female yet that kept me hard this long and had sex back to back. Look at what you did to me," he said.

"Wow. I can't believe you're rock hard."

He kissed me on my lips.

"You gonna have to stop kissing me like that. Come on, let's go see if everyone is still outside," I said.

He grabbed my basket and called a cab once we were downstairs. I walked outside and saw that everybody was still there, sitting on the front steps and talking shit. They looked at me and started clapping. I was guilty as charged. There was no way I could lie. We had been literally fucking our brains out for over three hours.

"Whatever. Y'all so crazy," I said.

Stanley came out a couple minutes after. He was glowing like a kid that just came from the candy store. You could look at his face and see how happy he was. We stayed outside, laughing and joking until the cab came. Stanley opened the cab door as Tonya and I got inside. He wanted a kiss, but I wouldn't let him. He gave me my basket and money for the cab and asked me to call him once I got home."

"So how was it?" Tonya asked.

"How was what?" I said, smiling.

"Don't play! I was watching when y'all crept at 7:30. It's now 11:30, and you just came out," Tonya said.

"Girl, I was up there smelling all these different scents of lotion. It's—"

But before I could finish, Tonya screamed, "I want details!"

"Okay, okay," I said. "Tonya, he was so gentle yet so rough. He dedicated his time to every body part. We had sex twice for hours, and just when I thought we were done, we had sex in the shower. If I would've stayed, we would be having sexual intercourse all night, but I had to go."

"Damn! What did he do? Purchased the entire bath and body works collection?" Tonya said as she took a few out for herself.

I got out the cab at my grandmother's so I could check on her. Tonya sat on the step while I went inside. The front door was open. I was surprised to see her sitting downstairs on her favorite chair. She had dosed of watching TV until she heard the screen door open.

"Where is everybody?" I asked.

"Everybody has gone home. Nathan went with his mother. Your mother just left, said she was going back down the house to play cards, I think."

"Oh, okay."

"Where did you come from?" She asked.

"Over some friends house with Tonya. She's at the front, sitting on the steps."

"Don't be out walking those streets at night, Tonya," she said.

"I'm not grandma. We caught a cab back," I said. "Anything I can get you?"

"Yeah, you can get me a pickle out the fridge," she said. She always talked about how sour pickles were and how they gave her lock jar, but she liked eating them anyway. I went upstairs, slipped on a long maxi dress with flip flops, grabbed a V8 and two oranges; one was for Tonya.

"Grandma, I'm going down my mother's." It was almost 12:00, but as long as I checked in and stayed in the area, she didn't mind.

We walked into my mother's house. She got her new boyfriend and her old boyfriend, sitting around the table with my godmother and the rest of their friends playing cards. It was so confusing, but my step dad probably so doped out his mind right now- He didn't care what was going on. They didn't really have a relationship. She was more like his bank and his baby mother he can steal from so he could sell it or swap it. Whatever it was that he did to get his next fix. I found him balled up under the sink in our bathroom one day. He had overdosed. If it weren't for my mother and I, placing him in a cold shower and calling 911, he would be food for a legless larvae. I still loved him like a father because he was fun to be around and he always cooked because lord knows that my mother couldn't, but my grandmother never liked him. She said he came out of the army as a disrespectful drunk, telling my mother "fuck you, suck my dick bitch," shooting dope, and staying out for days getting high.

We went and spoke to everyone and as usual. They got their drugs of choice. Forty ounces of millers, boones farm, E&J, and a bottle of crown royal. I looked in the fridge, but there wasn't much in there—hot dogs, Bologna, potatoes, eggs, cheese, milk, and a jug of juice that said "Orange drink"

"See y'all later," I said.

"Where are you going at this time of night?" my mother said.

This particular night, I didn't feel like bringing back chicken boxes or sukiyaki subs from the carry out, so I simply said, "Down the street" as we left.

"Be careful out there this time of night, and don't be out too late."

"Okay, Ma."

As we walked home, I realized that I forgot to check my pager. There were three missed pages. One was from Jessica; she called twice from her mother's. I forgot that she wanted us to come down Eldorado's. The other number didn't look familiar. I'd call it back from the phone booth once we got on Harford Road.

As soon as we turned the corner, you would think it was a block party. You could tell it was the weekend, and it was hot outside. I walked over and used the phone booth. Tonya ordered for me.

"Three wings, salt, pepper, ketchup, and hot sauce," I said.

I dialed the number. It was a pager, so I left the number to the phone booth I was on. As soon as I walked away, the phone rang. This guy I knew answered it.

"Anaya, did you page somebody?" he said.

I walked back and grabbed the phone. "Hello?"

"Yeah, this is Pop. Somebody paged this number?"

If there wasn't so much noise in the background, he would have heard the guy call me by my name to get the phone. "Hey, Pop. What's up?

"Is this Anaya?"

"Yeah, that's my man pager."

"People were on this phone all day."

"All day . . . why didn't you just call me from your house?" I asked.

"I've been out here, watching my money all day, so I left a pager number for you to page. That way, I would know when you called."

The warning signs were screaming out at me, telling me to stay away from this guy and that he was not the one for me. But I was greedy and hardheaded, I did not even listen to my own thoughts. I did exactly the opposite.

"So how was your day?" he asked.

"I had a lovely day," I replied.

"What made it so lovely?"

"I just hang out with my girls. We did a little shopping."

"Oh, yeah! What did you get me?" he said.

"I didn't know I was supposed to get you anything."

"I was just joking. Why you gotta be so evil?" he asked.

"I'm not being evil . . . just being honest."

"Well, your day's gonna be even better after I pick you up tomorrow."

I forgot that I told him I would hang out with him tomorrow, but after the night I had, all I wanted to do was relax. Besides, he wouldn't be picking me up anyway.

"Well, I'm at the carry out and my food is ready. I'll give you a call tomorrow."

We walked back down to Tonya's house. I sat on the steps and ate my food while she got the house phone and brought it outside. I told her to call Jessica and made sure she was okay. Between that boyfriend of hers and that job she recently started, we hardly see her anymore. She didn't even invite us over her house anymore.

"And remember when we all went shopping out Towson instead of letting the cab drop her off home on Lock Raven which was closer? She came down with us and got picked up from her aunt's house."

"You know she acts nonchalant every time she gets a new boo," Tonya said.

"I don't know, Tonya. This time, it feels weird. You know I have the psychic intuition, and things don't look right in my crystal ball." We both started laughing.

CHAPTER 5

Is It Love

Jessica

"SORRY, I'M RUNNING late, George. I'm headed to the dressing room now," I said.

"Well, you need to hurry up. Edward paid me to let you work here, and he is out there waiting," George said.

"He's my boyfriend, George." I said.

"Yeah, yours and everybody else's. If he didn't pay me up front, you wouldn't be here. Don't make me feel like I'm wasting my time with you, Jessica. My time is money," George said.

I didn't know why he was complaining. Edward paid him, and his fat, nasty white ass still took a cut of my money when I started over a month ago. I bet if I was one of those white snow bunnies, he had running around he wouldn't say that. I'm tired of working here. I'm the only black girl, and he's been picking on me since I started. I normally work at Eldorado's on Fridays, but Edward said he didn't like the way all the black guys gave me too much attention. I didn't understand. I didn't need coke to relax there, and these white guys gave me just as much attention—if not, more. I tried calling Anaya and Tonya to tell them I wouldn't be dancing tonight. Edward told me not to tell anyone about us yet. He didn't want my friends to become jealous of me.

I changed into my pink bunny outfit. It already had all the private areas out. This way, I could be revealing but still sexy. The only thing

I'd be taking off was my top. I knew how white guys loved women with big breasts. That was why I faced forward most of the time when giving them a lap dance.

My stage name was *Strawberry*. Edward gave me that name. He said I was his chocolate covered strawberry—dark and sweet on the outside, and sweet and juicy on the inside. It was a full house tonight. Edward always sat by himself, but who was that light-skinned, fine-looking man that he was talking with?

I had never seen him before, I thought. Edward already gave me a line, so I took one more shot of Jack Daniels, and I was up next.

"We have fresh meat tonight, gentlemen. She's only been here for a month, but this is her first Friday. She has a body in all the right places. She's chocolate, she's sweet. Get y'all money together for the Chocolate covered . . . Strawberry!"

I entered the stage feeling like a superstar as I danced my favorite song "It's like candy / I can feel it when you walk / Even when you talk it takes over me." My hair grazed my hips as I worked that pole and dropped it down to a split. I closed out all the thoughts in my mind and imagined nothing but me, bouncing up and down on Edward's dick. I took my top off and swung it out into the crowd. These white truckers were loving my breasts. The entire crowd began to go wild. There was money everywhere. I saw my favorite white guy; he'd been coming to tip me nice regularly. He had a bottle of champagne at his table. He always sat close to the stage. I crawled toward him, rolled to my back, then proceeded to spread my legs wide, making them bounce as my outer thighs tapped the stage floor. He told me once during a lap dance that he admired how flexible my body was. As I slid my body closer to his face, he put a roll of money in my strap as he rubbed his finger down my pussy, which was not allowed, but he was the sweetest so I didn't mind. I then closed my legs as I rolled over to my knees, backing it up, giving him a little ass action. I stood to my feet and finished my routine. Once I was done, I picked up my cash, headed to the back to count, and wiped off so I could go out and make my rounds.

Thanks to my white regular for giving me one thousand stack, I made $1880 just on stage. I hadn't even did any lap dances yet. Tonight would be a good night, thanks to my Edward. The only way one could make this type of money at Eldorado's was if a football player or someone rich was in the building and picked you over the other girls who were hungry for money. On a night like tonight, I should be able to bring home over three grand easily. Being a newbie plus black had advantages white men could have their fairytale that would embarrass them in their real world.

After I freshened up, I headed straight over to my regular and gave him the first lap dance. He sat on a table and pulled me a half glass of champagne. I drank it as I climbed on top. He wanted to play with my breasts, but that was against the rules unless he paid for a private session in one of the four small private rooms. I allowed him to rub my thighs since no one could see under the table in the dark. He slid his fingers into my pussy as I went up and down, grinding as if it was a regular lap dance. The coke helped me get loose and made me feel at ease. He played with me until I came, then he slipped another roll of money into my strap. I kissed him on his forehead and proceeded to the next.

"Jessica." I heard Edward calling my name. I turned around, and he motioned for me to come where he was. Now he knew I would always go over to him after I finish my rounds. I met Edward in the strip club, so he already knew the routine.

"Yes, Edward."

"I want to introduce you to my man, Sean," he said.

"Pleased to meet you, Jessica. Ed told me quite a bit about you," Sean said, "but he didn't say you were beautiful."

What? I didn't understand why he said that in front of my man, but I didn't have time for that right now.

"Edward, I need to finish working. Nice meeting you," I said as I turned to walk away.

Edward grabbed my arm. "Baby, do me a favor," he said.

"Yes, Edward." I loved it when he called me baby, but he never said it in front of anyone. "Give Sean a lap dance for me?"

"What? Come on, Edward. Stop playing. You said you don't like it when I give dances to the guys you know. That's why I'm working here or at least trying to if you let me."

"I know baby, but he's from New York. He doesn't know anyone here," Edward said. "See if you let me tell your sister and Anaya about us, I could introduce him to Anaya. I bet he would love her, and he looks like her type."

"No, Jessica! And don't make me say it again. Now is not the time!" Edward snapped.

I started to wonder if there would ever be a good time. I turned around to give Sean a lap dance, but Edward stopped me. He looked over at George fat ass and gave him a signal.

"Baby, I want you to be comfortable. Since I pay George to keep you safe, he set up the champagne room for me."

What damn champagne room? I thought.

"Go on, baby. George will show you where it is. I'm coming right behind you. Love you, baby," Edward said.

"I love you too. You owe me, Edward, because you're messing up my money."

Before I got my words completely out, Sean threw a knot of money wrapped in a rubber band at me.

"This should cover you for the night," Sean said.

"Well, thank you," I said to Sean who looked like the Puerto Rican guy from *21 Jump Street*. I told George to wait while I ran in my dressing room to put my money away. My regular slipped another $600 in my strap, and Puerto Rican threw me two thousand dollars. He was right, it covered me all right. I made a total of $3880. Now, Mr. Sexy knew how to pay to play—but for a lap dance . . . really? Well, Edward was kind, gentle, and giving, and so was his friends.

George walked me back to the big double doors that were always locked. I assumed it was an office. I walked in the room, and it was lit up with red lights. There was champagne inside of an ice bucket with a glass already poured, which I knew was for me. There were small metal ashtrays on all the glass tables. Just how much did Edward pay Mr. Piggy? *That's my boo. I love him, and I can't wait to become his wife*, I thought.

I sat down on the white leather sofa as I put down the glass of champagne. The doors opened as my bald head chocolate drop walked in. He had to duck so he wouldn't hit his head on the entry way. I hopped and greeted him at the door with a hug and a kiss. Damn that was some good champagne, I was floating already. Edward and Sean came over to the sofas and lined some coke in the metal ashtray-looking objects.

"Oh, that's what those little silver-looking straws are for beside the trays," I said as they both snorted a line right from the tray.

I positioned myself to give Sean a lap dance. Edward pulled me another glass of champagne, stuck his finger in it, rubbed his finger in the coke, and told me to suck it.

"Now drink," he said.

Wow, now that was a rush. I felt extra sexy and horny. I had never seen this side of Edward before so demanding. Sean started to suck on my nipples. I couldn't believe what was happening, but my body felt so good, I couldn't stop him. Sean lifted me off his lap and sat me on the sofa. He took all his clothes off and stuck his dick in my champagne. He took a blue top of a clear capsule, sprinkled some white powder on the top of his dick, and pulled my head closer.

"Here, Jessica, lick it." Sean said. After I licked all the substance off, he made me suck it. I almost threw up a few times. He made me get to my knees facing Edward where he had one foot in the chair and the other on the floor. He had more coke on his dick. He pushed my head down and made me suck it. Edward wiped the tears that were rolling down my face.

"This is why I love you, girl," Edward said. "Suck this dick, my little coke head. Yeah! Suck it! Suck it! You like that, don't you? You've been a nasty little girl. You didn't think I saw that white man playing with your pussy during his lap dance, did you? He seems to be getting special treatment around here so . . . So should my man. Now spread those legs apart."

Sean licked his finger, sprinkled some coke on it, and stuck it in my ass. It was painful for a split second, I was so numb from all the coke they had been feeding me, I could barely feel anything. I felt high confused and ashamed. I only knew Sean's dick was inside me because with every pump, Edward's dick would go deeper down my throat. Tears rolled down my face.

"Yeah, my little coke head cry baby. I know you like sucking your man's dick," Edward said. "Now drink it, drink it."

My tongue was so numb, I couldn't taste it. I only felt the warm cum going down my throat. Once he was done, he pulled out then signaled Sean. "Come on, your turn. Feed her yo!"

Afterward, Edward cleaned me up and made me drink a glass full of water. I couldn't believe what just happened. *Was I dreaming?* I thought as I lied on the sofa and passed out.

CHAPTER 6

Who Baby

Anaya

THIS WEEKEND HAD been busy. I loved Sunday mornings. I got to lie in bed until noon. *What a beautiful day!* I thought as I lied in bed and tried to gaze at the sky, which the bright sun was covering. "Grandma!" I yelled, but there was no response. "Grandma!"

"What, girl?"

"Nothing!" I yelled back. I just liked to call her name. Knowing she was there made me feel good. I put my slippers on and went in the bathroom to get myself together. I heard my mother downstairs. I loved it when everyone was present. Most of the time, my mother came first since she lived directly down the street. As I walked in our little kitchen, I saw my grandmother sitting in her favorite yellow chair with metal arms, The chair was only about three feet away from the stove which had pancakes and bacon sitting on a plate.

"Do you want an egg?" My grandmother asked.

"No, I can just eat what's already here." I didn't like scrambled or the eggs with the yolk running out, and I didn't feel like waiting for any eggs to boil. My mother came in from sweeping the berries that constantly fell from the tree. I hated it when she'd do that. She always had to be cleaning, pushing, moving, or pulling on something.

"Oh! The princess has awaken," she said sarcastically. "Who do you think you is?"

I wanted to say, "No, it's 'who do you think you are, mother,' but I didn't feel like it.

"You think you're god's gift to the world. You think everybody owes you something. It's one o' clock in the afternoon, and you're just coming down to eat breakfast—oh, I'm sorry you call it brunch. You're supposed to wake up in the morning and do chores. There's more to life than just school and shopping, Anaya. You need a job," my mother said.

She was really on a war path today, I thought.

"Now, Linda, just wait. Why are you always picking on that girl? All she needs to focus on right now is her school work. This is my damn house. Leave her alone, and focus on that bad ass son of yours," my grandmother said.

Before my uncle Ron had a car, he would walk and get me wherever my mom and dad lived at the time. I finally came to stay. When I was nine, my father would argue and fight with my mother constantly. My uncle nor did my mother want me around all the abuse. Their father did the same to my grandmother; therefore, they knew what it felt like to go through it. But it was too late—I remembered *everything*. I saw the woman my father brought in the house whether my mother was there or not; I heard the way he called her 'whore' and 'bitch' even though she went nowhere and didn't have many friends; and if he wasn't locking her out for going outside, he was locking her inside and taking the phone cord along with him. His father treated his mother that way, and he did the same to mine. What I did not understand was why she waited long to get a divorce and leave. I told myself that I would never be happy and stay with a man because of kids.

I paid my mother no attention when she said things like that. I was too excited that my uncle brought me my own cordless phone with caller ID last night. He charged it, but he didn't connect the phone cord. After I hooked that in, I took the phone off the charger and went to walk outside.

My grandmother yelled, "Some boy called for you three times. I told him you were asleep, and he called again. Tell that boy to stop calling so much."

"Okay, grandma. I'll tell him," I said. I went upstairs and grabbed my pager and my food and sat outside on the steps. Stanley paged me three times, so I knew it was him. The other number must be Pop. It looked like the house number he gave me. Although I didn't want him to have my house number, he didn't seem like the type that would call if I didn't want him too.

The phone rang three times. I was about to hang up until someone answered. It was a little girl. *I don't know who's number this is*, I thought. *I was not about to have a conversation on the phone with a baby who paged me.*

Just when I was about to hang up a guy said, "Hello."

"Hello, did someone page Anaya from here?"

"What's up, Anaya? Hold on."

"Pop, Anaya on the phone."

"Hello."

"Hey, Pop what's up? I thought I had the wrong number so I was about to hang up. I thought someone paged the wrong number when a little girl answered."

"Oh, no. That was my daughter," Pop said.

My heart began to beat fast.

"Hello . . . Anaya?"

"Umm . . . I'm sorry . . . Did you say *daughter*?"

"Yeah, she's three."

"Don't you think that's something you should tell a person when you first meet them? Something like . . . 'Hi, my name is Pop. I have a daughter'?"

"Yeah, you're right, but you said you didn't want to deal with a guy that had a baby mother."

"You should've told me that first, Pop! That was supposed to be my choice to decide if I wanted a second date with you or not," I said.

"Anaya, don't be mad. You will love her, and you don't have to worry. I don't have any issues with her mother."

"Pop what happened at the night you said that you wanted to be honest with me and you'd tell me everything? I want us to be honest about everything!"

"That was for me to be honest not you, right—"

"Yeah, I thought so," I said, cutting him off before he could answer.

"No, Anaya. I meant it," he said. "That's why I wanted you to come over on Friday. I knew once you meet her, you wouldn't be able to get mad."

"Really, Pop? That's not something you surprise someone with. 'Hey, Anaya, I have you a gift a pair of shoes and a daughter!' I'm only seventeen. I don't think I'm ready to be a parent right now. I'll call you back a little later, okay?"

"Anaya, don't. Don't act like—"

I hung up. I couldn't believe I liked this guy, but he had a daughter all along. Maybe she wouldn't be in the way . . . No, I don't like kids. Maybe he didn't get her that often. It seemed like he had enough money for the both of us. *How much money would she need? She's only three*, I thought. If he was capable of hiding a daughter, what else could he hide? All these thoughts went through my head. If I didn't like him, this decision wouldn't be difficult.

My phone rang. I had to read the directions so I could hook the caller ID up.

"Hello. Can I speak to Anaya?"

"What is it, Pop?"

"Anaya, please don't hang up? I'm sorry I didn't tell you. It's just that I really like you, and I didn't want 'having a baby mother' to be my first impression. It would've been easy for you to walk away if you knew nothing else about me."

Son of a bitch, I thought. He was right because it worked.

"Won't you come down here today, give her a chance before you call it quits? You can leave whenever you want, and if you would like to stay, maybe the three of us can go shopping."

Damn. He was good. He thought he knew how to get me already. I never let a man feel as though he knew my next move. In the game of chess you always protect the queen.

"Not today, Pop, but I'll call you. Please don't call this number back. I just needed some time to think," I said.

"Okay make sure—"

I hung up before I let him finish. My mother was bugging. Pop wanted me to play house. What was next?

My phone rang again.

"Boy!" I screamed.

"Anaya."

"Who is this?"

"Stanley," he answered. I couldn't believe that after calling three times, he didn't wait for me to call him back.

"My grandmother is going to kill us both if you don't stop calling like this."

"My apologies. You didn't call me last night, and I was trying to catch you before you made plans because I wanted us to hang out today."

"Stanley, I can't lie. Sex with you last night still make my legs shake when I think about it. And now that I know it's like that, I can have sex with you often, but I know it wouldn't be anything else but . . . I was digging the friendship we had. First, you showed me your daredevil side and ate me out in the hallway," I whispered, "then you gave me the most appreciated gift ever. To top that off, we had amazing sex."

"Okay, everything you said was positive, so what's the problem again?" Stanley said.

"Absolutely nothing. There is no problem for me. I just don't think you can handle us hanging out, being cool, and fucking all at the same time. And the last thing I want to do is hurt a friend."

"You never really put it like that, Anaya. I always thought I would be a man, and go after what I want. Okay, I'm cool with us being friends," he said.

"So no more sex, just friends?" I asked.

"I didn't say all that, Anaya. You never know . . . maybe it will lead to more," he said.

"Stanley!"

"I'm just joking. Won't you come over? We can hang out with my brother and them, if that'll make you comfortable. Bring Tonya with you if you want. I just like hanging with you," Stanley said.

"I think Tonya is going somewhere with her mother. I might come with Jessica, but let me get myself together and put some clothes on," I said as we hung up the phone. I was actually glad he called. That way, I had something to do instead of thinking about calling Pop back and playing "step mom" at the mall.

I looked at the time. It was a little unusual that Jessica hadn't called, not even to throw in our face about how much money she made, how many ballers were down Eldorado's, and so on. We should've been there as her friend and checked out how good she was in action. I still didn't get why she wanted to shake her ass for money in front of a bunch of strangers. I knew her father left her mother for another woman and moved to Atlanta over a year ago, but her mother made good money working at social security. She took really good care of Jessica, especially since she's the youngest, and her brother has been in jail for the last five years.

I knew that I worry a little too much about my friends, but crazy things do happen. Most of the time it was by people you knew. It didn't matter better being an "exotic dancer" as she liked to call it. The last time I checked, sliding your naked ass down an infested metal pole wasn't under the word *dancer* in the dictionary. Besides, I was sure there was one guy that looked at throwing his money on a stage as a pussy investment. Let me see if Tonya was back yet and if she talked to Jess.

I called Tonya, and her mother answered on the first ring.

"Hello, Mathew's residence," she said in her southern accent. This woman had to be the phoniest person ever.

"Good afternoon, Ms. Diane, can I speak to Tonya?" I waited for her to tell me that she putting taw on the roof next.

"Hi, Anaya. Tonya is asleep. I think, she came down with that flu that's going around—"

"I have it, Ma!" Tonya said. Her mother hung up.

"Are you, okay Tonya? I didn't hear about your flu," I said.

"Girl, you know my mother is lying and making up shit."

"What you say you were doing today?" I asked.

"I'm supposed to be driving up south Carolina with my mother. We been calling his black ass all morning. I told my mother that I haven't talked to him since he dropped us off at the shopping center yesterday. Did he say who he would be with or where he was going?" she asked.

"No, he just said he was going down the strip club later," I told her. "He would be out there messing with all them chicken heads, but not one of them have their own place."

"And normally, her perfect child is here on a Sunday by the time she wakes up. Girl, ain't no telling where Edward's wild ass at, but speaking of strip clubs, have you talked to Jessica?"

"Nope, she hasn't called me all day today."

"Yeah, she hasn't called me either."

"Okay, we'll go ahead and find Edward. I'm about to call Jessica house."

"Okay."

"Okay, bye."

Okay she's not at her aunts. *Something doesn't seem right*, I thought as I called her at her mother's.

"Hello," some guy answered the phone. "Can I speak to Jessica?"

"Jessica is not here. She left with her mother earlier. May I ask who's calling?" the guy said as he started laughing.

What was he laughing about? Was this the mystery boyfriend she claimed to love her so much that she'd introduce him when the 'time is right'? Or maybe, her mother got a new boo. "Let her know that Anaya called. Make sure she calls me back, please."

He hung the phone up. *So rude*, I thought.

I went upstairs and figured out my ensemble for the day. *It was a tough job, but someone had got to do it*, I smiled and thought to myself. I loved smelling good and playing dress up. That was the best part of my day aside from seeing my grandmother home on the weekend. I had this long black tank top dress that was fitted up top and began to flare out at the waist, sleeveless half jeans jacket from express, and black penny loafers. I dazzled it up with my fourteen-karat gold accessories. I unwrapped my hair and put a French braid on the side. That way, both my earrings would show. I had big hoops in the first hole and smaller ones in the second. I put on a watch and grabbed a clutch, sprayed on some lemongrass body spray from Stanley's collection, then rubbed it in with the lotion to make the smell hold. I lifted my dress up to give my panties and ass one last spritz.

As I walked in the kitchen, I saw my grandmother lying her head down on the table and my mother rubbing her back.

"What's wrong grandma?"

She raised her head, trying to be strong for me as if everything was okay.

"I'm all right. I just need a glass of water. Can you grab me some water, Anaya?"

"Sure, grandma," I responded.

"Maybe she should go to the hospital, Ma."

"Grandma is just fine. There's a lot of heat out there, and you know she likes to turn her air conditioning on at the last minute," my mother said.

She was right. Grandma would sit in the kitchen, sweating, adding, and subtracting to come up with one lottery number to play.

"She could at least open up the back door to get some air in here," I said. "Maybe she still should go to the hospital. She could be having a heat stroke, but she hadn't been outside since yesterday. What were they not telling me? I knew my mother. The way she was answering and looking at me. She was holding something back, it was hard for her to keep a secret, so it must be something serious.

"No, really, I'm fine. I think it was the lunch meat sandwich I brought home from work. I ate it yesterday. It must've been bad."

"Just a little food poisoning, is it?"

"Let me lie down. Can you bring me a glass of warm coke, Anaya? That should ease my stomach," she said.

I called Stanley and told him I would call him in about an hour. I wanted to sit with my grandmother for a while in case she needed me to do anything because she was not feeling well.

About half an hour later, I went and checked on her. She said she felt much better. She just stayed in bed and watched some TV. She seemed perfectly fine now. That coke must've really helped. I was going to stay home and watch some TV with her until she said, "I'm not turning of no MacGyver."

There were three more episodes coming on back to back. I had no idea why she was interested in this white men running around saving the world with as little as a paper clip, but what I did know was that I wasn't about to lie there and watch it. Valley of the Dolls came on next Sunday.

"You can watch it with me," she said, "if you could keep your *hyne ponce* still."

I started laughing every time she used one of her old-country-back-in-the-day granny phrases. "Okay, grandma." I can manage to keep my butt still. I gave her a kiss and asked if she needed anything for the last time; then, I went downstairs and left her to dose on and off while MacGyver watched her. As I went into the kitchen to let my mother know that the soda I gave grandma earlier helped, I heard a lot of commotion going on from the back of the house on the next block. I walked out front to the corner and saw Tank, standing in the corner of Garret Avenue. He lived around the corner and was a good friend of ours. He was one of the guys getting money in the area. He always had a crush on me, but after trying so long and getting nowhere, I became more like a little sister. He was one of the many who referred to my grandmother as 'grandma.'

I walked to the top of the hill and as usual, Tank was picking with the same boy with the deformity, his arms were almost longer than his body. The boy was cool with all of us. They both were jokesters, but

Tank went in hard when he joked, so you could tell that Tank's jokes were getting to him.

"Leave him alone, Tank," I said.

"You're my nigga. You know that I'm just be fucking with your ugly ass. Give me a handshake," Tank said. He finally stopped teasing. The boy went home from embarrassment.

I stayed and talked for a while. Everyone kept joking, saying the next time he gone just squeeze all the life from Tank with his long arms, they just started laughing but I didn't think it was funny- even though he was a sweet heart and wouldn't hurt a fly.…. people do crazy things when embarrassed in front of people! "See y'all later, and Tank, leave that boy alone."

"Y'all don't say that when he be cracking jokes on everybody else, but once it was done to him—"

"Leave that boy alone."

"Yeah, you're right."

"Well, I'll catch up with y'all later."

"What, your boyfriend with the land cruiser is coming to get you?"

"No! Tank!" I said as I was walked down the hill. As I turned to the corner, I heard everybody laughing. The boy walked up the hill with a tan trench coat on even though it was hot outside. *Poor boy*, I thought. As I put one foot on my step, I heard the loudest bang I ever heard. I ran to the corner and saw the boy running back down the street. I ran back up the hill and couldn't believe what I saw.

They said he had a shot gun, and it lifted Tank off his feet. Tank was lying on his back in the gutter in a puddle of blood with his arm resting on the side walk. He had a hole in his chest the size of a golf ball. I kneeled down beside him, held his hand, and told him not to talk, thinking he was losing way too much blood.

The police finally arrived and asked us to clear the area and step back. They asked us his name, age, and where he lived. They then kneeled down to Tank. "Who did this to you? What's the person name who did this to you? Where does he live? Can you give us a description?" the officer asked.

"Leave him alone! Can't you see he can't talk?" I screamed.

Tank lost so much blood that every time he tried to speak, he would gurgle blood as it poured out of his mouth. The officer paid us no attention. They questioned him until his eyes were closed, and he was gone.

The officer came over to us and said, "It would have helped if we could have gotten something from him. Sorry, we knew he wasn't going to make it." They finally began to ask the people in the crowd. They got the answers they needed, and the boy was shortly arrested. My family and I couldn't believe what had just happen.

"It was just so sad that it had to result to this," I told my mother as tears came down her face. Even though my grandmother didn't like the kind of business Tank conducted, he was respectful, and she liked him as a person, but she didn't cry. I couldn't recall ever seeing her cry.

It was 5:00, and I thought I needed to relieve some stress. What should my stress reliever be . . . shopping with Pop or sex with Stanley? I didn't want to run into the arms of Pop after the stunt he pulled. What if we started a relationship later. I didn't want him to think that as long as he gave me money, I forgave him. I decided to hang out and have some stress-relieving sex with Stanley.

Tonya needed to know what happened to Tank earlier. I called and checked if they ever left to go down South. I called, and Tonya answered.

"Oh you still here? Edward never came home?" I asked.

"He did, but my mother was too upset and didn't want to take the drive, so we just got back from my aunts."

"What happened around there? I heard somebody got shot, but didn't hear who."

"I'm on my way. I'll tell you once I get there."

She wouldn't believe this. She really loved Tank. I met him from being around her house. He lived right up the street from her since a child. I got to her house and told her that it was Tank.

"Well, what hospital are they taking him to?!" she screamed.

"I was right there, holding his hand. He died on the scene, Tonya."

She almost fainted. It made me cry all over again. We sat there for almost an hour. We cried, we laughed. We finally got ourselves together and decided to save some tears for the funeral.

"Where was Edward at all that time?" I asked.

"Girl, I have no idea. He snuck in here smelling like a liquor store, and I think I saw little specks of blood on the bottom of his shirt."

"Blood?"

"Yup."

"You asked him where he'd been?"

"He yelled and told me mind my business."

"What?"

CHAPTER 7

Denial

Jessica

MUST HAVE been pretty fucked up because I woke up at home on the sofa, sore as fuck. I heard a lot of noise upstairs. I looked at the clock, it was 1:00 in the afternoon. Who could be upstairs banging on the walls? Where is my mother? I yelled for her, but got no answer. There was always so much going on outside that if somebody would break in and kill us, no one would even know. I hate the fact that my mother started using that shit heavy like that, "Everybody knows, don't get addicted."

She was so stupid. She lost her job at social security. She lost our home on Loch Raven after my dad left. If it wasn't for Edward helping us, we wouldn't have a place to live. He got a house on MontFord and Federal where he stashed his supply and took care of most of his business, but he only came by for a couple hours some nights to spend time with me. That was why I had no idea where all the noise was coming from upstairs. As I'm walking toward the steps. I faintly heard the voices of what sounded like two different men. I softly walked up the stairs, being careful not to let the steps squeak. The noise was coming from my mother's room.

As I got closer, I heard a man saying, "Shut up, bitch! You like to suck that glass dick. Then Suck on this! Yeah, man, she got a fat ass.

Turn that ass around this way. That's a nice tight hole you got back there."

"Yo, gag that bitch with your dick!" Another guy said, bossing the other.

"I see why you're making her suck your dick for that shit. Old bitch got some good ass head and ass. Let me get some more of that head. You can take over this ass."

As what sounded like them switching as I got closer, I heard a familiar voice said, "Yeah, bleed on this dick. No mercy. I'm bussing this ass wide open."

I bust in the door. The room was ransacked like somebody broke in, looking for something. My mother's belongings were all over the floor.

"Edward!" I screamed. "No! What are you doing? Why?"

My mother wanted to say something. I saw tears pouring down her face as Sean was ramming himself in my mother's mouth, it had to hurt. Edward looked at me as I if I wasn't there. He continued from behind. He had blood on the bottom of his shirt. What have I done? What have I gotten us into?

"Get off my mother!" I yelled as I hit on Edward hurt and confused. I heard Sean, why he said he made her do things for crack? Did my mother had it that bad? Was she turning trick for that shit? Neither one of them stopped until they were done. Sean looked at me with that dark look in his eyes.

"If I hear a word of this from anyone, I swear I'll come back and kill this crack head whore you call a mother." He then looked over at Edward. "The next time this base head steal and smoke some dope of mine, you better kill this bitch before I kill you. Now, make sure they clean this house up. If the police ever have to come to this house for any reason because of your whores, I don't want them having reason to search for my shit. No more slipping. Now, I'm going back up state, only contact me if it's an emergency. Otherwise I'll be in touch."

A lot of last night was a blur, but I remembered Edward and Sean doing what they pleased with me. They took my body—was that not enough that they had to abuse my mother? I couldn't do anything but cry as Edward walked over to me and kissed me on my forehead.

"I know how much you love me, that's why I love you so much. Now help your mother get cleaned up, then clean this place up. I'll be back later. Make sure you be here," Edward said.

He left out the room, but they were still here. I heard him and Sean talking. My mother was lying there on the bed, helpless and crying with her face on the pillow. I wanted to console her, but the closer I got the angrier I felt toward her. We couldn't leave if we wanted to. My mother turned and looked at me with her beautiful coal black eyes. "Jessica, listen to me baby. That man is the devil. You know your mother and how much I hate what drugs do to people. Edward had this planned from the very first time he stepped foot in my house."

"Ma, just stop it. No, there's no excuse for what he's done, but you put him in a tight situation with Sean when you decided to take something that didn't belong to you," said Jessica.

"If it wasn't for Edward, we wouldn't have a place to stay."

"Jessica! Listen to me. And please don't say anything to Edward . . . I never wanted to tell you this, but you listen to me! That weekend you went over Tonya's for a sleepover, I was at home listening to some music and drinking wine. Edward knocked on the door, he was charming and respectful just like how he was when you introduced him.

"How you doing Ms. Irene, is Jessica here?" asked Edward.

"No, she's gone to a sleepover and won't be back until tomorrow."

"But Ma, Edward knew where I was. I was at his house."

"Did he come there Jess? No! Well, listen to your mother!"

"Do you need anything Ms. Irene?" Edward said.

"No, baby. That was sweet. Thanks for asking."

"Do you mind if I use your bathroom?" Edward asked.

"Sure. It's one in the basement."

After he was done he said, "Thank you. It looks like your running low, Ms. Irene. The liquor store is literally two minutes away. Please let me be a gentlemen and grab you another bottle. I insist!"

"So I thought nothing of it and said sure. He came back with three bottles. He put two in the fridge."

"I really like your daughter. I hope I'm making a good impression. Now, I wouldn't be a gentlemen if I didn't open the bottle and pour your first glass."

"I was impressed, and since he has been over more than once, I sat on the sofa and told him where the wine opener and glasses were. He poured my glass and started talking about how much he cared for you and he needed you to be within reach at all times. Before I knew it the bottle was only half full, but I didn't feel like myself. I was getting hot and drowsy. As I sat on the sofa, I thought to myself because I couldn't form the words to actually say them. I only drank half of the bottle he brought. Why am I feeling this way? Then all I heard was him saying how much he liked my body and how I had nice breasts. It was like I was hearing what he was saying, but couldn't respond." my mother said as tears streamed down her face.

"I could hear, see, and feel, but I could not move. That's when I knew he must've put something in my wine. He started caressing my breast and the next thing I remember was waking up on the sofa with nothing on. There was a lighter, a spoon, a needle, and a tourniquet on the table and my arm was sore. I felt extremely high, and I had the jitters. Edward came over to the sofa and scared the hell out of me because I thought—well I hoped—that he was gone."

He said, "Go get yourself cleaned up, then come back down, and we can talk. Don't try and reach Jessica. If the authorities come to the door, I'll tell them I found you in here high with the front door open, then I'll show them all the shit that's on the table. This is your house not mine."

"It's like he was a different person, Jess."

I couldn't believe what my mother was telling me. I was in such shock. I didn't realize how much blood my mother had running down her leg, or how she kept wiping her mouth from the little that was coming from there as well.

"Come on, Ma. Go in the bathroom, and get cleaned up, and put on some clean clothes while I straighten up. I'm driving you to the hospital."

We proceeded down the stairs. I noticed Sean and Edward, sitting in the kitchen. Edward was kissing ass, telling Sean he should stay and check out all the fine ass girls down Eldorado's tonight. All I could think was, *Good! Stay the fuck away from me tonight.* Thank god we were able to type the code in the doors for them to unlock to use the spare because we didn't wanna have to stay in that house any longer, not one more minute looking for the keys.

I flew down the street, thankful that Johns Hopkins was pretty much around the corner. Once registered, we got sent to a room where they took my mother's blood work. she took her clothes off and put on a gown. After the nurse was done, they hooked my mother to an IV and said she was dehydrated from all the drugs in her system. My mother was so weak, but she wanted me to know everything. When the nurse left out, I let her finish. Once I cleaned up, I came back downstairs.

"The area where he stuck the needle was tingling so bad. I couldn't stop scratching."

"You have dope running through your veins. It's starting to wear off, that's why your scratching. I don't want Jessica ever catching you getting high. Oh, and trust me you will need more. I want you and your daughter to need me, Ms. Irene. I want to be here for you both," Edward said. "Now, this is a pipe. It's simple. You just place a rock inside, light it, and smoke it. No more needles. I can't have you walking around with track marks, okay? I'll leave this right here on the table with my number. I'll wait about thirty minutes. If you don't want it, flush it. I'll break your poor daughter's heart and stay away from the both of you," Edward said.

"I was so happy to hear those words. I couldn't wait for him to leave. As soon as he left out that door. I locked the room, grabbed that trash, and flushed it down the toilet, but not even fifteen minutes later, I felt like I was going crazy. *I had to have it!* I called him, and he came right back. I'd been using ever since privately until he stopped returning my calls and I had to get it elsewhere and pay for it."

I sat there and looked at my once beautiful mother. Her features reminded me so much of Anaya—long, thick black hair; small waist, big ass, and caramel skin. I have the hair, but I got the dark skin from my dad. Oh, how I wished he was here right now. Since he moved to Atlanta, I barely talk to him anymore.

The doctor finally came in to explain her blood work. The only problem was that there were too much and too many different types of drugs. She agreed to use all the ones they listed except for the drug called Rohypnol. Working in the industry, I had heard about people slipping Ruffie in drinks; it was some type of date-rape drug they use when they wanted to take advantage. Hearing my mother's story sounded kind of familiar, just never been slipped the drug before, except till now. The only thing was, I didn't pass out immediately. It could've been all the coke they gave me, but I wouldn't tell her. She had enough to worry about.

The doctor went in, saying she had some rectal tissue damage which should heal on its own. "Get a stool softener. It will help with the discomfort. She has damage to her tonsils. I controlled the bleeding, but she might have to get them removed if the inflammation won't go down within seven days. Due to the amount of narcotics in her system it's the law for us to only release you to the care of a NA three day facility."

"Mrs. Johnson," he called her. She still hadn't yet gotten a divorce from my dad. "You are a beautiful woman." I thought if he saw her three months ago. "You have a beautiful seventeen-year-old daughter who needs you. Stop allowing anyone to do these things to you. If not for yourself, for your daughter. Now she is seventeen, she's old enough to be at home by herself. And since you stated that this did not happen at your residence, I'm going to assume your home is a safe environment for her to stay at for the three days, and the family listed for your emergency contact still lives close by at this address?" he asked.

"Yes," we both said, not wanting him to report this to the authorities since I am under eighteen.

They gave my mother some ointments to take along with her. She'd apply them three times a day along with a prescription for antibiotics. I was glad that my dad never took the three of us off his insurance. I got the prescription filled while at the hospital. They said that if she was not checked in within an hour of checking out the hospital, the police would come to the address listed, and she would be arrested and taken to a facility required her to stay longer than three days. I sat outside of the drug clinic on North and Gay and waved bye to my mother as she walked inside and the closed door behind her. It was six o'clock by the time I dropped her off. It had to be one of the worst days other than when my father left and my brother was taken away.

I was starving, so I drove back down to Broadway and monument to get something to eat. Once I got there and smelled the food, it gave me an upset stomach, so I just got a slice of pizza to hold me over until I got back home. We always had food with my mother getting food stamps. All I had to pay for was gas for my mothers car, electricity, and my mother's car payment—which wasn't a problem since Edward always gave me money and surprised me with stilettos and watches. He even brought me my first black and white MCM bag with a hat to match. That was why I didn't understand why he acted like this. He was a good man. I was his only girl. He paid the rent for us. If only my mother was strong enough not to use again. He gave her a choice, he even stopped giving her drugs, but she kept choosing that glass pipe. I waited till I got home to eat my pizza. Hopefully this feeling would be gone by then.

I walked in the house and sat at the table. Before I can take my first bite, I vomited all over myself. *What is wrong with me?* I thought. *Why are my hands shaking?* My girls and I were too smart, so we always let our boys use condoms no matter the situation. The rain coat came first, that was why we all had one more year of high school, and none of us had ever been pregnant or had a STD. Anaya always said, "Money can be the root of all evil. Never let it take over your life. A house, your own car, and a two-karat diamond comes first."

Maybe there was too much of that shit he put in my champagne last night. I showered. I'd ask him about that and my mother's situation when he got home tonight. I knew I needed to leave him after what he did, but without him, we wouldn't have a place. I knew I could change him to the man I knew he could be. There was no excuse for what he did, I know. I also knew Sean made him behave this way. In the last two days, he acted like a puppet and Sean was pulling the strings. He met Sean in a strip club and said he came all the way down here from New York to go to a strip club. He didn't know anyone here, and he just happened to befriend Edward's dumb ass.

Something ain't right with the whole Sean situation. I just couldn't put my finger on it. *He got something up his sleeve, and Edward fell right into his trap*, I thought as I jumped in the shower and washed my hair. After I was done, I put my robe on.

I forgot that Edward always left us a little white powder in the drawer for whenever we wanted some. After the last twenty-four hours of stress, that was just what my body needed right now. I pulled out the folded fifty-dollar bill, grabbed my straw, and did two lines. Instantly I felt better. I turned the music on downstairs to drown out the outside crowd and emergency sirens that were always speeding down the streets. I rinsed off some previously cleaned wings while the grease got hot when my phone rang. All anxious from doing a line, I answered.

"Hello."

"Hey, baby," Edward said. He knew what calling me baby did to me.

"Hey, Edward, I don't understand what's going on so we need to talk."

"Okay, baby, it must have been the drugs, baby. I'm sorry, it will never happen again. Go get something out the draw to calm you down, baby," he said.

"I already did, Edward. We need to talk about earlier, and we need to talk about Sean."

"Relax we should be there soon." He hung up.

We? I thought. I really don't want *Sean* to come back in this house. The thought of him made me sick. I couldn't believe how our lives turned upside down in the last twenty-four hours. I wanted to tell him not to come here, but this was his place—not mine. He didn't even ask if my mother was okay. We had to move!

CHAPTER 8

Who is this guy

Anaya

N HOUR HAD passed by the time we finished reminiscing about how flirtatious and funny Tank was. We sat there, laughing at the memories. Suddenly, a black Mercedes E190 with tinted windows and gold BBS rims pulled and stopped right in front of Tonya's door.

"I have no idea who this could be especially with those New York tags," Tonya said.

"Girl, Edward had blood on his shirt right? Maybe the person in this car have something to do with it, and we should get up now," I mumbled.

Before we got a chance to get up Edward singled the car to park.

"Oh, shit. My heart was in my draws . . . *well if I had some on*," I said.

"I thought it was about to be a shootout. If so, we would've been dead," Tonya added.

"That's my homeboy, Sean, from up state. Once he has parked, just let him know I'll be out in a few."

"His smart ass must be talking to you, Anaya."

"I'm sorry, baby sis. I just wanted to get in the house before Mommy saw me. I didn't want her getting upset over period blood," he said then went in the house.

"Your brother is so disgusting."

"I know," Tonya said. The guy, Sean, parked and got out the car.

"Damn! He is sexy!" Tonya said. "I guess light skin brothers are back because that's all we seem to be running into now a days."

"And he is a cutie," I said.

He came over with his gazelle shades on and just stood there at first and just stared. *Weird,* I thought.

"Hello, ladies. How are you doing on this beautiful Sunday?"

"We're all right," Tonya said. She was always loud and ghetto. "I like your accent." There she went, flirting with her brother's friend. *She knew Edward would have a fit,* I thought.

"Well, thank you," he said. "You must be Tonya, Edward's sister. Y'all favor. And you must be Anaya. I heard a lot about you,"

"Oh, really. Why is it that you're hearing a lot about me? What exactly did you hear?"

"That's what I heard right there," he said as he started laughing. "I heard you were a beautiful tiger that didn't take no shit."

"A little woman with a big bite—yeah, that's her ass," Tonya said.

I wasn't impressed. This Cuban-looking motherfucker got duplicitous written all over him. I heard about them New York cats. The only time they really came down Baltimore was when shit was not right. Otherwise, these soft Baltimore niggas run straight to their boat-looking asses. Looking at the submarine Rolex on his wrist, Edward was not a friend by choice.

"So Anaya do you have a man? I'm flattered, but you didn't know, I like tatas," I said as I grabbed Tonya's breasts. She didn't know what else to do. She bust out and laughed because she knew how much I loved a strong man with a capital M and a big dick with a capital D. Pussy wasn't on my options of delicatessens.

"I can change how you feel about that." Sean said.

This burrito won't give up, I thought.

"You have your own car?" He asked me.

"No, I don't."

"See, that's because you're fucking with the wrong cats. I'm hanging with my man, Edward, tonight, so I'll be here in Baltimore until tomorrow night. Check this out. How about we take a ride tomorrow and let you pick out a nice car you can get around in? Don't be stressed. You don't have to worry about paying. Tonya can ride along with us if that will make you feel comfortable."

"Sounds like a plan to me. What time should we be ready?" Tonya asked.

"Excuse me! No matter how flattering that sounded, I'm not for sale. You really should stop thinking every female is," I said.

"You know what mommie, even though I was dead serious, I like that. I respect the way you carry yourself. You're a classy tiger. How about this . . . instead of me going with Edward tonight, I can take you out to dinner. Now, that's not buying you—that's being a gentleman."

Okay, I'm trying not to be rude, but this guy won't give up. "Look, I appreciate all the gestures, but I'm just not interested."

"Okay, mommie. If you ever change your mind, here's my card. Call me."

The card read: "BIG Apple Computer Repair"

"Yeah, I have my own business," he said. "If you need your computer fixed or rearranged, that's my direct cell number."

I didn't know how Edward got his connection with this one, but his banana-peel-looking ass was getting so much money, he needed a store front as a cover up. When I thought about it, why would he want to waste his time taking computers apart and putting them back together. *Light bulb*—he transported drugs and money. He was taking the house apart, stuffing it with packages, boxed it, and shipped it. He was too big for me. Dealing with somebody like him would have you laid out in a body bag. Tonya needed to talk to her brother; he had to stay far away from him, but Edward probably was so far in, he couldn't get out.

Edward finally came outside, smelling like Drakkar. I always hated that smell.

"Where y'all off to, Ed?" Tonya asked.

"Going down the strip club. Y'all wanna come?" Sean asked.

"Naw, man. They're good. I don't want my little sister down there. They're too young for that shit."

"Speaking of strip clubs, have you been seeing Jessica, Edward? She works down Eldorado's. Do you ever run into her while you're there?" I asked.

"Well, nice talking to you ladies. Anaya, don't forget. I'll be in the car, Edward," Sean said as he gave Edward this weird look.

"I think. Maybe once or twice, but I haven't seen her in a while," he said as he walked off with a small trash bag tied in a knot. It appeared to be clothes.

"I called her earlier. Some guy answered and said she left out earlier with her mother. She should be back by now. It's after 6:00. Let's call," I told Tonya.

Tonya dialed the number and put the phone on speaker.

"Hello," Jessica said.

"Jessica!" we both screamed at the phone. "What's up? Why haven't we heard from you? Are you okay?"

"Yes, yes, I'm great," Jessica said with slurred speech.

"Why do you sound like that?"

"I'm just tired. I'm about to go lie down. Can I call y'all back later?"

"No, Jessica! Jessica, where is Mrs. Irene? Put her on the phone."

"She's not here."

"Well, we're on our way over."

"No!" Jessica yelled.

"Jessica, we're your friends. We love you. We're not worried about your house not being clean if that's the problem. We all have a messy house at one point or another."

"No!" Jessica yelled and slammed the phone in our ear.

"Wow!" I said as Tonya and I looked at one another in such dismay. Tonya quickly called a cab before taking the phone inside. "I can't believe what was going on. First, my grandmother was not feeling good, then Tank, now this. This is too much in one day. What do you think is going on with her, Tonya?"

"I don't know, Anaya, but ain't no telling with her working at that strip club."

"Well soon as the cab comes, we're going straight over there. Before I came around here I had intentions on going over Stanley's to relieve some stress, but it doesn't look like that's going to happen."

"Look at you, turning that boy out back to back sessions. You know that boy can't handle that."

"Well he's a big boy. He said he's fine with it, and I'm glad I told him that friends is all I wanted us to be—Oh, here's the cab."

We hopped in the cab and pulled off. "I can't believe she yelled and slammed the phone down like that. Something better be wrong because I will be choking her smart ass out if not," I said.

Making a right on Edgewood road off Lochraven Boulevard, we pulled up in front of her house. I knew it had been a while since we had been over here. Was this the right address?

We told the cab driver to wait as we went and knocked on the door several times, calling her name louder each time. There was no answer. We peeped through the torn blinds.

"There's no way this could be Jessica's house. Everything was in shambles—broken glass, court notices on the floor, and her mother's maxima wasn't out front. She said her mother wasn't home," Tonya said. From the looks of it no one had been here in a while.

"I think we had the wrong house," I said as we walked down the steps. The neighbor came out; it was the older ladies' granddaughter.

"Hi," we spoke. Remembering seeing her face from being over Jessica's, we waited for her to point us to the right house, but instead she said, "Jessica and her mother moved." *No way*, I thought. She would've at least told us that much. "They moved almost three months ago. I think the house is in foreclosure."

"What!" I yelled.

We thanked the neighbor and got back in the cab. We were both lost for words. Our friend was in trouble, and we had no idea how to help.

CHAPTER 9

Ménage Five

Jessica

"BABY, WAKE UP, Baby! Baby!" Edward yelled then smacked the back of my ass hard as hell.

"Edward, what?!" I yelled back. I felt like I had been hit by a truck. What time was it? Damn, it must be late because he was home and he smelled like pussy. "Get off me, Edward. I'm tired. I can barely open my eyes. What was that shit you gave me. I feel paralyzed, and I don't feel like getting up."

"Just lay with me. We need to talk anyway."

"Hell no!"

"Stop stressing me out, Jessica. I don't wanna keep talking about that bullshit!"

"But Edward, Edward—shit! We got company downstairs."

"Come down or stay your ass up here and sleep. I don't need you fucking up my high!"

"But Edward—" He stormed out the room, slamming the door behind him. I couldn't believe after everything that had happened, I still loved him, and I wanted to be with him. I just wanted to go to sleep and wake up from this nightmare. Edward said we were going to get married. This was not the same Edward.

Wait . . . *do I hear females downstairs laughing?* He said he had company, but I didn't think he meant females. What was it that he put in that fifty-dollar bill? I could barely get out the bed. I forced myself out and made my way downstairs.

"Oh, no! Edward they gotta go! Leave!" I knew this was not my place, but this was just disrespectful. Three girls sat on my mother's sofa with Sean sitting in between, drinking and smoking like everything was okay. Karma is a bitch. Everything was beginning to make sense—so this was how the female felt when I first met Edward, and he brought me to this house. A girl was there carrying on because she was mad that I was there. He told me she was a crack head. My mother was right. Edward didn't care about me like he said he did. He was the devil, and I was in hell.

"Sit down, Jessica, or go back to bed."

"How you gonna be telling me who I can have up in my crib? I let you and your mother stay here because your mother became a base head and neither one of you had nowhere to go. Don't you forget that! Now, act like a good girl, and go join the party."

His words cut like a knife. I wanted so badly to tell him that I knew everything. How he forced my mother to get high then violated her body by having sex with her while she was sleep, but she made me promise not to say anything so I wouldn't—at least not yet.

"Hey! Go change from those pajamas before you join us." I knew now that if I didn't listen, he would cause a scene and get abusive. I was already embarrassed enough, so I went upstairs, cried, and wished my brother Stacey was home. With all that had been going on with Edward, I just realized that my brother hadn't called in over a week. We had our old number transferred to this house. This way, we didn't have to explain to him or anyone else why or where we moved too. He was supposed to be home in six months, and he would flip out if he knew what was going on. That was why my mother had to get clean, and we needed to get the hell out of here. I didn't want my brother going back to jail as soon as he got out. I went downstairs before Edward flipped out.

Walking back down these dreadful set of stairs, I could smell the marijuana. It instantly made me sick. I had no appetite, and the last thing I wanted was drugs. I entered the living room, and Edward sat on the sofa with this hoe sitting on his lap kissing her passionately the way he kissed me. My insides turned. I wanted nothing more but to beat his ass and hers too. Edward was supposed to be mine. What happened to our happy fairytale? He motioned me to come over, sit next to him, and demand that I do a line.

"No, Edward!" I told him. "Edward, we thank you for letting us stay, but when my mother is released on Tuesday, we're going to my cousin's. My mother needs to get herself together, and so do I."

"Look, girl. What did I tell you about talking that shit? You're not going any—motherfucking—where! Stop fucking up everyone else's high with that bullshit! Now, snort this shit, and stop talking reckless."

I feared Edward. There was no telling what he was capable of. I desperately wanted to call Tonya and let her and their mother know, but I knew I couldn't do that. As I snorted the first line then the second, nothing seemed to matter anymore as I sipped on some Moet. Edward decided to introduce me to the rest.

"Jessica, say hi to Monica, Tia, and that's Keisha."

Keisha couldn't speak since her mouth was occupied with Sean's dick. She squatted on her feet while he stood up in the kitchen. She appeared to be enjoying it more than he was.

"Come here, Tia," Edward said. After Edward put the blunt to her mouth, she went down south. Was this really happening? Was Edward, as they put it, trying to turn me out? First drugs, now this. I had never been with a woman before or never had an interest too. I didn't know if it was from all the drugs and alcohol I had in my system, but she was giving me head better than Edward. Next thing I knew, we started a train. While Tia went to work on me, Sean went in on Tia. Monica gave Sean a head, and Edward was straight giving it deep to Monica. The coke mixed with the champagne had me so horny that I literally came in Tia's mouth three times before Sean came over and fucked my walls open. We fucked, sucked, got high, ate, and slept on repeat way into Monday.

I woke up. It was 9:00 Monday night. Looking around, I was the only person there like everything had been a dream. From the looks of it, it wasn't. Stuff was everywhere—liquor bottles and bottles of Moet that hadn't been open yet. Damn, near an eight ball of coke sitting on a mirror, I saw why he would always sell out of the stuff he started getting from Sean. That shit had me feeling extra good last night. Think I'd do another line just to get rid of this headache. I needed some energy any way so I could get this house cleaned up and pick my mother up in the morning.

I was not sure what Edward's agenda was—why he wanted to keep me and my mother in here, getting high, trapped like hostages; but I have my own agenda whether he liked it or not. After I straightened up, I grabbed my clothes off the floor then went upstairs to clean up. I thought it was time to call my aunt. I just hoped she would greet us with open arms. The phone rang several times, then my aunt answered.

"Hi, auntie."

"Hi, Jessica. How are you?" she asked.

"We need a place to stay auntie. My mother lost the house. I could explain everything later, but I was hoping we could come over this weekend and stay for a while. I know you and my mother are not in good terms, but we really need you right now. I can pay you whatever you need."

"That won't be necessary we're family and I have nothing against my sister. Of course y'all can stay."

My mother stopped speaking to everyone—including my aunt—after my father left her for another woman.

"Thank you so much, auntie."

The only thing I'd bring my mother here was to get what little things we had; then, we'd go to a hotel for a few days. I had enough money saved up from dancing and the money Ed gave me before he turned into this monster. We needed to figure this out together.

Suddenly, I heard a door slam.

"Hello?" I said.

I looked out the window and saw Ed, hopping in a car. *Shit!* I had no idea he was here. I hope he didn't hear me talking to myself.

CHAPTER 10

You Heard What

Anaya

"WHY DIDN'T SHE say they moved months ago? I mean . . . really? It had to be something pretty bad for her not to tell us that she was moving," I said.

I knew something didn't feel right. We hadn't seen much of her lately except the day I dropped her off at her aunt's house. She was acting weird then.

"Maybe her mother got fired, Anaya. She was too embarrassed for us to know where she lives," Tonya said.

"Yeah, maybe you're right, Tonya. But either way, we have some investigating to do. What are you doing today?" I asked Tonya.

"Nothing really."

"I told Stanley I was coming down today, but with all the commotion, I never made it. You still wanna go?"

"Okay, cool."

"Call a cab. I'm on my way around," I said as I hung up the phone.

I finished some last touches to my hair so by time I got around Tonya's, the cab was coming down the street.

"So what's going on with Pop?"

"Don't think I'm ready to talk about that one."

"Why?"

"Girl, he got a whole daughter."

"And?" Tonya said.

"What do you mean *and*? I just found out today! He lied. He knew I told him I didn't want a man that had kids."

"Well maybe that's why he was afraid to tell you. It's not like y'all been dating for a long time. You've only been on two dates, Anaya. I think you should give him a pass."

"Yeah, well you know how many passes come after I give him this one? I don't know, Tonya. We're here," I said.

"Can you beep the horn again?" I was surprised they were not outside.

"Anaya, no one is home, they must've left. When was the last time you talked to him?"

"Earlier, but he said they would be here. Girl, they in there," I said. "Let me get out and knock on the door." I raised my hand, but the door opened. *I thought* I *heard a horn.*

"What took you so long little girl?" Stanley asked as he picked me up and wrapped my legs around his waist.

"You don't want to know," I said as I kissed him deeply we were about to make out in the doorway until Tonya screamed

"Excuse me."

The cab! "Oh, I forgot to pay the cab, dear. It's still not a problem that Tonya came right?"

"Never! That's my girl." All the guys loved Tonya because she was just as gangster as they were.

"So where's everybody? It's like ghost town in here," I said.

"We're all in the basement. Come on."

We walked down the basement, and it smelled like they grew it, bagged it, sold it, as well as smoked weed down here.

"Y'all a bunch of pot heads. Now, put me a little bit in some top paper. Don't give this white girl none, All she's gonna do is waste it," Tonya said.

"No, I'm not. I'll take one or two puffs now, and save the rest for another time. And yes one puff does *D*, all of the above. Goofy, horny, and hungry in that order."

"I got some top paper for you baby," Stanley said.

"That's because that's all you smoke," Tonya said. We all started laughing.

"Let's play double dare. Anyone who doesn't want to do the dare have to go through the patty wagon then take a shot of boons farm at the end of the wagon," I said.

"That ain't too heavy," Stanley's brother said.

It was only five of us down here—Stanley, his brother, and our nerdy but cute friend, Paul. Everyone agreed. I had the best ideas. The game was fun so far, everyone went through the patty wagon several times. Bobby had to tongue kiss Tonya. We were all tipsy from the boons shots then Tonya double dared me to put my hands down Stanley's pants and French kiss at the same time in front of everyone. She thought she was slick. *She knew I didn't really like doing that in public with Stanley, but we're having fun so this won't be a problem today,* I thought to myself. I walked over to Stanley and climbed on top of his lap. I didn't just put my hands down his pants. I straddled his cock and put my tongue down his throat. We kissed for almost five minute straight. They called our name, but we didn't stop. With me on his lap, Stanley stood up palming my fat ass as we exit the basement going up the steps.

I whispered in his ear, "Get a condom and a pillow. Let's sit out back."

He started laughing, but that was what he liked about me. I was spontaneous and never transparent. He sat down on the pillow as I climbed on top of him. We kissed a bit and sucked each other's necks for almost half an hour. He then pulled the front of his sweatpants down over his dick and put the condom on. He pulled my tank dress up just enough so my ass wouldn't show.

"Hmm . . . no panties . . . so smooth," he whispered as he stuck his tongue in my ear and softly rubbed his finger back and forth across my soaking wet pussy right before pushing his big hard cock inside of me—and boy was it big. I felt every inch as I went up and down, working my pelvis in a circular motion. My ponytail bounced, tapping the back of my shoulder with every movement.

It was a little dark. The back was lit up with nothing but one distant street light. I felt like I was in a scene of a love movie. He wrapped his arms around my body and held me still and tight as he pushed deeper inside me like he knew it was gold he was digging for. We kissed hard and moaned together until our bodies went into convulsions as we both released. We went inside, wiped off, and decided to go back downstairs. I sat beside Tonya, staring across the room at Stanley. He was staring as if he could talk with those eyes. His eyes were so sexy, I was getting turned on. Just sitting there made my vagina feel like she had her own heartbeat. I tightly crossed my legs. The more he stared, the harder my nipples became.

We continued to play the game. Stanley's brother dared me to let Paul grab my breast. He should've dared Paul to grab my breast because I chose the patty wagon. I think Bobby just wanted a chance to smack the ass of the woman his brother was fucking. It was cool and fun. After, I stood up and took my shot. Stanley picked me up in the air and pinned me to the wall with my legs around his waist.

"Oh." He couldn't get enough. He would've taken it if people weren't there. I palmed his head with my hands and he sucked that strawberry Boones flavor right off my tongue. He took me upstairs to the bedroom. This time we took all our clothes off, got under the covers, and had sex till our bodies were soaking wet. We layed there, talked, ate, and had sex again. Before I knew it, it was almost ten o' clock. I showered and got dressed.

"I needed this stress-free night, Stanley."

"Well I'm glad I was able to help you with that, Anaya."

"Yeah, me too. Now let's go back downstairs and see what these fools are doing," I said."

"Speaking of fools, what's going on with your girl, Jessica? I heard she was working down the strip club and using that shit."

"What? Wait . . . Yeah, she is working down the strip club, but what shit are you talking about that she's using?"

"That 'yay yo.' My homeboy saw her putting some in her nose."

"I guess that's the reason she never calls or answers when we call her."

"Yeah, y'all need to check on your girl. She was seen several times with some Spanish-looking guy. He stood out because they could tell he wasn't from around here."

We went back in the basement. They were watching "Yo MTV Rap."

"Tonya, guess what Stanley just told me?"

"What? He wanna marry you?"

"Funny! No, silly. He said one of his homeboys saw Jessica doing coke and was seen several times posted up with a Spanish dude from out of town."

"Anaya, I'm not surprised. Mostly everyone working in those clubs gets high one way or another."

"Tonya, listen. He said the guy stood out because they could tell he's "not from around here." Maybe that's the same guy she was hiding from us. Just ask your brother. Is there anything he's not telling?"

"I don't know. I'm tired. There's school in the morning, I'm going to bed once I get home. I bet you are," Tonya said. I started smiling

Rethinking this entire week, I could be overreacting. If they were seeing each other, what's the big secret for? He's cute, and why would he try so hard to get at me? He knew we were friends. Yeah, that was silly. He was not the only "Poppy" that would be hanging around these parts. Most of the Baltimore guys connect came from upstate anyway.

I said I was going to stay in this Sunday and relax, but I couldn't help but think about Jessica.

CHAPTER 11

The root of all evil

Anaya

"WHAT'S GOING ON with Jessica and her mother?" Jessica didn't come to school this week. I heard she was supposed to be getting high, but I was not sure how true that was. Her mother lost their home. Her mother was so excited about purchasing her own after dealing with the fact that Jessica's dad left. Something was wrong, and I would find out what it was. I tried calling her, but got no answer. Guess I'd try and call back later today. I checked my pager, and Pop had been blowing it up all week during and after school. Did I want to call him back? It had been a week since I last spoke with him.

Well, it couldn't hurt. Let me see what he was talking about. He called me from his house phone. *Knowing him, he probably left out already*, I thought as the phone rang.

"Hello," he said on the first ring.

"Hi, Pop. I'm returning your page."

"You mean pages?" he said.

"So you wouldn't have called me if I wouldn't have paged you all those times?"

"To be honest? No."

"Come on, Anaya. Are you still mad about my daughter?"

"Am I not supposed to be?" I asked.

"What can I do to make it up to you? Name it, I'll do anything!"

Did he say *anything?* A week ago, that statement wouldn't have mattered, but I felt like he used me. He knew how serious I felt about being second. When—and if—I decided to have kids, I wanted my kids to be our first, so I didn't care about using him when his money was concerned, and I had a feeling that this wouldn't be his first lie.

"Well, you know the word 'anything' leaves me open for possibilities. As of this moment, I saw some gold and diamond hoops that I want to out my name in from the jewelry store down Howard street, They were like $1600. If I could think of anything else, I'll let you know later."

"Okay you ain't said nothing," he said, "but first, I need you to come down here before my daughter leaves at six so you can meet her. Also, I got you a little gift while I was out last week."

"Okay, Let me take a bath and get myself together. Make sure you're out front when I get there."

"I will," Pop said. After I got out the tub, I put on my Ralph Lauren khaki shorts and white button up shirt with the big collar. I tucked it in, put on my red leather coach belt with the matching loafers, and sprayed on some Elizabeth Arden Red Door. It was only twelve o' clock, so I grabbed a cushion, went out front to sit on the steps with my grandmother, and listened to my aunt talk about what was going on with everybody in the neighborhood. I would be a part of the discussion if I wasn't standing right there. After about an hour, grandma went in to watch what's happening, and my aunt walked home. I called my cab and grabbed my red coach bag. Once the cab came, I called Pop and told him I was on my way.

As I pulled up in front of his house, he walked over, paid the cab, and opened up the door for me. His daughter was sitting on the steps.

"Anaya, this is my daughter, Yanika. Say hi to Ms. Anaya," Pop said.

"Hi pretty, how are you?" I said. Her mother must have brown complexion because she was a brown-skin split image of Pop without the light eyes. "You are a cutie. How old are you?"

"Three," she said.

We sat on the steps. Pop talked about how he really did want to tell me. He pretty much got to say everything he wanted without me hanging up on him. I just sat there and listened.

"Come upstairs with me, Anaya. I want to give you something."

Pop's brother came from across the street and squeezed me like he always did in school, then started playing with his niece. We went upstairs and into the room. He shut the door behind us.

"I see that you've been shopping," I said. He had diplomat, Simon Harris, kazons and barney bags on the bed. He handed me a kazons bag. I opened the box and pulled out the softest cream leather bag with leather fringes dangling from it.

"This is sexy. All I need is some tan leather boots for this fall to match."

"Okay," he said.

"Oh, I wasn't saying that for you to buy them, but thank you . . . It's super cute!"

"No problem," he said smiling. He passed me this small gift bag. I would have a heart attack if it was a ring. Thank you, Lord—the box that was inside was too big to be a ring, but I could spot this red and gold box from anywhere. I already knew what it was. It was something that I wanted, but I didn't have.

I opened the box. It was the prettiest gold Cartier watch I'd ever seen. He sure did hit a home run with this. Now, this was the type of shit that make you rethink your last thoughts.

So what if he was older than me and he had a daughter? He was cute with a great since of humor. He's a protector; he's giving; he really liked me; and he got hella bread.

"Oh wow!" was all I could say with my mouth open.

"Put it on and make sure it fits your little wrist."

"Pop, this costs too much. I can't accept this."

"Why not? I like you . . . I do! While I'm hoping it manifests into something more, I understand that we're just friends. I'm just giving you a glimpse of how your life would be if you were my girl, but if you don't go that route—no hard feelings. What I give you is yours. I don't want anything back. Now, put it on before I bite you."

How could I say no to what he was proposing. I still had some hard thinking to do, but I did put on the watch and it fit like a glove. I saw that you liked watches, and I couldn't let your other boyfriends outshine me."

"Ha! You're funny. You're the jealous type, and did you say boyfriends? I'm too young for that word to be plural. Or am I?" I said as I started laughing. "I'm just teasing."

"Well I don't care how many boyfriends are there or if you even have one at all. I want to take care of you as a man should," he said.

We spent the rest of the day laughing and talking. His daughter had been picked up by her mother earlier than originated. Thank goodness, they had a good relationship. I couldn't handle any baby momma drama. Before I knew it, it was seven o' clock. It was still early, but I'd been here since earlier. I had plans to watch *Valley of the Dolls* with grandma, so he called me a cab. As the cab pulled up, he walked with me. I opened the door as I climbed inside.

"Here you go Anaya," Pop said. "I know you said that the earrings you want are $1600, but this was all I have on me right now. You should be able to find a nice pair with that," he said as he handed me a knot of money folded in half with a rubber band holding it together.

"No, Pop. You really don't have to. Take this back. The watch was enough. Really!"

"Naw, a deal is a deal. Don't worry about it, take it. It's cool."

"Thank you, Pop. You're too sweet."

"No problem, baby" he said as he kissed me on my forehead then shut the cab door.

What was up with this guy? He gave away money like it grew on trees. It didn't even matter how much money it was, but as I counted it, it was $1300. "Unbelievable."

The sound of the alarm made my teeth clench. I absolutely couldn't stand getting up in the morning, especially with the air on. It was so nice and cozy under these covers, but I hated being late for school as well. Glad I had something hanging up in my small closet already put together. I hit okay on the tape deck and began singing to Hi-Five "'Cause I like the way / You kiss me when you're playing the kissing game." I always take a bath at night and another in the morning to make me feel rejuvenated, but this morning, I just did a bird bath at the sink. I put on my green button up shirt with the collar, my red plaid shorts with the suspenders, my red and gold flip flops, and the gold watch Pop just brought me (I definitely had to hide this.) I sprayed some perfume, put my black MCM back pack on, and went out of the door.

Tonya's door was open as usual. I was about to go in, but she was on her way out. As we walked to school. I said, "Today will be a good day. Oh, did you get a chance to ask Edward about that guy, Sean, and Jessica?"

"Anaya something is not right."

"Why, what happened?"

"Girl, his ass just acted weird. First, I told him I was running low on my shit and I needed to re up. He gonna tell me I'm gonna have to get it from somewhere else. He won't have any for a while. His ass made me mad because I saw a whole heep of that shit in his room last week. He ain't selling that shit that damn fast. I would ask him about Sean. Rumor was Jessica might be dating him. I thought it was farfetched, but I still asked him," Tonya said. "Girl, he grabbed my arm and told me he don't wanna hear anything about Jessica. He's too secretive. There's no way he don't see Jess as often as he go down Eldorado's. And the way he acted just for asking him about her. She gonna tell us something today when we see her in school. She won't be able to lie in our faces. By the way, where did you disappear to yesterday? I thought you were supposed to be staying in the house. I called twice. Your mother answered and said you weren't there."

"This sure felt like a long walk to school this morning," I said as I ignored her.

"Oh no, you will not, Anaya! Where did you go? Back down at Stanley's?" she asked. "You might as well give that boy a chance and be his girlfriend. He genuinely makes you happy, and y'all look so cute together. Your short ass only reaches his chest."

"I wasn't with Stanley yesterday," I said as I covered my mouth looking guilty.

"Wait a minute, bitch. I know you got a lot of shit, but where did you get that watch from?"

"That's a . . . Cartier," I said.

"Yes, that! Oh, hell no. That's a five-thousand-dollar watch. Who brought that? And don't say your uncle."

"No. What happen was . . . Pop called me yesterday."

"I thought you were done with him for lying about having a child?" Tonya said.

"Yea, but I let him explain. His apology was very sincere, and it came with gifts. He said he would do anything I wanted, and it didn't include this watch because he had already purchased this over the weekend. We had a nice time talking. I met his daughter—she's really cute."

"Well, shit! Gifts like that will make his momma cute, and we both know she's torture to the eyes." We both bust out laughing.

"Girl, you're crazy," I said.

"So you finally gave him some, Anaya. And if you didn't, I will!"

"Shut up, Tonya. No, not yet. I was going to, but I didn't wanna feel like a hooker."

"Shit sounds good to me. That's one expensive hooker. Call me what you want!"

"Tonya, you're a mess. Anyway it's perfect timing. I'm good. Stanley put it down so good this weekend, I had no need to. Shit, it seems to be working. Plus, I didn't wanna have sex with two different people, so the longer I have sex with Stanley, the longer I can make Pop wait."

"Yeah, you hope so. He wants you bad. One more gift like that, and I'll let Stanley know he's history for you." We gave each other high fives and made our way to school.

Soon as we walked up the steps, Stanley came. Why do we always manage to run into each other right here almost every morning whether I was running late or not?

"You're waiting for me, Stanley?"

"No . . . Naw," he claimed.

"Come on. Walk with me Stanley. Aww . . . you waited for me," I said playfully. "Aight, Tonya. I'll see you in the cafeteria. Make sure to bring Jessica with you."

There was something about the end of the school year. Time was going by pretty quick as usual. Next period was lunch, but I needed a pass to the laboratory now. I had to go badly.

Feeling relieved, I exited the bathroom. Stanley grabbed me from behind and began biting me on my neck.

"Oh, Stanley, we have to calm down with this."

"What are you talking about, Anaya?"

"I don't want us to get confused about our relationship," I said.

"What do you mean confused? We spent time together after school and on the weekends. My family likes you . . . so you're right. It's a little hard for me, but I know we're friends. You won't seem to let me forget that. But really, Anaya, all I did was grab you in an empty hallway. So I'm good enough at my house, but I can't even touch you outside. Is that what you're telling me?"

"Stanley, why are you getting so upset? I thought we had this conversation already. Every time I turn around, its like you're right there grabbing on me, even when I come out the bathroom. It's starting to feel kind of creepy."

"You know what, Anaya, you're right, I need to calm down, and right now, I will," he said as he turned and walked away. I went back to class. The bell rang before I was able to sit down.

I was so hungry. I had a taste of a Greek salad with extra olives. I was glad when Pop paged me earlier the words 'I miss you.' I called him back from the office and asked him to bring me one if he wasn't busy since I wasn't driving and couldn't leave out to go grab one myself. By the time I got to the cafeteria. He paged me with '??,' letting me know he was outside.

He was right on time, and he even brought me a jumbo iced tea. I loved Mama Mia's salad from Thirty-Third and Greenmount.

"Thank you, babe. I really appreciate it," I told him as I reached in the car and gave him a nice moist kiss on his forehead.

"No problem," he said. "I know this is your lunch break, so I'm not gonna hold you up, but call me when you get out of school. I have a surprise for you."

"You're spoiling me, Pop."

"I know," he said. I started smiling.

"Okay, I'll call you later."

I walked into the cafeteria. Everyone is in line, getting their food. I sat at the usual table and saw Tonya coming over but didn't see Jessica.

"Where did you get that salad?"

"Pop just dropped it off to me."

"Damn isn't he just your knight and shining armor?"

"Tonya, I said make sure you bring Jessica with you."

"I would have except that she didn't come to school today."

"Are you serious?"

"She missed majority of fourth quarter."

The rest of the day, I couldn't help but think about Jessica. The bell rang, and I waited in the usual spot for Tonya's slow ass.

"Hey, Anaya, why are you looking like your best friend got ran over by a truck? Here I go," said Mona. We both laughed.

"I got a lot on my mind. Homeboy got killed this weekend, my grandmother hasn't been feeling too good, and we don't know what's going on with Jessica. I heard she was getting high, hoping it's not true though. We went looking for her at her house, but the neighbor said they had moved months ago . . . I don't know where to. She's not returning our calls. We don't know where she is. We went around her aunts, but she and Jess's mother don't really speak, so they couldn't tell us anything either."

"Have you seen DJ?" Mona said.

"No, not today. Why?"

"I talked to him on the phone this weekend, and he asked me if Jessica lived down the hill. I think near Federal Street somewhere? I told him I didn't know her like that, but I remember y'all use to visit her of Loch raven at one point"

"Really? Why would he think she lived down there instead of visiting somebody? Maybe her boyfriend lived down there."

"Oh, I don't know. That was all he asked me."

Tonya and DJ arrived.

"Hey, sexy."

"What's up, DJ?"

"DJ, where did you say you saw Jessica this weekend? We'd been looking for her little ass."

"I see her all the time down on Montford and Federal," he said.

"With who?" Tonya asked.

"I have nothing to do with that one. I gave y'all the street and the crossing street. What I can say is, I'm surprised y'all don't already know the answer to that," he said and stared at Tonya as he left out the school door.

CHAPTER 12

It's a Set-Up

Jessica

REALLY DIDN'T feel like cleaning this damn house, but I knew Edward would flip if he came here later and I didn't. I did a couple more lines of coke as I cleaned. I turned the radio and listened to my song. I just wanna dance with somebody who loved me. I love Whitney Houston. As I sang along, the phone rang.

"Hello."

"Yea, Jessica, who you got up in there?"

"What are you talking about, Edward?"

"I sent my man there to give you my money and a package. He said he got no answer, but he heard loud music playing."

"No one is here but me Edward. I'm in here cleaning this mess you left here. The music must've been up to loud for me to hear the door."

"Well, he's coming back. Make sure you answer."

"Okay, Edward."

"The eight hundred dollars he owed me you can have that, but put the package in your room."

"Why my room?"

"I'm going up New York for a few. You don't have any plans to go anywhere do you?"

Why would he ask that? Was he in here eavesdropping on my phone calls? I'm too scared to tell him. He might not leave. "No, Edward."

"Hmm, aight. I should be back in two or three days."

"Okay," I said, thinking *yes, he won't be here when I pick my mother up on Tuesday. We can take our time and get all our shit and leave this hell hole.*

Why was I so afraid to tell him that? There was nothing he hadn't already done to me. I hang the phone up and waited for the guy to knock. I got the money. It was more like a sandwich bag of rocks. I guess this was the package. I put it in my bottom drawer under my pajamas. I turned the music back up and poured a glass of champagne. I ran some bath water. It felt good to stay in the house since I didn't have to see or talk to Edward anymore. I'll go down Eldorado's to make some fast cash. Maybe I'll meet another guy to take care of me . . . the right way this time.

Relaxing in the tub filled with bubbles, I floated on cloud nine while I listened to Natalie Cole sing "I live for your love." Suddenly, the phone rang.

"Hello, Jessica speaking."

"Well, who else would you be? Edward's voice came through the receiver. Are you okay baby? Do you need your daddy to come save you?"

"Edward, I thought you were leaving for New York?"

"Ha, ha. I'm fucking with you. We on the road now." *Shit he scared me; he almost blew my fucking high.* "You miss me?" Edward said.

"Edward, this past week has been too much for me to handle. I need this time to myself. My mother needs to get cleaned. My brother will be home in six months, and we can't be staying here when he do."

"Fuck your brother! That pussy ass nigga. So for everything I've done for y'all, you're just gonna say 'fuck me'?"

"Edward, we appreciate you letting us stay here, but the truth is we wouldn't need a place to stay if it wasn't for you. Now I know why you never wanted me to tell anyone about our relationship because we never had one. Bye, Ed. I'm sure you can find someone else to manipulate. Call Monica, Keisha, or Tia. They seemed to really enjoy you this weekend."

"Bitch, you should be thanking me. If it wasn't for me, your mother would be dead for stealing. If she wasn't a junky, she wouldn't be in a rehab center. She would be still sucking on this dick willingly while you're in school. Fuck both of y'all ungrateful asses. If I hear you talking about anything that goes on in that house, y'all both will end up in body bags. I know your moves before you do, Jess. See, you're too stupid to plan anything without me knowing. I got something for you and your crack whore mother. You'll be back, one way or another," he said then hung up.

His threats don't affect me anymore. If my brother was home, he wouldn't be saying that shit—if my brother even had an idea. He would be the one in a body bag and that nigga Sean! But he was right . . . It was okay. Every dog has their day. The phone rang twice more, but I didn't answer because I knew it was Edward, and l wasn't about to let him or anyone else blow my high. I got out the tub, put on my push up bra with my knee-length body dress, grabbed a few of my outfits out the closet for tonight, and jumped in my mother's car. I made sure to have the rest of the coke from earlier because it was time to celebrate my freedom.

I pulled up at Eldorado's. It was pretty busy for it to be a Monday night. I walked inside. There were a lot of people sitting, drinking, and chatting. They didn't seem to be interested in the dancers, but I wouldn't be either. The Monday night dancers looked like they should be paying them to watch. I slid in pass everyone without being seen. I wanted everyone to be shocked when I walk up on the stage. I checked with the manager, making sure it was okay for me to perform tonight since I never performed on a Monday. Of course, he was happy to say yes, and told me he hope I would liven the place up. He didn't have to worry about that since dancing was my specialty. If I couldn't do anything else, I damn sure I could slide all this ass up and down a pole.

I stopped pass the bar. They always gave us our first drink on the house. I grabbed my drink of choice and headed back to the dressing room. I brought three costumes with me, but from the looks of things, I'll only need one time on stage. The rest will be spent on the floor. I'd be making majority of my money doing lap dances tonight. While changing, another dancer just arrived. Her name was Star. She was a little shorter than me with real light skin. Her mother was white, and her father was black. Guys loved her small frame, big D cups, and long brown hair with blonde highlights.

"Hey, Star."

"Hi, Strawberry. You're just getting here too?" she asked.

"Yeah, I decided to come at the last minute. I've never been on a Monday before."

"Yea, me neither," she said. "But my father is driving me crazy. I swear, one day while my mother is out, doing what she cares about most, her damn drugs, I'm gonna be in there, cutting his dick off."

"Why, your father rapes you?"

"It started when I was seven. I just kind of got use to it, but now, the only time he has his way is when I come home stoned and passed out. I gave up telling my mother. All she would say was 'what is wrong with you, Sophie? Are you trying to take your mother's happiness? He's your father. Why would he want a child when he has a woman, anything he does is because he loves you.'"

"Girl, I'm here to tell you, that's not love. That's sick!" I said. I thought, *Damn, white people. I got enough issues. I can't get myself involved with her fucked-up shit. I have enough fucked-up shit of my own.*

I took a sip of my drink, lined some coke on the mirror, took it back, then took another sip.

"Oh, girl. Damn! Where did you get all that shit from? Can I do some?" asked Star. Everybody knew no one wanted to drink or get high alone.

"Sure, help yourself. Drink some of your drink afterward to get the taste out your throat."

I put my costume on. It had the strawberries which covered parts of my breast. It was a bikini-type bottom which had no sides; a strawberry covered each ass cheek with a green leaf in the front center. I slipped on my thigh highs, put on my black garter belt, and clipped it to the top of my stockings. I put on my six-inch see-through heels and covered up with a black silk robe. I tied a perfect bow in the front, put my hair in two ponytails, and had my school girl glasses on. Now, who can say no to this?

I turned around, and Star sat in the chair naked, staring at me with her big ass titties, rubbing her body down with oil in slow motion like she was in a porn video. That coke got her just like it had me the first time. She better enjoy it because she'd never get that same feeling again.

"Damn, you look good," Star said. "Do you want to go on stage together, Strawberry?"

"No, thank you I want to be the *star* of the show."

"Please, come on. I always go by myself. It will be fun. Please?"

"Okay, do another line first."

"Done!" she said. That didn't take much convincing.

"Okay, get dressed. You go on first. They play your song 'You Do Your Thing' for ten minutes. When the song 'Candy' comes on, position yourself in the chair. Hang your head over the back of the chair, arch your back—one leg straight out the other on your tip toe—while holding on to the side of the chair. Got it?" I asked.

"Yup, it sounded like a scene from a *Flashdance*."

"Yup, you got it."

We started laughing. "Once I came out, you sit there and let me do all the work. You don't mind getting splashed with water, do you?"

"Nope."

"Cool. Shoes off."

"Okay," said Star.

This ought to grab their attention. The DJ did exactly what was instructed. Star was good. She work that pole to the tune of "I love Rock and Roll / Put another dime in the jukebox baby." The song slowly started to fade out as "Candy" played. Star sat in the chair, looking like a perfect silhouette. I placed my strawberry shaped bowl on top of my head—that I occasionally fill with chocolate syrup—filled with water. I walked out slowly, swaying to the beat with every step. As I bent over to place the strawberry bucket on the floor, I spread my legs wide open to give the crowd a peak. I then picked up the bucket and splashed Star with the water. She went right along with the program, whipping her pretty hair from front to back as the water splashed on my body. It looked just like a scene from *Flashdance*. She laid back in her chair as I danced around her wet body. As I stood behind her, I caressed her breasts and took her top off. We had every pair of eyes staring directly at us. Now, this was the type of attention I was looking for. I worked the front of the stage, and Star worked the pole. She slid down the pole nice and slow with her hands between her legs, landing on her stomach with her ass in the air. I started at the top of the pole twirling, twisting, and sliding down with my ass landing perfectly on Stars.

I had to admit—we were two bad bitches on stage. We worked the pole like no other. The crowd was loving our act. By the time we finished rolling around on the stage together, they couldn't wait to pay for a lap dance. Several guys brought us drinks. We were so fucking high from the coke. I gave this guy a lap dance, and Star came over, climbed on top facing me, and wrapped her legs around my waist. We both started grinding our bodies on one another. The guy got so turned on. He lifted Star's ass off his lap and pulled his dick out. Star sat back down, allowing him to enter her. She bent over and touched her knees, bouncing up and down as if she were giving him a lap dance. I danced over her one leg as he grabbed her breast with one hand and played with my pussy with the other. I came instantly. We knew the owner had strict rules—no touching and no sex in the club—but he was nowhere around. I could only imagine what Star was going through at home. It still didn't give her a right to have sex with a stranger. His nasty ass didn't even put on a condom.

I looked at the time. It was still early. They threw a lot of money on stage, but they were mainly ones. With that and the lap dances I gave, I had about $420 in two hours. Not bad for Eldorado's on a Monday night. I couldn't help but look around at all this. The money was good, but the experiences were life-threatening. Once I pick my mother up tomorrow, I'd be done with this life style—the dancing, the drugs. We'd move and find a place of our own. I'd never bring another guy where I lived. As a matter of fact, I was done with dating for a while. I had one more year of school—nursing school . . . here I come.

I left the two alone. Star was a big girl. I heard that she always had sex with the customers. I walked around, checked out the scenery, trying to see who looked like I could get the most money from; then, I heard somebody call my name. I turned to see who it was. It was an old friend of my brother's. He got caught up for beating a nigga to death. He didn't get as much time because he pleated self-defense, but shit, he still got enough time. I didn't know he was home. Damn! I know my brother's gonna find out about me working at the club now. I didn't want him worrying while he was in there.

"Hey, Damon," I said. "When did you get home?"

"I got out last week."

"Did you happen to see my brother while you were inside?"

"We haven't talked to him in a while."

"Yea, he was about to bust a nigga's head to the white meat for talking about you working up in here. Your brother was really hurt behind this shit, lil shorty," Damon said with a serious look on his face. "Lucky for him, he was on good terms with a few of the guards. They put him in maximum security to keep him from getting in trouble so he can make it up outta there in four months."

"Four? I thought it was six," I said.

"Naw," said Damon.

"Well, this is my last night working here anyway."

"Yeah, I hoped so because he's already mad about a few other things he had heard about. That's why he don't want to see or talk to anybody until he gets home."

"What other things, Damon?"

"You'll find out when he get out."

Lord, please, I hope my brother didn't find anything about what has been going on with me and my mother. He just messed my night up and blew my high. I haven't even figured out how I was going to explain to Tonya that I had been dealing with her brother for eight months, and I didn't want to explain it to my brother. Well, I made enough money for tonight $420 plus the $150 each the guy paid for the double the pleasure lap dance. I went home and changed.

I hadn't slept like that in a long time, knowing that I made the decision for my mother and I to leave today, and knowing Edward was out of town had me feeling at peace last night. I must've been tired. It was twelve o'clock noon. I needed to shower, get dressed, and call the Holiday Inn on Lochraven to make sure they had rooms available. My mother could check us in once I pick her up. I grabbed the phone to call my mother; I hadn't spoken with her all weekend.

"Hi, can I speak with Irene Johnson, please. It's her daughter."

After they put me on hold, she spoke, "Hello."

"Hey, Mommy, I miss you."

"I miss you too, baby. I tried calling you the other day, but they told me no phone calls."

"Yes, I know." she said.

"Well you sound better. How do you feel?"

"Great! I can't wait to get out of here and come home."

"Okay, your release time is one o'clock. I'll be there. We can go straight to the hotel and check in, then come back and pack. Since Edward is out of town, we can take our time and make sure we don't forget anything. I don't wanna have to go back there."

"Wait, wait, wait one minute, Jess. Hotel for what?"

"Ma, we can't stay there at Edward's place anymore. You need to get yourself together so you can get another job. We can have a place of our own. Did you know Stacey was coming home in four months? We can't live there when he gets out. You know how overprotective Stacey is."

"So we're just gonna stay in a hotel, Jessica? It will take time for me to get a job, Jess. How are we supposed to pay for this hotel?"

"Ma, it's only until Friday. I know once Edward gets back he will be looking for me. Right now, I'm weak when it comes to him. I figured that once he can't find me in a couple days, he'll stop looking."

"Well, what's next? Where are we supposed to go after Friday?"

"Ma, relax. Can we worry about getting the room so we can come back here and pack our stuff and get out of there? I'll explain everything once we get all our belongings and get back to the hotel."

It had only been three days, so I knew that she still got that itch. If I told her we were going to her sister's, that would be her excuse not to leave. She didn't care what Edward did to her as long as they fed her drugs.

"Okay, and we can also talk about why you're not in school." *Wow.* What a difference. When she was doing drugs, she cared less about what I did.

"Okay, Ma. Anything you want." I said as we hung up. I got dressed. Might as well do a line. There was no need to throw it away. Once the rest of this was gone, it would be my last time using anyway. I slipped on my shirt, sweat shorts, and my high top Reebok's. I grabbed my mother's keys and made sure I had my license.

It was amazing what four days of detox did to the skin. My mother looked lighter and happy. I missed seeing her like that. I felt like it was all my fault that we were in this situation. If my eyes weren't closed to the truth, we wouldn't have been in this situation in the first place. Tears fell down my face. All I wanted was for Edward to love me. Just because a man said he loved you didn't mean he really did, and just because he was giving didn't mean you should accept. I should've known something was wrong with my mother a long time ago. I was going to make sure things got back to the way they used to be . . . or better. This was my wake up call. *With more time, she'll look better than ever. She'd start to gain her weight back,* I thought as I watched her walk down the hall of the detox clinic. I gave her the biggest and longest hug I ever gave her. We needed each other when my dad left, and I realized we needed each other more than ever now.

"I love you, Ma. I don't know what I would do without you."

"I love you too, Jess." I loved when she called me Jess.

Once we got to our hotel room, we checked it out and found that everything was nice and clean. On our way back to the house, she tried asking me questions about where we were going to stay, but I changed the subject by telling her I wouldn't be dancing at the club anymore and how I wanted to make her proud by finishing school so I can go to a nursing school so I can help people. I parked the car in front of the house. We went inside and started packing right away.

It might be a bad idea that I brought my mother back here. She looked nervous, and I knew that she had a lot of bad memories here, but they'd be gone soon.

"Ma, are you okay up there? Do you know where everything you wanna take is?"

"Yeah, its in my room. I'm okay. I can go pack it. I had to use the bathroom."

"Okay. Well, please try and hurry up. Make sure we don't leave anything. Edward said he'll be back tomorrow, but I don't trust him."

"Jessica, did you tell him we were leaving?"

"Yes, Ma. I told him."

"What exactly did you say to him? You didn't tell him anything I told you, did you?"

"No, not really. He called us 'ungrateful,' and I told him if it wasn't for him starting you on drugs in the first place, we would have never needed a place to stay anyway."

"Jessica, I asked you not to say anything to him about what I told you! He told me he would kill me if I told you or anyone else."

"Ma, calm down. Don't worry about Edward." I assured her. She was so scared that she was shaking. "I promise you. Everything will be okay," I said as I walked down the steps. I felt like I was the mother with all that had been going on. I finished packing. My mother was still upstairs, taking forever.

"Ma!" I yelled, but she didn't answer. What could possibly be taking her so long? While waiting for her, I went down and checked the basement to make sure there was nothing that belonged to us. There were a few plants my mother brought from our old place. There was no use in taking them since they were dying due to lack of water. As I went back upstairs, the phone rang.

"Ma!"

"Yes, Jess."

"I forgot to get all my pajamas out the bottom draw. Can you pack them with your stuff?" I told her as I answered the phone. "Hello, you're still there, I see. How's your mother doing?"

"We are packing now. Since when did you start asking about my mother?""

"You know that I care about Ms. Irene. So, okay, you're leaving for real. Can I speak to her?"

"No, Edward. Bye. I have to go."

"Well, can you tell her something for me?"

"What is it . . . your sorry?"

"Tell your mother that I hope she enjoy. She really deserves it—to be clean, that is."

"What?" He was so high all the time, he barely knew what he was talking about. "Boy, Bye" I said as I hung up.

"Ma! Do you have everything?" I asked as she came down the steps.

"Yes, thanks for packing some of my things for me, Jess."

"What are you talking about, Ma?"

"I didn't pack anything."

The phone started ringing. I knew it was Edward. I did not answer, but I knew that if he was on the phone, he wasn't on his way here.

"What do you want, Edward?" There was silence on the other end, but I knew someone was there because I heard them breathing. "Hello," I said again.

"Jessica, this is Anaya. Did you just say Edward?"

My eyes got big; I felt ashamed, and I couldn't say a word.

"Jessica, what 'Edward' are you talking about? Please say you're not talking about Tonya's brother. Jessica answer me. We know where you're staying. We're on our way," Anaya said.

I hung up.

"Come on, Ma. It's time to go."

I didn't want Anaya and Tonya to find out like this. I wanted to tell them when I was ready. We took one last look around and left his key on our sofa.

"To new beginnings." I locked the door, and we drove back to the hotel. I sang every song that came on the radio until we pulled up at the front door. We grabbed all our bags and put them on the carrier; then, I parked the car. I was excited about the decision we just made, and my mother's attitude seemed to have shifted as well. She seemed happier about it also. I'd figure out how to deal with the girls later.

I layed across one of the beds.

"What are you doing, Ma? There's no need to unpack. We'll only be here for three days . . . four days max."

"I'm just unpacking a little bit, Jessica."

Wow. She didn't ask me where we were going to next. Good . . . because I didn't feel like explaining right now. My mother's finger tips were rough looking from vialing up Edward's shit. How could I have not seen this before? I guess I didn't want to. He use to make her stay up all night while I was sleep for school or out working at the club. To vial up his coke and dope, she did it as long as she stayed high.

"I'm going to the bathroom, Jess."

"Okay, Ma."

She went in the bathroom and shut the door.

"So where are we supposed to go after here Jess?" she asked.

"Well, first, just so you know, I have a little over eight thousand dollars saved up. That should hold us over for quite a while. But now that you're working on getting better, it won't take you time to get a job. You have a college degree."

"Wow, Jess! You saved all that money. I'm happy you got something from shaking your ass at that damn club."

I hurried and snorted a line of what I had left and rubbed a little on my gums before my mother came out the bathroom. "So until you find a job, and remember it won't take long, we'll be staying at aunt Gene's house." I covered my ears and got prepared to hear her yell.

"Ma?"

"Yes, baby."

"Did you hear what I said?"

"Yes, baby. That's great news. Mommy loves my big girl."

What? She sounded delusional. I sat there thinking, but all I heard was Edward's voice in my head—*Tell your mother that I hope she enjoy. She really deserves it—to be clean, that is.*

"Ma! Didn't you say there was a bag that was already packed in your room? Where is it? Ma!"

There was no answer. I tried to open the door, but it was locked.

"Ma!" I screamed. I moved back and tried to slam the door hard with my shoulder, but that only worked on television. I started crying and screaming. "Open the door, mommy . . . "

I heard a loud thud then a drop—

"Ma!"

CHAPTER 13

Anaya

Anaya

"WHY DID DJ look at me like that?" Tonya said.

"Why are you in denial? I told you that Jessica must be messing with that no-good-ass tortilla named Sean."

"You think that's what he meant?"

"Yes, I do. Edward just not gonna tell you."

We called Jessica to see if she was home, but we wouldn't tell her we knew where she stayed.

"I hope she answers. Shit, I would like to know what's the damn secret for."

"He's not even from around here. Shit, I would let the world know if I was fucking with his pretty Spanish looking ass," Tonya said.

"Okay, okay. I think I get the point, Tonya. I think those guys over there want you."

Tonya started laughing as she walked toward them. She sold weed almost to the entire school. One thing was, definite, she always kept a hustle going.

"Hurry up!" Mona and I walked so we could catch up.

"So you think Jessica's getting high?" Mona asked.

"I don't know, but I hope not. It's not even about who she's messing with that scares me. It's where she's staying and why."

"Where is her mother staying?"

"I would think they're staying together, but girl I don't know."

"Well, I hope everything is okay. Be careful if your white-girl ass goes down there."

"Whatever."

We both started laughing.

"Okay, call me later so I'll know everything is okay," Mona said then walked in her direction to go home. As I walked down Saint Lo Drive, Tonya came behind me.

"I just made fifty dollars that quick," she said. Tonya knew everybody. On our way home, she would stop and talk to everybody. By the time we got to her house, she made $150 by selling dime bags of weed, not counting what she made during the course of school hours.

I went inside her house and sat on the sofa while Tonya called Jessica.

"She should be home. It's not like she came to school today. I was really not worried about her, now I know that Mr. New York is the big secret, but I'll call her one more time." There was still no answer. "If I were her, I wouldn't answer either because we would be too busy in the sack," Tonya said.

"Girl, if she calls you back, just page me. I'm going down Pop's house later. He said he had a surprise for me."

"Damn! Why you gotta be lying, Anaya? You know you gave that boy some ass!"

"Shut up. No, I didn't."

"So no Stanley's today?" Tonya said.

"Nope. He's not speaking to me anyway."

"Why?"

"Because I told him he has to chill out. He's grabbing me every time he sees me in the hallway."

"Anaya, you're confusing that boy."

"No, I'm not, girl. Bye . . . Don't forget to call me if she calls you later," I said as I walked out the front door.

My cousin was the only one there when I walked in.

"What's that bag on the sofa, Nathan?"

"Oh, uncle Ron said it was yours."

"Where did he go?"

"To pick momma up."

"Oh, okay." I opened the bag. There were two Nike tennis skirt sets and two pairs of huarache—the green and the purple ones.

"What did you get?" I asked Nathan. "I know you got something. He got all of us Jordan's. Nice," I said as I took my bag upstairs.

After I used the bathroom, I grabbed my book bag, sat outside, and finished my homework. I knew I told Pop I would call him once I got home, but he was giving a little too much too fast. My grandmother always told me: "Don't be out there accepting gifts from boys. They'll do anything to get in your pants" (even though I liked Pop and I was the one who wanted to get in his pants).

The term "nothing comes for free" didn't always mean that it was sex you'll end up giving. It could be your life or just self-respect. To me, it was a little scary to know that he was getting money like this. What if they raid the house with me in it or do a drive by while we sat on the front steps? I was too smart not to take all of this into consideration. Well, I was glad I did majority of my homework in school. I finished up this last paragraph for Mr. Murphy, so I was done.

It was perfect timing when uncle Ron just pulled up.

"Hey grandma, how was work? Thank you for my gift bag, uncle Jim." I smiled and held him around his waist as we went in the house.

"Anaya, why do you always ask that?" My grandmother had a mean streak to her. She felt like work was work. "It's the same every day."

I guess she was not as excited being a nurse anymore maybe she was just tired.

"Retire, Grandma," I said.

She gave me the strangest look. Well, I wouldn't say that again. The house was paid off, and she didn't have a car—why was she working so hard? *I don't know*, I thought.

I heard my pager from upstairs. "Nathan, can you bring my pager down off the night stand pretty please with a cherry on top?"

Pop had paged me twice. I grabbed the phone and called him back. "Hey, Pop. What's up?"

"You?" he said. "Did you enjoy your salad?"

"Yes, it was delicious. I ate it all."

"Are you coming down here?"

I walked outside with the phone. "Look, it's pretty obvious you're making pretty good money doing what you do, but I don't want to get caught up in the things that come along with that. I feel like I'm putting myself at risk just by coming down there. Haven't you heard the quote 'Don't shit where you lay'?"

"Anaya, stop playing. You have nothing to worry about. Didn't I say I was going to take care of you? You are safe with me. You don't have to worry about that. You think I would let my daughter come over here if it was something to worry about?" I went silent because he said exactly what I wanted him to say. "So stop worrying, call a cab, and come on down. Now, Anaya!"

My uncle just left, and my grandmother went to take a bath. She was going to lie down and watch TV if she felt a little tired. She didn't need me to do anything, so I called me a cab.

After waiting twenty minutes, the yellow cab finally pulled up. I sat on the steps and waited so he wouldn't have to blow his horn.

"Nathan, let momma know I'm going to a friend's house. I'll be back later."

Damn, the cab man smelled like he just got straight off the slave ship. Didn't he trust deodorants? I rolled the window down and rode with my head hanging out the entire ride. Thank god his house was only ten minutes away. I jumped out the cab before it was fully stopped. I didn't wait for Pop to open the door for me this time.

"Are you okay?" Pop asked.

"I am now," I said as I inhaled and exhaled fresh air. "So what are you up to today, Mister? Just chilling on the steps?"

"I was sitting here, waiting for you. Come on upstairs with me," he said as he opened the door, letting me enter first. We went in, and he shut and locked the door behind us like he always did. He had this big box on the bed that was wrapped up with a bow.

"Pop, what is this? You just gave me a very expensive watch yesterday. You could have at least waited a couple days." We both started laughing because everyone knew I loved the finer things in life. I now realized nothing was turning me on more than surprises from someone I like that paid attention and knew my taste.

"Open it!" Pop said.

I couldn't stop blushing. I never had a man do these things for me before, except for my uncles. I always said to myself, *I would never find a man that could hold my attention and spoil me like they do.* "Looks like I might be wrong," I said as I opened the box. *Haaaaaaaaa* was all I heard. The light from heaven shined down on this beautiful, nice, genuine leather Dooney and Bourke luggage set. "My favorite!"

Most girls my age were into lots of MCM, Louis Vuitton, and Gucci, but Dooney had class written all over it. Besides, I never liked my labels posted all over my attire as long as I knew what I wore was all that mattered.

"Open the luggage," he said, and I did. Inside was the softest, prettiest, brown leather with pink trimming D&B satchel; a makeup case; and matching silk scarf. I felt like I was dreaming.

"Pop what was all this for?" I was in awe at that moment. He stole my heart.

"Look inside the zipper."

"Oh, come on. No more, please!" I couldn't believe I knew how to say that phrase when gifts were involved. "How were you able to pick out everything so perfectly?"

"I have my sources," he said.

"Oh, okay"

Big Shot! Inside the zipper of the luggage was every apartment brochure there was. "Now, I'm nervous," I told him.

"Don't be. There's no rush. I just want you to know that I'm not bull shitting you. Whenever you're ready, just let me know."

"I will," I said, "as soon as I'm ready."

I jumped on his lap, squeezed my legs around his waist, and kissed him with all I had; but I still wasn't ready to have sex with him. I mean, I was turned on and ready—just not ready.

"Anaya, I don't want you to rush and do nothing you're not ready to do."

Shit, that just made me want him even more.

"Hey, my man's birthday is at the end of June. He got a cabin up deep creek Maryland. It has a kitchen, indoor and outdoor pool, and three hot tubs. If you can get away, I want you to go with me. It's gonna be a lot of fun—good food and good people."

"Okay, I'll let you know."

"Good, then we can fill that luggage up," he said.

"Okay," I said as I revealed a big Kool-Aid smile. I started kissing him again. We played across the bed, kissing and talking for hours. "I can get use to this."

"Good. I want you to. You know, once a girl gets accustomed to the life she's living, she'll never want it to end. And why should she?" he said as he grabbed the back of my head and pulled my mouth to his.

Tuesday was going by so slow, but I was up for school on time. I even beat the alarm clock. I felt so good since I had such a great night with Pop. I felt like I had a new walk. I thought I'd be pink and preppy today. It was so beautiful outside, pink should be the only color that should be worn when the sun shined. And who else was better to rock it? Me—of course!

After my bath, I sprayed on some Champs Elysee's—one of my favorites—went over to my draw, and took out my quarter length Calvin Klein baggy jean jumper and my chocolate tank with the pink satin bow I made and sewed on a while ago. I put on some thin white bobby socks that came a little pass my ankle, slipped on my shiny pink heels, and carried my bag that Pop gave me last night. I always had gold fever, so I topped it off with my gold Cartier. It was everything my baby brought me.

I smiled, thinking about him. He had a hell of a way of apologizing when he did something I didn't like. What else would he like to do wrong? I smiled as I grabbed the keys to the red Suzuki sidekick my uncle let me drive. There was no music needed. I just wanted to feel the wind blow through my long black hair. I beeped the horn for Tonya, letting her know that we're driving today. Since I got so caught up, I wasn't able to talk to her last night.

Okay, bitch, the 4-1-1. Who was I kidding? I didn't need music because I knew she would talk over it, but hell, that was my rode dog; I was excited to tell her everything.

"Girl, please," Tonya said. After everything I told her, all she could say was, "If it's not a college dorm, your grandmother will not be letting you move in with a man, a boy, or whatever. I couldn't blame her."

She was right. "I wasn't thinking about moving with anyone anyway. I just liked the fact of how he presented everything."

"So does this mean you have a boyfriend now?"

"No, not just yet. I need to make sure I can shake Stanley's sexy ass and his sexual pleasures. First, I don't want to start a relationship if I'm not ready. There's no rush to dive in head first for a commitment," I said.

"Girl, you and your quotes . . . you'll say anything, so you won't have to say you belong to someone."

"I do belong to somebody—God and my momma."

"You know what I meant."

"Come on. Get out let's get in here before we're late."

There were no signs of Stanley this morning. He must be really mad at me.

"Oh, did Jessica ever call you back yesterday?"

"Nope."

"Well, hopefully we'll see her in school today."

"Did you ask Edward?"

"He's not home. He's gone to New York. He won't be back till tomorrow."

"Oh, okay."

"Ah!" Tonya screamed as Stanley came from behind and grabbed her waist. "Boy, you play too much. Now, if I had a gun, you would be shot." Tonya said. "Now where's your money at? Buy some of this good chronic from me."

"Tonya, you know I keep my own shit. I'm not buying those leaves you bagged up out your yard."

"Oh, okay it's like that?"

Stanley and I started laughing, but Stanley didn't look at me or say anything to me either. I wasn't hurt—just a little disappointed feel like I'm slowly losing a good friend. I understood that he needed to do whatever he needed to do to keep his heart intact. I see that he's starting to now realize that we can't have great sex while just staying friends. I told him from the beginning when I threw this pussy up in the air, it turned to sunshine.

Tonya walked in the opposite direction to class while Stanley and I had classes across the hall from each other. I couldn't walk down an empty hallway side by side and not say anything. It was just stupid.

"So you can't even acknowledge my presence now? Our friendship we had is over too?" I asked.

"No, I just need a minute so we can get back to that point."

"Okay, Stanley. I understand. Shake on it?" I stuck my hand out. He shook it then walked into his classroom. Damn, he always smelled so refreshing. The way he acted was turning me on; I like a chase. I was such a freak when I wanted to be, but I gave him all the space He needed He seemed hurt enough, and that was the last thing I wanted to do.

The day was going by rather quickly, and Stanley said nothing to me all day. To be honest, I kind of missed the attention he used to give me, but I didn't want to send him mixed messages. I thought the sex he thought he could handle was enough.

It was lunch, and as usual, Tonya came down to sit with me.

"Don't tell me Jessica didn't come to school again today?" I asked Tonya.

"If she did, no one has seen her. What's he doing in here?"

"What's up, ladies?"

"What's up, DJ? Do you ever go to class?"

"Yes, I do, Anaya. Y'all remember the guy, Damon? He got locked up for beating a nigga to death with his hands."

"Yeah, he used to hang with Jessica's brother Stacey," I said.

"Yea, him. Well, he just came home. He was down Eldorado's last night, and somebody heard him talking to Jessica about how her brother was mad about her shaking her ass in the club and some other shit. He said he'll be home in four months. He said Jessica packed her shit and left."

"Yeah, Stacey's crazy ass is overprotective especially when it comes to her, so I hope nobody's making her do something she doesn't want to do," I said.

"So I guess she won't be making out with girls on stage either," DJ said.

"What?!"

"Yeah, my man said that she and this chick named Star put on a good ass show last night. I'm mad that I missed it," DJ said.

"Jessica and another girl? What is going on with her? I can't believe this Tonya—Tonya!" Tonya clear across the cafeteria, making her rounds. "She didn't hear anything you said, DJ. Well, we're going down there during the weekend, but we're gonna drive down where you saw her at today if She doesn't answer the phone."

After lunch, we went to our last classes. Once the bell rang, I went and waited for slow poke at the same spot near the office. Mona met me there. I told her all about my visit with Pop yesterday.

"Girl, tell him that your ass is spoiled enough! So, is he your boyfriend now?"

"No, not yet."

"You know your overprotective ass uncles not gonna let you move with him."

"I don't want to, but I do want him to get his own place so I can visit him somewhere other than Greenmount."

"Hi, Mona," Tonya greeted.

"Hey, Tonya."

"Aight, Mona. I'll call you later," I said. I was glad that I drove. I had to use the bathroom.

On our way home, I tried to explain what DJ told me during lunch, but she really wasn't paying any attention. She was too busy counting money. All she heard was 'Jessica had sex down the club with a woman,' and that was not even what I said.

"Alright, Tonya. You and your money . . . Get out. I have to go to the bathroom. I'll call Jessica before we leave out, but either way, we're still going," I said.

"Hey, Nathan."

"Hey, grandma gonna be home late. She had another doctor's appointment. Your mother went with them."

"How many appointments will she have? She went to the doctor several times this month. I knew she was not feeling sick from the cold 'she picked up at work' as she claimed."

"Oh, he just said it was a doctor's appointment."

I grabbed the phone off the charger and took it in the bathroom with me. Pop had paged me, so I called him while I soaked in the tub. We talked for almost an hour. I told him that I didn't think his mother liked me very much. Every time I spoke, she gave me a cold wave.

"She doesn't like anybody."

"Oh, okay. I guess that makes me feel a little better. Well, I'm about to get out the tub. My toes and fingers are beginning to look like prunes."

He started laughing. "Okay, call me later," he said.

We hung up, and I called Jessica. The phone rang twice then she answered.

"What do you want Edward?!" I was flabbergasted. *Did I hear her right? Did she say 'Edward'?* "What Edward?" I thought she was messing with Sean, but that outburst had meaning, like it was Edward she had been talking to. I slipped on some ripped up jean shorts and a white tank that had black leather trimming and a pair of white pumpkin seeds. I called Tonya and told her to be out front.

Driving down Broadway, I tried to tell Tonya that it was her brother I thought Jessica was dating, but Tonya just wouldn't listen. She claimed that her brother would have told her if it was.

"All the more I know something is not right," I said. "Think about it, Tonya. Why would she want to keep someone from New York that we didn't even know - a secret? It doesn't make sense."

We drove to MontFord and Federal, but we didn't know what house or if we were even on the right side of the street. Guys started whistling and yelling out. We got red tops and blue tops, like we were there trying to cop some drugs. Shit, I was ready to go already.

"Excuse me," I said to a guy I saw sitting on the corner steps. "Do you know a girl named Jessica that moved around here a while ago?"

"Naw," he said.

"You might have seen her driving a white maxima . . . or her mother maybe?"

"Oh, yea. They're four doors down that way, but I think you just missed them. They were loading bags in the car. They looked like they were moving."

"Okay, thanks."

We kept on knocking, but we got no answer, so we left.

We decided to go to the Rec at Kirk Avenue and play some ping pong. But We just watched instead, then we decided to go around to the court, and watch the fellas shoot a few hoops. We were there for about thirty minutes when we decided to go outside and walk around to the outdoor court. I heard somebody call my name, so I turned around, but I didn't see anyone.

"Anaya," it called again when I saw Stanley was coming up the grass hill.

"Oh, I thought you weren't speaking to me," I said playfully. Damn, Stanley! Why does his bowlegged ass gotta come at a girl, looking all sexy and shit with his chocolate linen pants folded up past his ankles, a pair of Saucony, and a short sleeve pink polo shirt? I just wanted him to do me right on the lawn, but I snapped out of it.

Stanley kneeled down in the grass, took my hand, and started singing. *What in the hell is going on right now? I'm confused*, I thought. "You may be young, but you're ready / You're not a little girl, you're a woman / Let me tell you, baby / I'm yours for the takin' / So you can do what you please / Don't take my love for granted / You're all I'll ever need / Hold me, hold me in your arms / Oh . . . baby, never let me go."

Keith Sweat, really! I couldn't believe that he came here on a mission. How did he know I was here? I was so embarrassed, I didn't know what to do. He did sound good, but I just wanted him to stop.

"Aww, Anaya. Now, that was so sweet. He is in love with you, girl. What you gonna do?" Tonya asked.

Nothing! There's nothing for me to do. I've had this conversation with him so many times. He told me everything was alright, and this wouldn't happen.

"Stanley, I'm sorry that I can't give you more than what we already have, but we talked and both agreed that we were fine just the way things were." I hated to sound cold. "I really don't know what you want me to say. Besides, I love Keith sweat, and you did sound good singing it to me."

He looked at me and walked away.

Tonya and I walked around to the court to watch the basketball game before we left. Toward the end of the game, I decided it was time for me to go and take this jeep home before it got any later. Tonya had her eyes on a little cutie on a dirt bike. Since it was only 7:00, she decided to stay and walk home later.

I really wanted to get home so I could see what was going on with my grandmother. This was her third doctor's appointment in a week, and something don't seem right to me.

As I pulled up, I noticed both of my uncles cars were parked out front. It took me almost forty-five minutes to get home due to everyone asking me—What did you do to Stanley? Never seen him act like that before. What do you have between your legs? I didn't know y'all were messing with each other. Blah, blah, blah.)

They were normally home around this time. As I walked in the house, I didn't see anyone but Nathan. I saw cars outside.

"Where is everyone?" I asked.

"Grandma was pretty sick that they had to help her up the stairs. My mother and your mother are up there too. I was on my way up there but they said to wait downstairs, and to tell you the same when you get in."

What kind of crap is that? We sat and waited for what seemed like forever. After a few more minutes of getting impatient, everyone finally came downstairs.

"Why y'all looking like that? It's time grandma gets a new doctor. She's had that cold long enough," I said as I was about to go upstairs again.

"Sit down, baby." My mother said.

"I was going upstairs to see grandma."

"I know, just sit down for a minute first. We have something we need to tell you and Nathan . . ."

CHAPTER 14

Seeing is Believing

Jessica

I RAN TO the phone and dialed 911. I then called the front desk to let them know that my mother was locked in the bathroom. It sounded like she fell and might have hit her head because she was not answering me. Hopefully they could get here sooner so we can at least get the door unlocked. I waited, still yelling for my mother, while trying to pick the lock. After a few minutes, I heard some loud bangs at the door. I ran and opened it. It was the ambulance. I couldn't believe that they had arrived before the hotel management. Damn Holiday Inn!

I began to cry as I opened the door. Reality was starting to sit in more and more. *Lord Jesus, I need you right now!* I prayed that my mother was okay. *Please, Lord, don't take my mother away from me.* Someone from the hotel finally arrived right before they got a chance to knock the door down. As they put the key in the hole and pushed the door open, my heart dropped as I saw my mother lying on the bathroom floor beside the toilet. I pushed the man out the way and grabbed my mother's head.

"Ma!" I screamed and cried out, but she was irresponsive. She had white foam coming out from her mouth and a tourniquet tied around her arm. There was a burned soda top inside the sink and a needle on the floor behind the bathroom door.

"Come on, ma'am," the emergency medical technician said as he lifted me to my feet. "Let us do our job. What is your mother's name?"

"Irene!" I screamed.

The others rushed in and checked for a pulse. It seemed as though everyone was moving and talking in slow motion. All I heard someone say was "We have a slight heart beat in here. We need the defibrillator and a stretcher."

An officer came over to me and said, "We don't know if she's unconscious because of the fall which caused her to hit her head, or if she overdosed off some bad drugs." I sat stiff as if I had no idea of what was going on.

"Miss,"—a female officer came over and sat beside me—"Are you okay miss? Do you have anyone you would like for us to call?"

In a blur, I saw them rolling my mother out on the stretcher while constantly working on her. I wanted to speak, but I couldn't; I wanted to cry, but I couldn't. All I saw was Edward's face, and all I heard was his voice . . . *Tell your mother that I hope she enjoy. She really deserves it—to be clean, that is.*

Edward tried to kill my mother, and he probably succeeded. I should be with her right now, holding her hand; but instead, I sat here on this bed, frozen, feeling like my wind pipe was closing. I couldn't breathe! Oh, God . . . Please help me!

CHAPTER 15

The Visit

Jessica

ALL I SAW were bright lights. Everything was white. Did I die? If so, I shouldn't be in heaven. I heard beeping sounds. Something was connected to my arm. *Oh, I'm in the hospital.* Bright lights and machines were everywhere. A tall handsome white man took my blood pressure.

"Sir, my mother was brought here by the ambulance, and I need to get up so I can find her to make sure she's okay."

"Miss, you need to lie still for observation for forty-eight hours. You passed out due to lack of oxygen to the brain. You have quite a bit of alcohol and drugs in your system. Since you're still a minor, the police, along with child protective services, will be in here to talk to you," he went on, saying. "You are extremely dehydrated, so you are hooked up to an IV for fluids. I'll be back in a while to give you a replacement once that's gone. Hold on tight, everything will be okay."

I'd be damned, I thought. I was not sitting here to wait for some damn child protective services. I wasn't afraid of needles, so it wasn't a problem for me to remove the IV and apply a little pressure to stop the bleeding. I got the hospital bag, and put my clothes on. I hurried and got in the elevator before anyone stopped me. Since I was only seventeen, they had the right to detain me until an immediate relative over the age of twenty-one came to my rescue. I took the elevator down to the main entrance and walked to the front desk as if I just arrived.

"Hello, I'm looking for an Irene Johnson."

"When was she admitted?" the receptionist asked

"Today." I tapped my fingers on the counter while waiting.

"And who are you?" asked this fifty-pound white lady with Coca-Cola bottles ass glasses on her face. They looked like they wore more than she did.

"I'm her sister," I said.

"One second. Someone will be down in a second," she said as she dialed on her phone. As I went to sit down due to light headedness, a black doctor, looking to be in his late fifties with salt and pepper hair, walked toward me.

"Hello, Miss. Are you the sister of Ms. Irene Johnson?"

"Yes. Are there any other family members here with you? No, just me at the moment. They're on their way," I said nervously, thinking the reason for all of these questions is because he was asking for child protective services.

"Would you like to wait for their arrival?"

"No! I would like to go talk to my sister, please. If you could tell me what room she's in, I can call and let everyone else know. Thank you."

"Well, Miss, I'm sorry to inform you, but your sister passed away on her way to the hospital. The paramedics did everything they could. I'm so sorry."

It felt like someone just plunged a knife in my stomach and constantly kept turning it. All I could hear was my mother's voice . . .

Jessica, don't go outside till your homeworks are done.

Jess, baby are you hungry?

Jessica, spend some time with your mother, and let's have movie night.

Jessica, there's something strange about Edward . . . it's in his eyes.

I instantly felt sick as I vomited all over the hospital floor. I realized I'd never hear my mother's voice again. I ran out the hospital down Broadway as fast as I could. I wanted to kill Edward and Sean myself. I needed to watch them suffer. I fell to the ground, screaming and crying. I couldn't believe that my mother's gone. Thinking maybe the doctors were wrong, I called my aunt Gene from a payphone on Broadway and Monument. I cried so much on the phone that she couldn't understand me.

"Calm down, Jessica" my aunt said. "Where are you?"

"John Hopkins," I cried.

"I'm on my way," said my aunt. Once my aunt arrived, she talked to the same doctor. My aunt grabbed her chest and immediately took a seat. As she put her face in her hands and cried, I wrapped my arms around her and cried too. Her husband consoled us both. We went to the room where mother lied, looking as if she was sleeping peacefully.

I laid my head on my mother's chest and held her one last time. I whispered in her ear, "They will pay for what they've done. They will pay." My aunt was devastated. She hadn't seen or heard from my mother in quite some time. She wanted time alone to talk so me and my uncle stepped out the room.

Even though there wasn't much sun coming through the small window in my aunt's basement, daylight was still too much for me to bare. I just wanted to soak in my own sorrow, but I couldn't. The small radio clock that sat on top of an old brown end table read 6:15 a.m. I was sweating and in pain. My stomach was in knots. I was bent over in bed in so much pain, thinking *what could this be?* I hadn't eaten in the past twenty-four hours—that has to be it! I forced myself up and got myself together in the bathroom. It had a small wall mirror, and it had just enough space for one person only. Even though I had no appetite, I needed to put something on my stomach. The closer I got upstairs, the more nauseated I felt.

My aunt was cooking everything—bacon, sausage, fried fish, cheese eggs, grits, fried potatoes, and biscuits. I guessed she couldn't sleep either. Her husband was the only one sitting at the table with a suit on because he had to work this morning. He offered to stay home so he could be there for us, but my aunt told him it was okay and it was best if he went to work.

I sat at the table and ate some bacon and a small bowl of grits. I immediately threw up all over the kitchen floor and broke out in a cold sweat. My aunt touched my forehead, "Jessica you are burning up."

"But I am freezing," I said.

"Take two of these, go back downstairs, and get some rest. I'll let you know when it's time to leave to go visit your brother."

I went downstairs and try to lie down, but I was getting colder and began to shake. I got up and went through all my belongings we had gathered from the hotel, and there it was. It wasn't much but it was enough. I took one deep inhale into my right nostril then my left. I instantly felt better. Damn! I guess I really needed this with all the stress my body was under. I lied down for a bit, went upstairs, pulled myself a cup of coffee, and made a small plate with a little bit of just about everything.

"Wow! You're feeling much better quickly, Jessica?"

"Yes, aunt Gene. I guess the pills you gave me for my fever worked," I said.

"Well, that's good. Eat up, baby. You will need all your strength and energy. You have a long road ahead of you."

"I'm a big girl, Aunt Gene. Everything will be okay."

"Good," she said, "you're strong just like your mother. Eat as much as you like. The twins are gone off to school. I told them not to go downstairs and bother you. I did not mention anything about your mother yet," she said with so much sadness in her voice. I could tell that she was trying to keep her composure for me, but I could look in her eyes and tell that she wasn't taking it too good.

"Okay, baby. Let me go upstairs and try to put myself together."

"Okay, Aunt Gene . . . and thank you."

I stepped out on the front porch and decided to walk down to the corner store to get me some Alexander the Grapes for the road. Walking out the store, a guy said, "He had nickel dimes and twenty bags."

"Of what?" I asked.

"Whatever you need," he said. "Let me see your twenties of coke. Damn, that bag will last me a while.

Only twenty, I thought, *Shit, I'd take it*. I had too much stress to handle. This should help out until I got things in order. Shit, it was not like I was one of those junkies. I had money saved, and this was my first time purchasing. I'd only use it when I want, which wouldn't be for long now that I was away from Edward. Besides, I knew people that drink expensive liquor all the time, and it didn't make them an alcoholic.

The ride on our way to see Stacey was very awkward. My aunt kept talking in riddles. I knew what she was trying to get around to.

"When did my sister start using where as though she over dosed?"

"The autopsy haven't revealed anything as of yet." Anyway, now wasn't a good time. It just happened yesterday, and I wasn't ready to explain anything right now. We drove with the windows down and listened to my mother's favorite song, Whitney Houston "The Greatest Love of All" until we arrived.

I was nervous as the big doors slammed closed with a bang, and even more nervous about what we were about to tell my brother. We sat at the table and watched him as he walked out. He looked so handsome. He got his six-feet-three height from our dad. His Hershey-kissed skin and his thick black shiny hair and eyebrows were from our mother. Being incarcerated, all these years didn't change him much. It only gave him muscles.

"Oh, I'm scared of you," I said playfully, trying to smile as we hugged each other tightly. Oh, how I missed my brother, but he could tell something was wrong.

"Hi, Aunt Gene," he said as he hugged her and sat down. "So what's wrong?" He came right out and asked. "You know, these walls have been talking, Jessica," he said as my aunt looked at me with a confused look. Therefore you know there are some things that have to be handled when I get out in three months."

"Really that's cr—"

"Where is mom?" he asked as he cut me off. "Why didn't she come? Oh, she had to work," he said nonchalantly. I sat there with a ball in my throat, wishing I could run in the bathroom and do some more coke, but I couldn't.

"Jessica . . . Jessica," he kept saying.

"Stacey."

"What's wrong, Aunt Gene?"

"We didn't want you to find out over the phone."

"What is it, Aunt Gene?"

"Your mother passed away yesterday, baby."

"What?! Who the fuck—what the fuck happened?!" he yelled and kicked his chair as he lifted the table in the air. "Not mommy! What the fuck did you do, Jessica?!" he screamed as the guards took him away.

CHAPTER 16

The Battle Continues

Anaya

"OKAY, MA. SO what is it?"

"Your grandmother . . . " she paused and bust out crying.

"My grandmother what ma?!"

"Look at me," uncle Jim said. "Momma's cancer came back. It's now lung cancer.

One tear so big that it could have shook the entire east Baltimore rolled out one eye and down my cheek.

"We've known for some time. Grandma didn't want us to say anything, but she's now getting radiation along with her chemo. Her hair is starting to fall out again, and she's becoming extremely weak. They refuse to allow her to go back to work right now."

This was the first time I saw my cousin Nathan cry.

"So what do we need to do so she can get better like the last time?" I asked.

"Nothing. The doctors are doing everything. I just want to let you know. Look at me, you two," my uncle said. "There's a great chance momma might not make it this time. Not definite, but I want you to at least know that it's a possibility. Okay?"

"Okay, so can I go upstairs now?"

"Go on, just don't mention anything to her right now."

"Okay," I said as I ran up the stairs. He turned around to finish talking to Nathan.

My grandmother was tucked tightly in her bed, dosing in and out like she always did while watching TV. I had so many emotions and feelings that nothing would come out. I climbed to the other side of the bed, gave her a kiss, and balled up under her as if we were having a regular movie night till I dosed off to sleep.

I woke up after my mother telling me to take my clothes off; and, get in my bed.

I was not sure if I awoke from the alarm or from the smell of a combination of Maxwell House's coffee mixed with Pall Mall cigarettes (which meant grandma was home today). I took my bath as usual, pampered myself a little by doing a short but well needed foot and body scrub, slid my hair up into a sloppy bun, put on one of my Nike skirt sets and a fresh pair of kicks, and ran downstairs.

"Good morning, grandma." I would've thought that everything that was said last night was a dream except the fact today was Wednesday and she was here instead of at work. She looked great, and she didn't look sick. Once her treatments were over, she'd be back. "Grandma, you should let me stay home just one day and keep your company."

"Anaya, you better carry your butt to school. I can't wait to finish these treatments so I can go back to work myself," she said as she coughed after taking a puff from her Pall Mall.

"Grandma, really?"

"What, Anaya?"

"I think it would be best if you stop smoking during and after your treatments."

"Anaya, don't think I'm gonna sit around here so y'all can tell me what to do. Nothing's changed. I'm the same person. I smoked before and I'm gonna smoke now."

"Grandma, you didn't have to get radia—"

"Anaya!" she yelled as she cut me off.

"Okay, okay. Grandma, you're so hard headed. So can I stay home?"

"It's supposed to be a nice day today. We can catch the bus down Lexington market like we used to do. Please, please, please . . ."

"All right, Anaya. Stop it with all that please stuff."

"Yes! She must be sick! I wanted to feel her forehead as a joke, but I didn't want her to change her mind. Normally it had to be a serious reason for her to let me miss school. After grandma got dressed, we walked up to Harford Road and caught the nineteen bus. She never had any desire to get her driver's license, and we only caught a hack from the market if we had too many bags to carry. I didn't know from whom I got my wits from because I would have a chauffeur at times if I could afford one (which made me think of Pop).

We got on the bus and got off in front of Lexington market. It was crowded at ten in the morning. You could tell that food stamps were out. I loved the hustle and bustle of downtown. Once in the market, I always got the half lemon with the peppermint stick inside. My grandmother got some salted cod to make cod fish cakes for dinner. She got herself some fried chicken, fried gizzards for Nathan, and an Italian cold cut for uncle Jim. Uncle Ron was too picky, so she didn't get him anything, he didn't stop over every day any way. Uncle Jim comes every day when he get off like clockwork. If It was for ten minutes or an hour, it didn't matter, he still dropped by. We had a nice day going in and out of different stores. On our way home, we stopped in Sears on North and Harford. I got two more pair of pumpkin seeds and several colors of tube tops. We went across the street to Goldenberg so she could get some toiletries. She thought about going to Big B super market on Broadway, but we had too many bags already. We got home around 2:30 right before those bad ass school kids got out. My grandmother had time to rest before cooking dinner. I put the food away as she went upstairs.

"I love you, Grandma!" I yelled.

"I love you too, Anaya!" she yelled back.

I'm glad we spent today together because her treatments will only make her worse before it makes her better, I thought. I didn't realize how tired I was, so I lied across the sofa as I watched reruns of what's happening. I dosed off and took a nap.

I woke up, feeling rejuvenated. I looked at my watch and couldn't believe I slept this long. Nathan was sitting on the sofa, watching Wheezy lay it on George as the maid sat there and did nothing on *The Jefferson's.*

"Where is everybody?" I asked.

"Grandma just finished cooking. She's gone upstairs now, said she was tired."

"Oh, okay."

"Your pager is upstairs. It went off several times, and Mona called twice. She said for you to call her when you wake up. Tonya called, and some guy, but he didn't leave his name.

"Okay," I said. I went upstairs to use the bathroom, peaking in on my grandmother. She was watching *Sanford and Son*. I grabbed my pager then shut the bathroom door. Tonya paged me once, while Pop paged me three times. Really? I hoped he was not one of those stalking clingy type. That was the last thing I needed. I got the cordless phone and called Mona.

"What's up, Mona?"

"Shit, just sitting here listening to my music. Girl, D'Angelo can get it," she said.

"He got that perfect crease, don't he?" I said.

"Yes, yes. Speaking of D'angelo, why you weren't in school today? You played hooky over Pop's house, didn't you?"

"Now, you know good girls never tell. Naw, I'm joking. My grandmother let me stay home with her today."

"What? Did somebody die? She never let you stay home from school."

"You're crazy. No, we hung out downtown and did some shopping. It was something we haven't done in a while, and since her chemo makes her weak. We took advantage of her strength while she still has it."

"Chemo? Chemo for what? Her cancer came back?"

"She has lung cancer, apparently, for quite some time. My mother and everyone knew. They just told me and Nathan yesterday."

"Oh my god! I am so sorry, Anaya. If anyone of y'all need me for anything, you know I'm here. Are you alright?" asked Mona.

"I know you are, and yeah I'm fine. She's going to pull through just like last time. Once the treatments are over, she'll be back to being her old regular self—smoking her cigarettes and drinking her coffee while doing her lottery numbers in the kitchen."

"Cigarettes?"

"I know."

"They told her to stop while doing her treatments?"

"You know they did, but she won't listen. She was smoking with her breast cancer, and God still blessed her. She'll be fine. So what's your 411? What have you been up to? Who have you been creeping with?"

"Oh, you already know. I've been chilling with just him lately. He'll be over here after he get off from work," Mona said.

"Umm hmm. So is he your baby now? Are you getting some good dick?"

"Yup! You nasty!" We both started laughing. "What's up with you and Pop?"

"He paged me earlier while I was taking a nap. You the first person I talked to all day."

"Aww . . . I feel special. Well, go ahead. Call him."

"If I don't call you back, I'll see you in school tomorrow."

"Okay."

We hung up then I called Tonya.

"Hello, can I speak to Tonya?"

"What's up, Anaya?"

"Hey, Edward. Did you just get back today?"

"Yea."

"Oh, okay. Have you seen my girl, Jessica?"

"Anaya, why y'all keep asking me about that chick like I'm her keeper or some shit?"

"Don't be getting all salty with me. Somebody finally spotted her down the hill and told us what house she was staying at. I called her first to make sure she was there and what do you know? She picked up saying 'What do you want Edward?'"

There was silence.

"So what? What that gotta do with me?" He stuttered.

"Your name's Edward, right? Dumb ass," I mumbled. "When did you start stuttering?

"Whatever, Anaya. I'm not the only Edward in Baltimore."

"Your sister and I went down there. Some guy said we just missed her and her mother, and they had the car packed like they were moving. Where did she go Edward?"

"Anaya didn't I say—"

"Relax, boy. I'm just teasing you, but if you see her down one of the clubs you gonna let us know, right?"

"Tonya! Come get the phone. It's your bossy ass boujie friend.

"Hey, what's up, Anaya? Where have your ass been at all day, missing in action and shit? You hooked school over Pop's house, didn't you?"

"Wait, let's rewind to when you answered the phone. How did you know it was me?" I asked.

"You're the only boujie bossy friend I have."

"Oh, so you think I'm stuck up now?"

"Now? You've been boujie. Stop playing. It's cool. You don't mean to be it's just you. Now, stop trying to ignore my question."

"Why y'all keep asking me that? No, I wasn't with Pop." I heard in Tonya's voice as she began to cry when I told her about my day with my grandmother. "She will be fine, Tonya. I'm not worrying. She's gonna be fine," I repeated with a little worry in my voice. "Well, let me call you back. Pop paged me a couple times while I was taking a nap."

"Yeah, and when did you start taking naps?" Tonya asked.

"I know. There's a lot on my mind, I guess. There are so many mixed emotions and thoughts. I needed that nap, but I'll call you back. Let me call him real quick."

"Okay," Tonya said.

I called Pop's house phone first.

"Hey, you" Pop answered on the first ring.

"Hey, yourself. Were you on the phone?"

"No."

"Oh, you picked up pretty fast."

"Naw, I've been waiting for you to call. I paged you several times, and my brother said he didn't see you in school all day. I was just making sure everything was good with you."

"Aww that's sweet. Everything is fine. I was with my grandmother all day, but I'm okay. I just had family problems."

"Anything I can help with? When am I gonna see you again?" he asked.

"No, there's nothing you can do. Thank you, and I can come down tomorrow—I guess."

"Okay good. We can go out to dinner."

"Umm . . . no."

"Anything else you would like to do?"

"Umm . . . nope, I don't think so. I just want to chill, but you can have a lobster tail and a baked potato for me when I get there. A bottle of Boones Farm of any flavor will do. If you're not too busy . . . " I said.

"Of course, I'm not. That's why I like you, Anaya."

"Why?"

"Because most girls try to be cute by being fake. They act, even talk, one way when you first meet 'em, but it just be a front—a cover up—but you've been the same since day one. You got your own hair, your own nails, your own color eyes . . ."

"So you're saying that you don't like for a girl to wear those things?"

"No. I'm saying I like you because you know you're beautiful even without it. You can wear what you want. I'll even buy it for you. A man just like to know he can also be happy with what's underneath when it comes down to it."

"Okay, Mr. Edgar Allan Poe . . . Hold on, Tonya's clicking in on my other line—Hello?"

"Anaya, you are not going to believe what I'm about to tell you!"

"What?"

"Girl, girl, girl," Tonya said.

"Why do you always do that when you have something juicy to say? Hold on. Let me tell Pop I'll call him back." I clicked over, then I clicked back. "Now, spit it out."

"Girl, it's not juicy, but it's sad. Jessica's mother, Ms. Irene, passed away. I think it was two days ago."

"What? Are you serious?"

"Yea! DJ called me like a half an hour ago and told me. He didn't say how or what happened or anything. He was acting all weird as if he knew her. I didn't know if he was upset—or nervous. It seemed like he wanted to tell me something, but couldn't. I don't know what's going on with him. He's been acting strange these past few weeks anyway."

"This is so sad. No one still haven't heard anything from Jessica? I mean, has anyone even seen her?"

"Nope. This not making sense. It's like she disappeared."

"I know. Jessica's mother wasn't talking to her sister, but we need to go knock on Ms. Gene's door. Something isn't right. Maybe her mother got sick, and that's why they had to move," Tonya said.

"I don't know, but we've gotta find out. I feel so sorry for Jessica. What can be so bad that she's too embarrassed to tell us?"

"Not sure, Ms. Inspector Gadget," Tonya said. "Inspector Gadget, let's make your way around my house so we can walk up to Ms. Gene's. Jessica should be there. She doesn't have any other family here."

"Make sure you're out front. I am not in the mood to deal with your mother, telling me something extraterrestrial stole you out your room!"

"Haha, you're funny. Just cuss her out. She'll leave you alone," Tonya said.

"Whatever. Bye. I'm on my way."

We walked across Kirk Avenue to Carswell and knocked on Ms. Gene's door. One of the twins answered.

"Hey, little lady. Is your mother here?"

"Hi Anaya, hi Tonya. No she's not here. She and Jessica went to go visit Stacey to let him know about Ms. Irene. Y'all heard?"

"Yea, we heard. What happened?" I asked.

"We don't know. They're not telling us anything."

"Okay. Tell Jessica we came looking for her. Sorry about your aunt. Tell your sister we said hi, and we're here for y'all if you need us."

"So what are you thinking, Anaya?"

"I don't know what to think. I know Stacey's gonna flip once they tell him." I said. "Hope there was no foul play. I think I heard Stacey was coming home soon and you know how protective his crazy ass is about Jessica and his mother," Tonya said.

"Yup. Well, now we know where she is. We can come back tomorrow after school."

CHAPTER 17

Come Here, Boyfriend

Anaya

"**N**O, MOMMY! PLEASE don't go, Mommy! Stay in my room and sleep with me! Daddy is always mad at you when he comes home late. Mommy, please don't go! He's just drunk. Mommy, please!"

I woke and sat straight up in the bed, drenched with sweat. It was amazing how much I could remember as a child. I hated those nightmares.

Well, one more day of grasping all this knowledge then it was the weekend. I loved popping tags off new clothing. I was told to use scissors, but I didn't. I loved everything about it. The way it sounded to the way it popped on my hand. That was the "I'm about to put on something new" sound. I grabbed a pair of new underwear, a white halter top, and a low wasted black maxi skirt. I layered everything on my bed while I took my bath. The water was nice and warm. My grandmother must've just ran it not too long ago. I submerged my entire body under water.

I had a few things on my mind today. It just seemed like I was surrounded by a lot of situations, and they were falling right in front of me like dominos. Since it was early, I was trying to relax and cleanse my head. I inhaled and exhaled, letting out a soft sigh. I got out the tub after about ten more minutes and added mousse and pink oil moisturizer to my hair. I scrunched it with my hands and let it dry in the air. I put lotion then bathed in my Champs-Elysées perfume. As my grandmother said, "As much as it costs, you only need a little behind the ears and wrist," but I go overboard. *I know I'm extra*, I thought as I put on everything gold. I loved my hoops with my name with the fancy lettering going across. I smiled at myself in the mirror. *Gold fever Thursdays*—I love to overdose off gold.

"Good morning, Ms. Maxwell." My grandmother couldn't stand when I called her that, but she drank so much coffee she might as well owned stock in it.

"You're up early," she said.

"I know." I didn't tell my grandmother about the nightmares. She despised my father enough as it was. She said he seemed like a pervert, and he only married my mother for a green card. She never understood why my mother would run off marry and have kids with a foreigner.

"Singing The Best Part of Waking Up is Folgers in Your Cup—I mean Maxwell House."

"You're not funny, Anaya."

"You have chemo today, Grandma?"

"Yes, I have it every day. Now, 1:00 on Thursdays, so I'll probably be out of it by the time you get home from school."

"Okay, is there anything you might be needing as you drift in and out of la la land?"

"Not really. Maybe a Coca-Cola and a Mr. Good Bar. If you can stay awake long enough, get my pocket book off the dresser."

"That's okay, momma I have money."

"Where did you get money from, Anaya?"

"Grandma, that's barely $1.50, but uncle Ron gave me some money last week."

"You're getting older, Anaya, and I can't make you sit on the steps when the street lights come on any more. But that doesn't mean you should be out there taking money from those fast ass boys. You don't get nothing for free in this world. I like to work for mine. Your mother had a good job till your father came along and snatched the rug from under her feet. I still don't see how she can sit around and wait for a welfare check every month."

"Okay, grandma. I have to leave for school now. Love you, see you later. I hope you have a good day today, and the treatments won't make you too weak."

I blew a kiss as I left out the front door. Aww, boy. I had to hurry out of there before I had to lie and say, "No grandma, I don't take money from boys because I know I don't deal with a guy if he's not giving," but my uncle gave me money too so I didn't lie. I just didn't tell the whole truth. Besides, Pop was different.

Even though Tonya's mother had already gone to work, I sat on the steps and waited for her to come out. Summer was in three weeks. Right now, the spring's weather was nice and breezy. We talked about Jessica and her mother the entire walk to school. Once we got in school, we were in and out of classes.

The day was almost over. We didn't get much school work toward the end of the school year. Time was going by pretty fast. It was funny how I hadn't ran in to Stanley in a while, not even when we all meet up in the gym. I asked his brother about him, and he always said, "You broke his heart." I didn't mean to.

The school bell rang, and it was time to go home. On my way to meet up at the spot, I saw DJ walking down the hallway.

"Hey, DJ. Wait up. What's up?"

"Shit just chilling. I'm about to meet up with my man to play some ball down the dome. Y'all should come down."

"We're going down there this weekend. I'm going down to visit Pop today."

"Yeah, did or did I not say that he had mad bread?"

"Yeah, you were on point. What's up with him though? He's asking me to be his girlfriend already."

"That's because he likes your little pretty ass. He was dealing with this girl a little while ago. They used to live together. If you go down there enough, you'll run into her. She always stopping by, and been trying to get back with him. He be leaning on her, but her ass is crazy. She still be popping up."

"Yeah, I think that's who we bumped into at Mo's. I hope she don't come down while I'm there. I don't have time for drama. Anyway, how did you find out about Jessica's mother?"

"I knew you were about to ask me that. My man over heard some people talking about it while he was down Eldorado's."

"Why would people be down Eldorado's talking about Ms. Irene? This is not making sense to me. Who was it?"

"Look, you my girl, Anaya, but that shit is too messy. I don't want my name mixed up in any way, so I can't tell you that. I said too much already."

"I knew there was more to it. Jessica act like she scared to be around us. Come on, DJ. You know you're the go-to man for all the important info. I promise, I won't say anything."

"Naw, Anaya I can't do that. If Jessica doesn't tell you, I'm sure y'all will find out soon enough. I heard Stacey's supposed to be coming home in like two months, and you know how crazy his ass gets down. You're not gonna want to be around when that shit hit the fan."

"Want to be around where? Give me a clue at least. Damn!"

"I gave you a clue. Ask our girl, Tonya. She should know. Talk to you later," he said as he left out the school. I hoped Tonya was not withholding info because I knew Jessica was talking about Edward when she answered the phone. I just hope he had nothing to do with Ms. Irene, and if he did, he better count his days because he wouldn't be living long once Stacey came home.

I stopped at my mother's house on my way from school.

"Ma!" I call out to my mother as I went in the kitchen and made a bowl of fruity pebbles.

"Yes, Anaya," she answered as she came up from the basement, carrying a basket of clothes.

"Oh, you were washing clothes. Have you been down at grandma's today?"

"Yeah, momma and I walked up to Stars and got something to eat. She's gone to chemo now,"

"Someone needs to talk to her about smoking those cancer sticks. Her cough is starting to sound worst."

"You know that your grandmother is not going to listen to any one," my mother said.

"Ma, did you know Jessica's mother passed away a few days ago?"

"No, I didn't know that. What happened? Was she sick?"

"We don't know. That's what we're trying to find out. Oh, there goes Tonya. We're going up to Ms. Gene's house. That's where Jessica has been staying. They lost their house and everything."

"Oh my goodness. Let me know when the arrangements are," she said.

"Okay," I said as I left out the door and met Tonya before she walked in.

"Hi, Ms. Linda," she greeted my mother.

"Hi, Tonya," I said. "Was Edward home?"

"Yeah, his lazy ass is in there asleep."

"Does it seem like he's home more often now?" I asked.

"Not really why?"

"Tonya do you think Edward had something to do with Ms. Irene?

"Okay, now the Jessica part was enough, but now her mother. Really, Anaya?" she said, rolling her eyes as she walked up the steps and knocked on Ms. Gene's door.

"Hey, twin. I'm sorry about your aunt. Is Jessica here?" Tonya asked.

"No, she left with my mother to pick her father up from the airport so he can help with funeral arrangements."

"Okay. If she's not tired, tell her to call me when she gets in okay?"

"Okay," she said.

They were Jessica's twin cousins, and the only way you could tell them apart was because one decided to cut her hair Bob-length and the other kept hers long and thick like Jessica's.

"Aight, Tonya. I'm going home to check on my grandmother then catch a cab down Pop's house. You better give that man some and stop playing," Tonya said.

"Whatever. I'm giving him nothing. He's not worried about it, so you shouldn't be," I said playfully.

By the time I got home, grandma was in bed watching TV—or should I say that the TV was watching her?

"Grandma, is there anything you want or need me to do?" I asked as I sat her candy bar and cola beside her while she was on the bed; then, I softly kissed her on the cheek.

"No that was all. I'll eat it when I wake up. Thanks, Anaya."

"Okay. I'm about to go over my friend's house. Nathan is downstairs watching TV, and my mother is on her way down here. Love you."

"Okay. Love you too," she said as she dosed off to sleep.

Since it was hot outside, I took a quick bath and put on some black lace thongs and a matching bra. I always said that no matter where I went or what I did, if I felt beautiful on the inside, it'd show on the outside. I put on a long patch work skirt that I made a while ago. It hugged up top and flared at the bottom like a mermaid. I put on a short-sleeved jean half shirt with the elastic at the bottom that stopped right underneath my breasts. I'd always been curvy, and even though this outfit was giving my curves life, I still worked on embracing them. I reapplied my Champs-Elysées. Damn! I guess he'd ask me to marry him next. After seeing me in this outfit, I blew a kiss at myself in the mirror then called Pop and told him I was on my way.

There were always a lot of people outside. His brother and his friends ran in and out as usual. As I pulled up to the front of the house, a random guy came over, opened the door, gave me twenty dollars, and waited for me to get out.

"Pop's in the house. He said to come on up," the guy said

I went in to speak to his mother who said 'hi' rudely, holding her head down, looking at a piece of paper. I went upstairs as I walked into Pop's room. I saw that he was on the phone with his back turned, fussing somebody out.

"Didn't I tell you to stop calling me? Come over here if you want. Okay well, I guess you're dying to get your ass beat! That was a mistake . . . Look shorty, we're done. Something I told you yesterday . . . bye!"

"Bad timing?"

"Naw, not at all. I thought I smelled you. Come here."

I walked around the bed to where he was sitting at a small wood foldable table. On it was a razor blade big vials with blue tops in sets, wrapped in rubber bands and a fresh key of pure white uncut coke. *Damn! Another key,* I thought.

"I'm sorry do you mind me having this out in front of you?" he asked.

"No, not at all. Do you?"

"I'm about to wrap it up though. Give me a kiss. Are you hungry? You look and smell nice as usual."

"Thank you, and yeah, I can eat."

He put everything away in his hidden compartment in his draw except for the big sandwich bag that's filled with vials of coke. I'd be right back. Let me take this to my brother.

I looked around at all the boxes of shoes then went in the bathroom, checked my hair as I admired how neat he was for a single man, then sat down on the bed.

"So you said you just wanted to relax?" he said as he came through the door, holding a clear-to-go container of food and a frosted bottle of Don Perignon.

"Wow. That's my favorite. What are we celebrating again?"

"It's always a celebration when I'm with you. That is what I'm trying to make you realize," he said as he passed the container of lobster and the biggest colossal shrimp I'd ever seen with melted butter and cocktail sauce for dipping. This nigga was either really good or a certified player. Either way, I like the way he rolled. Every time I came down here, he'd gotten nothing but an A+ in my book. He grabbed the two champagne glasses he had on the dresser and grabbed a deck of cards.

"Let's make a bet," he said as he filled up both our glasses. Mine had more since he was more of a weed smoker than a drinker.

"Umm . . . Okay. What's the bet?"

"Let's play "'I D Claire War.' You win, you get whatever you want. I win, you give me a shot at being your boyfriend."

I couldn't stop laughing as I nervously sipped my champagne. "You're serious, aren't you? *I D Claire war is about to determine if I'm in a relationship or not,* I thought. *This is crazy.* Okay bet . . . I always win, so get ready for my expensive taste.

"Aight! Bet!" He said as he refilled our flutes. We talked, ate, and laugh as we played the longest game ever until he only had three cards left and he won. I was shocked because I always win. I was the game master.

"Now, come here *girlfriend,*" he said with a smirk on his face. "You know I was just teasing. You don't have to be my girl until you're ready."

I looked at his sexy ass, feeling all good inside from the champagne and said, "A bet is a bet! Now come here, *boyfriend.*" as I palmed his head with both hands and kissed him passionately. We rolled around, kissing, hugging, rubbing and gazing into each other's eyes for almost an hour.

Tears began to roll down my face. I had so many emotions. I thought of how good he felt, mixed with my grandmother being sick, losing a close friend, thinking that my best friend's brother might have something to do with our girlfriend's mother.

"What happened? Did I do something?" Pop asked.

"No, it's not you. I just have a lot on my mind right now, and I'm feeling a little emotional."

"I know you said it was family business on the phone yesterday, but can you let me in just a little?"

"Well . . . My grandmother has been diagnosed with cancer for the second time. She had breast cancer over a years ago, and now she have lung cancer. I try and act strong and not worry, but the truth is . . . I'm scared."

"You should be. That's a lot to keep in. Come here. You know I'm here if you need anything, right? Even if it's just to talk or a shoulder to cry on."

"I know you are. You almost seem too good to be true. I didn't mean to get all emotional. Must be the Dom P," I said as I climbed on top of him and pulled my shirt over my head. He flipped me over on the bed and began kissing and biting my neck from behind. It felt so good that I had chill bumps going through me.

"Choke me!" I said as I moaned.

"Oh, yes . . . Oh! You like it rough, huh?"

"Yes!" I took my hair out my ponytail and put his hands through it. I moaned. "Grab it, Poppy!"

Calling him Poppy must've turned him on because he pulled off my skirt and panties then he spread my legs apart as he lifted my ass in the air. He grabbed what little champagne we had left and drizzled just a little down the crack of my ass as he began to lick, suck, and nibble on my throbbing wet pussy, mixed with the taste of champagne. This was long overdue. He reached in his drawer then put a condom on as he rubbed his shaft up and down my throbbing clitoris. He put it in deep then pulled it out and then licked and sucked my clitoris until I came.

He made love to my entire body.

CHAPTER 18

A Fool Twice, Shame on You

Jessica

I WENT OUT of the car while aunt Gene tried to explain to the guard what had just happened, hoping they would have little sympathy to Stacey's feelings and that outrage wouldn't interfere with his release date. I grabbed my purse out the trunk, unfolded my twenty-dollar bill, grabbed a half straw, and did a quick line. I couldn't believe what just happened.

"Was he going to be all right? Will he still be able to attend the funeral?"

"Yes, they said he will be fine. The warden had already prepared them for what his reaction might be," she said as she closed the car door.

"I really messed up this time, Aunt Gene. I've never seen Stacey so angry."

"Jessica, it's time we talk. I need you to tell me what happened to my sister. I stared out the window as we passed the cars driving down the highway.

"Jessica!"

"Yes, Aunt Gene."

"How did my sister lose her house?"

"She started using drugs and got fired from her job."

"But I don't understand. Why would she? What led her to do such a thing? It just doesn't sound like my sister to me," she said as tears rolled down her face. I began to tell her everything that led to me calling, asking her if we could stay. Everything except the guy who was responsible for this. My aunt couldn't believe the words that were coming out of my mouth. She cried the entire way to the house. I was too coked up to cry. I couldn't wait to get back in the house so I could do more to keep me numb from this situation. It hurt too bad to face.

"You know that your brother is going to find out what happened to his mother, and I pray to God he doesn't come home and do anything that's going to send him back or cost him his life. Why didn't you tell this to the police, Jess? Whoever he is needs to be in jail after what he's done to you and your mother. I believe he would rather be in jail instead of waiting for your brother to hunt him down. So are you using too?"

"No!" I said defensively as I walked in the house. I was happy she knew nothing about my hospital incident.

I hated that I took the basement from one of the twins, but they assured me it was okay and wanted me to stay as long as I wanted to, but I didn't plan to stay long. My father was catching a plane here from Atlanta tomorrow and I thought it would be a good idea for me to go back with him and finish school there, but that's not going to happen. I'd be eighteen on the 23rd of May, and in less then two weeks my brother comes home. I'd be looking for an apartment before then. But for now, I just wanted to lie down. I know the twin said that Tonya and Anaya passed by, but I couldn't see them right now. There was no way I could look Tonya straight in the face and not tell her what her brother had done to us. I was scared to hurt her this way because I broke our girl code—Never mess with each other's ex. Never mess with each other's family member—but I'm more afraid of what Edward would do to me if he found out I told her. I knew it might sound stupid, but I still had feelings for this nigga. What if he didn't do this to my mother and he was just saying that my mother deserved to get her life back together? What if his homeboy, Sean, did it? What if she got it from somebody outside the house while taking bags out to the car and I didn't see? I put on some pajamas, turned the radio on, and laid across the bed until I dosed off.

The sun was too much for my eyes to handle so I got out the bed, went upstairs, and pulled myself a cup of coffee. If I could stay in the bed every day, I would. It was ten in the morning, and no one was home but aunt Gene and I. I was safe during the day. I knew that Anaya and Tonya were in school, and by the time they got out, it would be time to leave and pick my father up from the airport. We needed to make the funeral arrangements, and since my mom and dad never got a divorce, we needed him to help with everything. The more I thought about it, the more I cried. I didn't want to cry in front of my aunt. She was stressed enough, so I went downstairs to watch some TV and do a line to help calm my nerves. As I finished and was about to turn the TV on, aunt Gene called me, "Jessica, the door—"

All shit. Don't tell me they didn't go to school? I thought.

"I told him he could come in, but he said he'll sit on the porch," she said.

"He? Who the fuck is *he*?! I did one more line in the opposite nostril, rubbed a little on my gums, took a sip of my coffee then ran upstairs to see who *he* was. I walked to the front door, and I could not believe it. I had a feeling he would stop over eventually, but after everything that had happened, I didn't think it would be this soon.

"Edward what are you doing here?"

"Tonya told me about your mother, and I wanted to make sure you were okay."

"Oh, now you wanna make sure I'm okay? You already knew about my mother because you did this to her!"

"Jessica, no! I would never do a thing like that."

"A thing like what, Edward?!"

"I know people that work at John Hopkins, and they told me she overdosed off some bad shit. Jessica, look, I'm sorry for everything that has went on. I was doing so much drugs and drinking . . . so much alcohol that I couldn't control the things I said or did. Jessica, look at me. I love you, baby, and I want us to be together as soon as I finish cleaning myself up. Okay, baby?"

"I love you too, Edward, but—"

"Has the police been around here asking you questions about me? They've been all around the house we had together on Montford," Edward said.

"No, Edward. They haven't been here, and why would they be looking for you if you say you did nothing wrong?"

"You know people like to speculate, baby," Edward said.

"Edward, did you tell Tonya about us yet?"

"No, baby. I'll tell her. Just try and stay away from the girls for right now. Just worry about your man!"

"But I have to go to school."

"There's only three more weeks left. You're a smart girl. You'll be okay—Jess your nose is bleeding."

"Oh my gosh, is it? Let me go get some tissue."

"Somebody's been putting their hand in the cookie jar, I see" Edward said as I ran in the house.

When I came back, Edward was walking down the steps to leave. "Where are you going Edward?"

"I know you all have a lot to do with the funeral, so I'll stop pass another time aight? Oh and stop fucking around with that bad shit! You know only your daddy got that good candy, and you know I can take care of you if you want me too," he said as he closed the gate and got in the passenger's seat of a black Cadillac Deville with tinted windows.

I've never seen that car before, I thought. He was right. I did have a lot to deal with right now, and it was best if he was not around. I really didn't want his sister to know anything right now until I—I mean—*we* figure out the best way to tell her.

I was excited for my dad to come in town earlier, but now that we were on our way, I was not so sure. I didn't know if I could look him in the face and tell him why or what happened to mommy. I was not a crack head or a junkie or anything. I was afraid my dad will be able to look me in the face just like Stacey and tell that I was using drugs. He didn't understand that it was just temporary. No one will.

We arrived at BWI. Watching my dad walking toward the car just made me cry. I never realized how much I missed him till that moment. He looked so handsome—a split image of Stacey. *If he was still here, none of this would have happened*, I thought. Oh, how I missed him! I wanted him to stay and never leave.

"Hi, daddy. How was your trip?"

"Oh, baby girl. Never mind that. Come and give your daddy a hug. Oh, I've missed you Jess. Oh my girl, are you okay? You're getting to be nothing but skin and bones," he said as he squeezed me tightly.

He was right, my clothes had been fitting rather loose lately, and he would be the one to recognize that. We stopped at the funeral home and made all the arrangements. The funeral was supposed to have been arranged for that Friday, but we pushed it back till Monday so Stacey could attend. On our way to the house, my dad wanted to check into a hotel downtown, but aunt Gene refused to let him. He insisted, claimed that he didn't wanna intrude. He had a lot of business to take care of first thing in the morning, and he'd be here soon as he was done.

They sat in the kitchen and talked for hours—about how sorry he was to leave the way he did. How he wish he knew something was going on with mommy and how she knew she could call on him if she needed him for anything. By the time they finished talking, I fell asleep on the couch. He wanted to let me know he was leaving, aunt Gene said, but he didn't want to wake me.

The weekend had went by so fast, and I barely managed to duck and dodge Tonya and Anaya. They popped up just about every day like a damn jack-in-the-box. They didn't understand that I didn't want to be bothered.

Today was Monday, the day of the funeral. I was happy to see Stacey, but I was hurt that this day had to come. The twins and I were getting the house together while their mother was preparing the food for everyone who decided to come to the house after the memorial service. There were barbeque, fried chicken, roast beef, turkey wings, cabbage, black eyed peas, neck bones, baked macaroni and cheese, collard greens with ham hocks, deviled eggs, potato salad, macaroni salad, baked beans, homemade biscuits, my aunt's famous corn cakes, and the trout she said she'll fry when we return. My aunt had always been the type that overcooked. She would cook more than enough so she could feed anyone that was hungry.

After I finished cleaning the basement where I was sleeping at that moment, I cut up some watermelon, cantaloupe, honey dew, pineapples, strawberries, grapes, and maraschino cherries. I squeezed fresh lemon over the fruit salad for the acid to keep everything from browning—I got that from my mother.

My daddy came in with shrimp cocktail, a sandwich, and a cake platter with all sorts of sliced cake. This house had food for days. The wake was at three, and the funeral was at four. After everything was prepared ready for family and friends, we all got dressed and waited for the family car to arrive. Aunt Gene and the twins had on black skirts and white blouses, looking like they were on the usher board. My dad had on a regular black suit, and a black shirt with a satin black tie. My mother loved colors so I purchased a red fitting knee-length skirt and a black silk shirt with a built on oversized bow that I had to tie. This was the most dressed up I'd been in a while.

I still couldn't believe it was for my mother's funeral. I felt myself getting emotional and ready to break down. As the family car pulled up, everyone got themselves together to exit the house.

"I'll be right out. I have to grab my pocketbook from the basement," I said, went down, and grabbed my special bill out of my wallet. I went in the bathroom and did two lines of coke. Edward was right. This was nothing like the product he sold.

As we walked in and viewed my mother's body one last time, I couldn't help to say over and over again how beautiful my mother was. She looked like a black porcelain doll as if her black coffin with red accents was laying on a bed of flowers. Thanks to everyone that sent their gratitude. My brother looked handsome as ever, standing there with a guard in the suit our father brought him. Oh, how I missed us all together as a family. My mother was really all I had at the moment, and now, she was gone. I was actually happy to see all my distant family that traveled from different places.

My mother's friends, coworkers, and all my friends showed their respect. I didn't realize how much I needed Tonya and Anaya in my life at a time like this until I saw them. I wish I could tell them, but I couldn't. Once the funeral was over, it was time to go to the burial site. I was so coked up from doing coke during my bathroom breaks that I couldn't cry. I couldn't believe how irrational I was acting. I was fidgety and couldn't keep still. I was loud and obnoxious. Everyone said I was behaving this way because I was in shock, but my brother was giving me that look like he knew exactly what the problem was.

I couldn't wait to get back in the house. I went in the basement and put my slippers on. My feet were killing me. As I went in the bathroom to change my clothes, I did a line. I heard people coming down the steps.

"Jessica!" I heard Anaya's voice. *Okay here we go. I knew I couldn't escape them forever, I thought.* I rinsed my face with some water and came out the bathroom.

"Thank you both for coming," I said.

"You don't have to thank us. We want to be here for you, Jessica. We're so sorry about your mother. Someone told Edward that she had a drug overdose. Is that true?" Anaya asked.

"Yup, that's what happened."

I'm so sorry, Jessica. Whatever you need us to do, just let us know," Tonya said.

"Thank you both, but I will be okay."

"Where is your mystery man, did he at least come for moral support?"

"Anaya you're a trip. No he couldn't make it."

"Why not, where is he anyway? I mean can we at least get a name?"

"He's out of town. You will know soon enough. We just wanna keep our relationship private a little longer."

"Well, today is not the day for that, so we won't get into it," Tonya said. "We miss you, Jessica. You will be staying here for now on right?"

"Yea until I get my apartment. Stacey will be home this summer, so I'll need to get a place before then so he can have a place to come home to. There's just not enough room here."

"Oh, okay. It's good to know where you are right now after everything. Settle down in a couple days. We can talk about where you've been, what you've been doing, and who you've been doing it with."

We all laughed. We went and sat out front with our plates of food while I hugged and talked to everyone who was coming and going to pay their respects.

"It's been a month since my mother passed away, and we're still acting like were not in a relationship. I'm shocked your sister hasn't found out about us all this time, Edward."

Look, Jessica, why do you keep bugging out? Didn't I tell you I would treat you different? Haven't I been? Have I not been treating you nice? Keeping your fridge full of food, making sure your bills are paid . . . Did you buy that Honda Civic you rarely drive, or did I buy it with cash for you? Do I make you pay for that candy you keep up your nose? No! So get off my fucking case, and stop asking me all the damn questions!"

"Don't talk to me like that Edward. You're in my shit. You can get the fuck out!"

"Do you think I care, Jess? You wouldn't have this apartment if it wasn't for me. I pay your bills, buy your food, and keep you coked up. While all you do is sit in here all day. If I leave, your little savings will be gone by the time you finish shoving it up your nose. You don't do shit for me but open your legs and suck this dick! And you be so coked up—even that's getting terrible!"

"You think I need you, Edward? Well I don't! Why do you have to be so disrespectful to me? I thought you were supposed to love me. All I'm saying is my brother will be home in less than a month, and I would hate for him to think his sister is in a relationship with someone who can't even acknowledge that there is one."

"Because we're not in one! You don't do shit for me. I pay your bills because you let me keep my shit in this motherfucker and as a bonus I give you this here dick from time to time. But don't worry, not that I care. I'll have my shit somewhere else by the time your brother gets home. Everything seemed to be dying down with the police, and I don't wanna fuck with your brother. I know he's coming here to stay, and I'm not gonna disrespect him by having my shit where he lay."

"So what was all that talk about us getting married? You had me looking online for rings. You said that we would be able to tell our friends and family soon. Now you're saying that I made all that shit up, and we were never to tell them?! Now you got me thinking . . . were you dragging me along, making me feel good to cover up some shit?! What the fuck, Edward! I loved you! I trusted you! I believed that we would be making our own family. I even lied to the detective over and over again by telling them you didn't stay at the house on Federal Street because I believed everything you said. Now you got me rethinking everything! Did you even love me in the first place?"

"Jessica, calm down. You know I love you. I do want to be in a relationship with you. I just don't want you tied up in all my mess. I care about you too much to do that. I appreciate everything you're doing for me baby. As soon as I get my shit together and stack these papers and buy a house in the county, you gonna be the first one I come scoop to live with me. So calm down and stop spas'n out girl!"

We began kissing and one thing led to another.

CHAPTER 18

Lies and More Lies

Anaya

"**G**IRL I'M OVER it! Every time I tried to talk to Jessica, she would blow me off. And the times I did talk to her, she was all fidgety and couldn't keep still, never giving me a straight answer. She couldn't even look at me. I can't believe she stopped coming to school. I feel so sorry for her. It's obvious she's getting high, Tonya."

"I know. You see how small she's got? Her face was all sunk in the last time I saw her," Tonya said. "You know she's not at her aunt's anymore. She moved in those nice apartments on Northern parkway and McLean Boulevard."

"Yeah, I know, at Wellington Gates. But her aunt says she doesn't know her address, and I'm done with trying to help someone who doesn't want to be helped. Whoever her boo is, he's definitely doing his part because she's not working. He has to be paying all the bills. I even heard she got a red Honda Civic."

"Well let's hope her skinny ass ain't skinny no more and stopped using whatever shit it was she was using. Enough of worrying about Jessica. How your grandmother doing?"

"Not so good girl. She's doing the chemo with radiation. I swear it's eating her alive. I'd be glad when she's done so she can start gaining her weight back. They just delivered an oxygen tank because she was having problems with breathing. And I'm not lying when I say she literally takes the oxygen mask off to smoke her cigarettes. I swear, she's gonna blow us all up. But besides that, she's in good spirit, still talking the same. She can't wait to go back to work. She's not the type of person who likes to sit around and do nothing anyway."

"I'll be glad when she gets better."

"Yeah, me too, so she can make us some of those piled high good lunch meat sandwiches," Tonya said, which made me smile. "So how are you and Pop doing?"

"The two months we've been dating, it has been good. He's still showering me with gifts. We've been riding around looking at apartments ever since we got back from deep creek. I told him to stop waiting for me and just get it. I'm tired of going down his mother's house all the time. Besides, he doesn't need to be in that area, making that kind of money anyway. He'll be waiting forever for me. I want my first place to be mine."

"That's because you're crazy. Who wants to pay their own bills? Let that man take care of you," Tonya said.

"Oh, he's taking care of me, all right. I just don't want to get used to the fast life when it might not last. So for certain decisions, I want to be my own. I like him as a person—I mean, he's twenty two. I like what he does for me, but eventually, that has to come to an end and he'll have to get a real job. I'd rather it be sooner than later."

"Does he know this?"

"I've mentioned it. He said that it'll be one more year then he'll be where he wanna be financially. I'd be finished schooling. We have enough saved up to buy a house. Then, I can work on my clothing line while I'm going to school for design."

"Wow. I hear a lot of French being used . . . we, we, we, we," Tonya said.

My smile was so big, you could see all thirty-two teeth.

"So you really like him, huh? Y'all getting pretty serious, I see. Anaya, are you sure you're ready for what comes along with that?"

"I don't just like him. I think I'm falling in love. I mean, things can only get better with time, right? The main thing is to have a plan, and that's what we have, which actually seem to be going pretty accordingly."

"That's what I'm talking about Anaya. You know how I get down, but you don't have to get down like that. What makes him so special anyway? He's not the first hustler you dealt with, and all of them like to wine and dine your spoiled ass with expensive gifts. What happened to friends with benefits? You're falling too deep for this nigga. You said it yourself. What else could he be hiding?"

What's wrong with that, Tonya? I just have to make sure he stays on track, follows the plan, and does the right things with his paper. After this last year, we can go legit and open a barber shop or buy a few of these rundown properties or something. Then, I can introduce him to everybody. I know my grandmother and mother will like him, as long as he's not putting me in any danger. I'll keep him in hiding for about a year. There's no rush. My grandmother will need time to get better anyway."

"So if he loses everything he has today or tomorrow, you'll still stick by his side?"

"Look, I said I *think* I love him. Never in that convo did I say I was stupid!"

We gave each other high fives and continued talking as we went in and out of different stores in Towson mall.

The temperature was steady rising as mid summer approached., but as of now, I spent every weekend with Pop—going out to dinner, movies, and shopping combined with a lot of sex. Today, we decided to stay in and after I watched him put cocaine in mini sandwich bags (he must've had a good connection because people always asked how he gets to bag or vial up so much product for a cheaper price). I had a taste for cheese steak, so I placed an order over the phone. What we were about to do would absolutely be working up an appetite.

After giving the package to his brother to be distributed to others that were outside working for Pop, he came back upstairs and turned the music on. He poured me a glass of chianti. I sipped my wine as I went into the bathroom to shower and slipped on some lingerie Pop and I got when we were out shopping during the week. As I closed the bathroom door and turned on the shower, I got a chance to take an earring off.

I then heard all this banging and yelling downstairs and what sounded like horses galloping up the stairs.

"Open the door!" It was the police. Pop opened the door. "Put your hands in the air! Is there anyone else in here with you?" the officer yelled. I opened the bathroom door.

"Put your hands where I can see them!" the officer yelled. All I could think of was that I was glad that there were no drugs in here at this time. Well, at least I hoped not. They instructed me to turn the music off and told Pop to get up slowly and put his hands behind his back as they proceeded to cuff him and read him his rights. He was naked with the exception of boxers.

"Can I at least get dressed? And what am I being arrested for?" Pop asked, which was my question exactly.

One officer helped him step into his pants while the other three checked his pockets. *There were total of four officers. This must be serious,* I thought. One ransacked the room while the other went to different areas of the house.

"Do you have any weapons of any kind?" the officer asked.

"No," said Pop.

After they were done, they put Pop in the wagon and left. My heart slowly started to chip. It hurt to see my baby in handcuffs, and it hurt even more not to know what for. As I got myself together, I went in his secret compartment and got all his money he had put together for the two bricks he was about to buy. This couldn't have happened at a not-so-better time. After I called a cab, I locked his door and went downstairs, all I heard was his mother saying, "That bitch! I told him to stay away from her crazy ass."

"What's going on?" I asked Pop's brother.

"His ex-girlfriend has been popping up over here all week, trying to talk to Pop while we're sitting on the steps. He doesn't pay that girl any attention."

"Yea. He does that's what his ass get for getting in the car with her ass the other day. He ain't come back till the next morning. Can't play with people feelings."

"Ma, shut the hell up! She doesn't know what she's talking about."

"Boy, don't tell me what I saw," she said.

"You're always running off at your mouth. You like to hear yourself talk. Go in the room somewhere.

She was too scared of Bobby to talk to him like she treated Pop, so she went on upstairs, complaining how they tore her house up.

"Anyway, what's this have to do with him getting arrested just now?" I asked.

"She lied and said Pop put a gun to her head."

"What? Are you serious? So he stayed with her . . . I'm sure he fucked her, then she got mad because of what? He used her and played with her emotions maybe. He knows how she is. He brought this on his self."

"Don't listen to my mother. He doesn't want her crazy ass!"

You don't have to want a person in order to fuck them, I said. Deep down, I wanted to believe his mother, but I knew she was just saying things because she didn't like me. I remembered when she yelled outside, "Pop, stop lying to that girl! You're an old ass. You're not 22, you're 24!"

"Yea, okay. Keep me in the loop as to what's going on that's my cab. See you later."

CHAPTER 19

Release day

Jessica

TODAY WAS THE day. It was finally time. I swore it didn't feel like he was ever coming home. I excitedly jumped in my civic and drove down the halfway house on Madison and Pulaski to pick up big brother. He came walking out the door with his one little net bag. He was free, indeed.

"Hey, Stacey!" I screamed with excitement as I jumped into his arms like I was still a little girl, wrapping my legs around his waist. He always made me feel so safe. "Dad couldn't be here because he had to work. He's pretty consistent on asking us to move down to Atlanta. He said he can get you a job and everything."

"Naw, baby sister. Tell him what I told him before. We're good." Stacey said.

It was three o'clock on Friday. We went back to the apartment where I already had Stacey's room fixed up with a bedroom set. It wasn't much, it was new, but most importantly, we had our own. I had three Russell sweat suits, three Adidas sweat suits, a pair of all white and chocolate Air Force Ones, a pair of top tens, a pair of 990s, and some butters, with more than enough white T-shirts and boxers. Other things lied across his bed.

"Welcome home, Big Brother" was what the banner said when we walked in. I had cooked corned beef and cabbage, a pot of barbeque chicken, rice-a-roni, corn on the cob, and a big picture of Kool-Aid mixed with 20/20 mad dog. I knew I'd been pretty distant from Tonya and Anaya, but now that my brother was home, I didn't have to worry about Edward just popping up whenever he felt like it. Today was to be celebrated! Not to bring up the pass, I'd tell them eventually. As Stacey finished showering and getting dressed, I called my girls and his best friend. "Too many friends ain't good," Stacey used to say.

Never have a lot of traffic where you lay your head. Everyone arrived. They were excited to see Stacey. We all listened to music, talked, cried about our mother, but for some reason my brother got real reserved once Tonya walked in. His whole aura changed. Did he know I was dating Edward? Naw, Tonya didn't even know. Besides, he would've said something.

After we finished reminiscing, Damon decided for all of us to go down Eldorado's. Since it was my old stomping ground as of two weeks ago, why not? Surprisingly, my brother didn't mind me going, but he just came home and wanted to watch my every move. The last time I spoke with him, he said, "Jess, before I come home, I want you to be done with putting that shit up your nose and done working down the spot. I'll be taking care of us from now on just like mom would have wanted it."

I didn't know why we didn't all ride together, but the girls drove with me, and Stacey drove with Damon in his 4Runner. As we pulled up front of the club, there were two parking spots. We parked in one, but Damon drove past us and parked somewhere around the corner. *My brother with incognito ass*, I thought. We walked into the spot, and it was live as all-out doors. It made me want to go up and do my Josephine Baker. Girls were up there doing their thing. Even though I was strictly "dickly," I loved to watch woman dance. On the other hand, my brother didn't seem to be interested, I knew that look he had on his face; it worried me every time.

"Why are you looking so paranoid? Are you okay Stacey?"

"Yeah, baby sis. I'm good. I'm free and in a strip club, how could I not be? You know how much I love you, right? He said as he kissed my forehead.

"Of course I do. I love you too," I said as I smiled. Damon ordered two bottles of Moet, and Anaya ordered a bottle of her favorite Don Perignon.

"I got it, big spender," Damon said to Anaya. We all bust out laughing.

We had girls giving us lap dances. Guys *wanted* us to give them lap dances. Anaya was feeling her champagne, making it rain while dancing on table tops. She was not her normal self, but she was going through so much right now with her grandmother being sick, she needed this. *Where did Tonya disappear to?* I thought. I looked across the room and guess who I saw.

There was Edward, looking good like a tall glass of Hershey chocolate milk. I was feeling hotter than a firecracker and the champagne had me feeling a whole 'nother type of way. I walked toward him, admiring his Saucony sweat suit and matching sneakers.

"Hey, baby, I've missed you," I said.

"What's up Edward? I knew you would be in here," Tonya said as she snuck up on us.

"I was just asking Edward if he has seen you," I nervously said as I played it off.

"You're going home tonight, Edward?" Tonya asked.

"Naw, I got to meet up with some New York niggas. Be home in the morning. What are you doing in here anyway?" He asked as some light-skinned chick came over and kissed Edward smack in the mouth. He stood there, kissing her back as if there was no one in the room but the two of them. My stomach was in knots, my heart was crushed. Afterwards, she pulled a mirror from her Louis Vuitton bag and applied more red lipstick. Her cleavage shook with every move. She was pretty and had on the cutest pair of tight-fitting bell bottom jeans with the cutest gap between her legs. I walked off, so Tonya wouldn't see my tears. It was weird how Stacey watched us the entire time with that same look in his eyes. I ran to the bathroom, wiped my face, and saw a girl doing some coke at the sink.

"Can I do a line? I can pay you," I asked.

"No need. Here you go. Do both nostrils," the angel from nowhere said.

I went back out and partied. The angel came over to our table. We went back and forth in the bathroom at least two more times. We partied till the lights came on. We were all drunk and hungry, so we decided that we would all go to Paper Moon afterward.

"We're leaving!" I screamed out to Stacey. "We're going to the paper moon. Are you coming?" I asked him

"Yeah, y'all go head. Let me wait for my man. I'll meet you there," he said.

Happily, we parked out front. We jumped in the car and waited for some of the backed-up bumper to bumper traffic to clear up. We then made a U-turn. As we drove about three blocks down Baltimore street, we heard a loud boom. It sounded like a grenade just went off, but we were almost positive that it was a gun shot. Niggas never knew how to act. Thank God, Stacey was still inside. Everyone but me was so wasted, they barely heard anything. I was high but still alert from all the cocaine I snorted. We pulled up to Paper Moon. As we were getting out, Stacey and Damon were pulling up behind us.

"Damn, y'all must've been balling a hundred easy! What happened? Y'all hear that canyon?"

"Yeah, that shit was crazy. People were screaming and running everywhere. Some fool must've got blasted," said Stacey.

"Damn these pancakes and eggs melted in my mouth. It reminded me of diving in some crisp white sheets and a soft down comforter."

"Really, Anaya?" Tonya and I started laughing.

I had my brother and close friends around me. What else did I need? Fuck Edward—I hope his ass catch gaine green fucking with those bitches. I'm done!

CHAPTER 20

An Eye for An Eye

Anaya

DAMN, THAT'S WHAT I get, knowing I couldn't drink that much champagne without Gatorade and sex to help work it off. My head hurt so bad that I just want to take it off, sit it on the night stand, and say, "I'll holla at ya later." I needed to get up. It's eleven o' clock. Since I stayed at my mother's last night, she was always up at the crack of dawn.

"Good morning, Ma. Are you making breakfast?"

"I ate, but I can make you something. What do you want?"

"It doesn't matter. Bacon, eggs, and toast is fine. Anyone been down grandma's this morning?" I asked.

"Yea, we were all down there. This the last week of her treatments, so she has to get tests done to see exactly where she stands with it."

Thank goodness, I know she'd be glad. All it had done was make her hair fall out. She lost so much weight, and she was always tired and sick. She had been taking it long enough, way longer than before. I agreed that was enough.

"Well, you've been staying here pretty often. What are you running from?" my mother asked.

"What you mean? I'm not running from anything."

"Oh, you're hiding from something Anaya. You don't check on your grandmother as much as you used to. So what's wrong?" my mother said.

"It just saddens me to see her like this, and there's nothing we can do to help. It hurts hearing her say she can't wait to go back to work, and she can't right now. I'm scared, and I don't know what to do and really, ma, I don't think she constantly wants me to see her like that. Besides, it's almost over now. Once she's through with all the chemo and radiation, she will slowly gain her strength back. At least she was right when she said that. Well I'm going upstairs to take a shower real quick before the food is ready."

"Anaya!"

"Yes?"

"I won't drill you this time, but don't come in this house drunk again. It would crush your grandmother if she found out."

I was embarrassed. She was asleep when I came in so I didn't think she knew. "Okay ma," I said, full of shame. I turned my radio on while taking a shower, singing to the tune "Keep on walking / I ain't talking to you anymore / You can just go on / Keep on walking, keep on walking."

I had so much clothes—tons at my grandmother's and my mother's—but I always had a problem with finding something to wear. I finally decided to put on my cut-off jeans, white tee with my brown penny loafers, and my blue and white MCM bag. It was a perfect attire for the carnival. I went down and ate my food. My mother made the best breakfast as long as she kept it strictly pancakes bacon and eggs.

As I was leaving out, my pager went off for the eighth time. Pop just wouldn't stop calling me. It had only been three days since I'd seen him, but I talked to him yesterday. What the fuck! I dialed his number.

"What's up Pop?"

"What do you mean 'what's up?' Why haven't I seen you?"

"Boy, we see each other all the time. I'm actually on my way to the carnival up lake. I'll give you a call when I come from there."

"No! Don't call, just come down!"

"But I'm not sure what time I'll be leaving."

"It doesn't matter. I'll be out front. Just come"

"Okay."

Pop was in Towson county about a month before he went to court. No going outside, no sunlight—nothing. The bitch didn't show up for court, so the charges were dropped. Good thing she didn't. I went to visit him once. I told him from the beginning that I didn't do jails. He came home and continued to get money. He even ran into a cheaper connection. *More money for me,* I thought, but I wasn't seeing Pop as often as before. He continued to say that he had nothing to do with his ex even though she described his boxers down to the stitching. I knew he was lying, so I gave him time to be with whomever he wanted—if that was what he wanted. He asked for a relationship, not me.

It seemed like he was doing more suffering than anything because he was calling me nonstop. He knew he couldn't come to my house, so he would pop up around Tonya's when I didn't respond or when I was too busy to see him for three or four days. He would leave gifts around her house as well. I wasn't going anywhere. I just wanted him to hurt like he hurt me. Even though things finally got back to normal, I still slacked off from spending too much time. He never did admit to it; he just promised he would never put his self in a situation where I would have to be without him. I did miss seeing him as often as before, but I didn't take 'being taking for granted' too lightly. I might not have made a big fuss about it. I did love him, but it didn't change my perspective about his ass.

The carnival was jumping. Everybody was there. We knew we were cute as we passed through crowds since all the guys tried to 'holla' at us. I ignored them. Tonya sold her dime bags of weed. I swear that girl made every situation into a hustle. She was a hustler by nature, and that was my girl. I wouldn't have had her any other way.

"What's up, ladies? Haven't seen you all summer. Sorry about your mother, Jessica. How'd you been?" DJ asked.

"I'm making it. Thank you," Jessica said.

"Okay, that's 'what's up,' I wrapped to your brother the other day. Glad he's home. That's my man. He's still the same old Stacey. Ain't nothing changed. Tell him I said don't forget to 'holla' at me."

"Okay I'll tell 'em."

"What's up, Naya? I know you glad your boo home. He told me keep my eyes on you while you were here too."

Boy, please. Pop's ass is tripping.

"I told his slick-talking ass to be careful when he first told me he was falling for you."

"What do you mean 'be careful'? Never mind, I don't wanna know," I said

"Don't worry. That's a good thing," he said.

"I'm sure. I'm catching a cab down later after I leave," I said as I started laughing.

"Yeah, he told me you were supposed to be going down. I might go down myself."

"Oh, really. He sure do tell you everything. I shouldn't go."

"Oh, please don't do that—then we'll have to hear about you all night."

We all decided to leave once Tonya saw her neighbor. He said her mother wanted her to come home now. It was important. If I didn't already know how her mother was, I would've thought something was seriously wrong. We walked back up to Harford Road where Jessica had parked. She dropped Tonya off first, then dropped me off at Pop's.

As I got out the car, he picked me up, twirled me around, and started biting me on my neck. I swore that every time I see him it felt like we just met. He carried me up the steps and into the shower. His manhood was literally poking me in my stomach. He bit me again.

"Somebody missed me, I see."

We made love on and off for two hours. My pager was blowing up like I was selling pizza. What could Jessica possibly want? Whatever it was, it had to wait till I get home. What I was experiencing right now is mind-blowing.

I couldn't believe that it was one in the afternoon. It felt so cozy in my room with the curtains closed and my air conditioner on. I really couldn't tell. After I got myself together, I went to check on my grandmother who was upstairs, watching mash or was it watching her?

"Jessica called like five times. Please call her back. She sounded like it was important," my cousin said

I dialed her number. "Hey, Jessica, girl. Is everything okay?"

"No, Anaya. It's not, it's bad! Really bad . . . and I don't know what I'm going to do!" she said as she broke down crying

"What's wr—"

"Anaya! Hang up and call 911! It's grandma! It doesn't look like she's breathing!" my cousin yelled.

"Sorry, Jessica it's my grandmother," I said as I hung up. I dialed 911 my mother and everyone else. My mother arrived first. The ambulance was right behind her. By the time everyone else arrived, the ambulance was packing up to leave. They explained to us that her oxygen level was low, even though she was no longer getting treatment for her cancer and just medication for her pain, she still needed the oxygen tank. Her cigarette smoking was defeating the purpose. We all knew that, and so did she, but unfortunately she didn't care.

My grandmother finally dosed off to sleep as we sat around talking.

"Anaya is everything okay with Tonya?" my mother asked.

"Yes, why you ask that?"

"Police and detectives were at her house all morning."

"Really?" I thought back to all the times Jessica had been trying to reach me, and just a few hours ago how she broke down crying before she could get anything out. "At least I hope so," I frantically said to my mother. I grabbed the phone and called Tonya, but got no answer. I then called Jessica back.

"Hello, Jessica. What's wrong? Are you okay? My mother said the police has been at Tonya's house all morning. Did you talk to her?"

"No, I haven't talked to her, but that's why I've been trying to reach you, Anaya! It's Edward! He got shot last night. He's dead!" she screamed on the phone.

Even though my heart skipped a beat and all I could think about was Tonya, I still didn't quite understand why she was so upset. They barely had conversations. Something just didn't sit right with me, but I'd get back to that later. I decided to go around Tonya's instead of trying to call again. Her front was filled with people. I walked inside where Tonya was sitting on the sofa, sobbing with her head on her lap and her sister sitting beside her, rubbing her back.

"Even though Edward has done a lot of hurt to a lot of people, I still never expected this day to come. I can only imagine what he's done to deserve this."

"Sorry, I didn't call you, Anaya. There was just too much going on. How did you find out?" Tonya said.

"Jessica called me. She was crying."

"Oh, okay. Wait—what? How did she find out?" Tonya asked, looking confused.

"That's what I was wondering. Maybe her brother—you know he knows everybody," I said not wanting her to worry about anything else right now.

"But his name hasn't been released yet!"

CHAPTER 21

I Knew All Along

Jessica

COULDN'T BELIEVE what had happened. Not Edward! Not *my* Edward! The worst thing I could've done was call Anaya, crying, but I needed to talk to someone. I was hoping she knew already, hoping she had more information, hoping to hear that it wasn't Edward. Maybe it was just his car, or maybe the police that answered his phone really wasn't the police.

I loved Edward so much, how could he say he loved me one minute then turn around and treat me the way he did the next? My mind was racing! I had to drive down to Tonya's to see if it was true. I needed to check on my girl anyway if it is. But would I be able to handle it? Would I break down once I hear it all over again? If I didn't go, they would know something just ain't right. How could I call Anaya without calling Tonya first? I should've waited and not called anyone. Oh my head, I just couldn't think straight.

I slid some clothes on. I needed to find a dime bag first that would ease my mind. As I was searching for my keys, I found a small baggy in my purse. Oh, thank god, just what I needed. I opened and snorted straight from my fingernail.

"Where you going?" Stacey said. He startled me so bad that the contents from the bag emptied right unto my purse. Shit! "What happened?" He asked me.

"You scared me! Don't sneak up on me like that, Stacey!"

"Well, you must've been doing something you had no business doing! Have you been crying?"

"No!"

"Yes, you have. What's the problem? What's wrong with you Jess?"

"Nothing! I just found out that Tonya's brother may have been killed. Not sure yet. On my way to find out now—what?"

"Nothing."

"Well, why are you looking at me like that, Stacey?"

"Oh, nothing go ahead. Don't be too long. We needed to have a talk when you get back. It's important!"

"Okay." I didn't have time to worry about one of Stacey's lectures. Right now is not the time. I needed to stop first and get what I needed to get so I wouldn't go over there like it was all about me and Edward and act like a fool. I hoped Tonya wouldn't ask anything because I'd have to tell her. Right now just wasn't the time for that either.

I pulled up in front of Tonya's, and automatically, I knew it was true. People were on the porch, talking; some were crying. If I wasn't coked up, I probably would have passed out.

"Is Tonya here?" I asked a young boy, sitting on the steps as if he was the only one around and no one existed but him.

"Tonya's not here. She went to the funeral home with my aunt. My cousin was killed two days ago. Your name's Jessica right?"

"And I heard about Edward, that's why I'm here, so do you know what happened?"

"They found him in the driver's seat of his car outside of some club downtown with a hole in his chest that also went through the seat. He was shot point blank with a shot gun. He died instantly."

Wow, this kid was pretty raw and even pretty unbothered, but no drug in the world could make me that numb. Tears poured down my cheeks like flood was coming. The young boy stood and gave me a hug. To prevent a loud outburst, I covered my mouth as I got back into my car and snorted two out of my fingernail and rubbed some on my gums. That should calm me down. I didn't want Stacey to see me crying. After I got myself together, I walked in the house like everything was okay.

"Come here, Jess."

I heard Stacey call me from his bedroom.

"Move that money out the way, and sit down. So what did you find out?" he asked.

I explained everything as if I wasn't bothered.

"Okay, check this out," he said, "I didn't magically come back from the dead. I was in jail. I knew all about you and Edward."

My heart just dropped!

"You know New York Sean, I'm sure. That was my informant."

My eyes got so wide I felt them pop out.

"When I found out that you started to talking to Edward, I asked Sean to hang around the strip club and introduce himself as an old boyfriend of a stripper who no longer works there. I offered him some weight, befriended him, sold him the dream, etcetera. He never told me that Ed had you and mommy staying in his stash house, but Sean ran his mouth about everything that went on in that house to a dude that got sent to the joint several months before my release. There's no need to worry about Sean anymore either. His New York ass is floating out there in the Statue of Liberty somewhere in the New York river."

I couldn't believe what I heard. I instantly got sick. I covered my mouth and ran to the bathroom. Everything was blowing my high. To even think that he knew half of what happened in and out of that house. I needed more coke.

"Jessica, I'm going to tell you this one time and one time only. You gonna get yourself together, or I'm sending you away to a drug program. I refuse to let you end up like mommy! Every action has consequences. That nigga Edward decided to put rat poison in some coke and give it to our mother, so his ass had to deal with the consequences.

I ran back to the bathroom. My stomach was in knots.

"Yea, get that shit and his ass out of your system. Flush it! Because today is your last day walking around here and looking like a fucking zombie!"

CHAPTER 22

Who number is this

Tonya

"I COULDN'T BELIEVE that Jessica didn't come to the funeral. She seemed pretty upset. Have you talked to her?" Anaya said.

"No. I know she came down before the funeral, but I wasn't there. I haven't heard anything since."

"I talked to her over the phone, but she was in a hurry. She seemed a little different than before. I can't put my finger on it, but between my design course I'm taking and being stressed with my sick grandmother, I really haven't had much time to worry about anything else. I haven't been seeing Pop as much either. I'm so scared that something is going to happen. I stay at my mother's more than usual, and I feel bad about it."

"She's been done with her treatment. What are they saying?" I asked.

"My mother said that she has a doctor's appointment tomorrow. They'll get all the questions answered then."

"Oh, that's good." I said.

"Yeah, it is. What's going on with Edward's case? Did they find out who did it yet?"

"No. It's been almost a month. I doubt if they ever do just another black man off the streets. They called and said we could come down the station and pick up his belongings—cell phone and other items—they found in the car which they had needed for evidence. I'm driving my mother's car down later. Wanna go?" I asked.

"Sure."

We got back to the house with all my brother's belongings—keys, sneakers, cell phone. I began crying all over again as I scrolled through his phone, leading up to the night of the incident.

"It was a number that was in the log repeatedly," I said. "It looked so familiar, but so many people called our house. It could be anyone." I still wanted to call the number back. I put the house phone on speaker as it rang.

"Hey, Tonya."

"Jessica"! We both screamed at the same time.

"Um, yes. Sorry about my absence at the funeral. I've been going through a lot."

"Jessica, I'm calling this number because there are so many calls to and from this number in Edward's call log. Why? Did he and Stacey have something going on maybe?"

"No, Tonya. I wanted to tell you, but Edward wanted to wait for the perfect time. Then when this happened, I just didn't know how."

"Didn't know how to do what?" I said

"Edward and I have been dating for almost seven months. He's my secret Tonya, and I loved him more than I can say!"

"Almost seven months, Jessica, and after all that time, he still didn't want you to say anything? You knew my brother. You heard the womanizing stories. We're friends . . . you knew not to go there!"

"I'm sorry, Tonya. He persuaded me at the strip club. It happened so fast. I fell in love with his charm, but he slowly started to change. I didn't know if it was from all the coke he was snorting or stress because he owed New York Sean a lot of money."

"I told him not to fuck with those New York niggas. They came here did their thing then carried their asses back up North. I don't even know if Sean was his real name. Jessica, can we come over so we can talk? We have a lot of catching up to do without you running off this time?"

"When?"

"Now!"

"Umm okay."

"Okay good. Anaya and I are on our way" I said as I hung up fast.

"Let's hurry up. Walk to Harford Road, and catch a cab before she finds a reason not to answer the door." I said.

As we walked into Jessica's apartment, we saw all the pictures she had displayed—her mother and father, her and her brother, the three of us clowning around in Lake Clifton hallway and at the skating ring a trip that Cecil Recreation used to give in the summer.

"Y'all want something to drink? I know it's hot out there. I have wine coolers," she asked.

We were cool with just two cold Snapple's. We all went and sat on the sofa. She only had one chair with twin end tables, one that displayed the pictures. Her apartment was nice and clean. *It seemed not too girly, but perfect for her and her brother,* thought Anaya.

"So Jessica, did they ever find out exactly what happened to your mom?" I asked.

"She was poisoned, but we're not sure where she got it from."

"I never imagined your mother to be the type to use drugs, even after she found out your father was cheating then he left. Is that why she lost the house and moved down the hill?"

"Yup."

"Who were y'all living with down there?" Anaya asked.

"We were staying down there with Edward," Jessica answered, embarrassed.

"With who? Are you serious Jessica? And when exactly did my brother get a house that he could move y'all into? Are you sure it was Edward's?"

"Yes, Tonya. It was the house where he kept his drugs. Look, I really don't wanna go into any more details about that if you don't mind."

"Well I do! Because it seems like you knew more about my brother than I did! I thought he was out, staying over a female's house or hanging out with home boys, but all along he was playing house with another family, taking care of your mother like she was his own while our mother was at home, worried sick most nights. He paid for my supposed-to-be home girl to have a house and giving his mother nothing! He was—"

"Tonya, stop! Edward raped my mother, got her in to using so we would have to stay with him. He's the reason why my mother lost her job and our home. He kept us drunk and high so he could use us however and whenever he wanted. He told my mother that if she ever told anyone about this, he would kill me. If I ever told you, he would kill her." *I know they didn't want to hear this*, Jessica thought.

She sat and told them from the beginning to the end up to the time they finally moved out and her mother died. "I loved Edward so much that I blamed my mother for a while, saying it was her fault. After, I realized it wasn't, I still didn't want to leave him, so I let him pay me to keep his drugs in my apartment just to keep him around, hoping we were going to let everyone know how we felt about each other before we got married. Just like he promised."

"No, Jessica. You are lying! Why you never told me any of this while he was alive?!" I screamed.

As Anaya squeezed both of us tight, there was a knock on the door.

"You want me to get it, Jessica?" Anaya asked.

"Yes."

"Are you expecting company?"

"No."

"Who is it?" Anaya said as she yelled through the door. She looked out the peep hole. "Jess, it's the police." Anaya said as Jessica gave her the okay sign to open.

"Jessica Johnson!" the officer said.

"Yes."

"I'm afraid we have some not-so-good news regarding your mother's death. Is there somewhere private we can go and talk?"

"No, it's okay. They're my friends. You can say it in front of them."

"Are you sure?"

"Yes."

"When your mother was raped, we took DNA samples. We collected fingerprints from the bag of drugs that killed your mother as well as the substance. The DNA matches the same DNA from another rape victim which matched everything else. Edward Smith raped a young lady a day before he was murdered. He laced your mother's drugs with termite poisoning."

I put my head in my lap and sobbed uncontrollably. Jessica didn't want her to hear all of this.

CHAPTER 23

Cancer is the devil

Anaya

I SAW POP once or twice. Sometimes, I didn't see him at all. It had been a month since my grandmother went to the doctors, and they gave her two months to live. She was not the same as before; she just lied around a lot. Maybe if they weren't keeping her on so much medicine, she could focus on being stronger. I mean, she was not like she was when she was doing her treatments because she was no longer sick, so I knew in that due time, she would get better.

Doctors were not always right. They were wrong before about her not having cancer when in fact she did. What made them think that they could give a person a specific day to die? Who were they to put a time frame on a person's life? Who made them gods?

"Anaya!" my mother called me from downstairs.

"Yes, Ma!" I yelled back.

"Somebody wants you at the door."

Who could that be? Tonya had gone down South, and I hadn't seen or talked to Jessica ever since everything was revealed. I went out to the front porch, and I saw Hershey's black Land Cruiser before I saw him sitting on the step.

"So this is what we do now? The pop up at the spot game?"

"Girl, stop playing. I called you and you had no response. I was close by anyway. What, are you mad?" he said with that devious, devilish but all so sexy smile. I just loved the way his eyes squinted when he smiled and how his teeth would shine through all that black skin.

"How would you know if I already had plans or not?"

"You do, so go put a pair of those tennis shoes on I brought you, and let's go for a ride."

"Sir, yes sir," I said playfully with a grin as I watched his six feet two slim ass bop to his truck. I didn't know who was darker—him or his truck. I smirked.

"Go ahead, girl" he yelled through the window, smiling with his bright white teeth.

I met Hershey almost a month ago right at the beginning of the school year on Saint Lo Drive while walking home from school by myself. I totally ignored him the first time, but two days later, there he was again. He parked this time and waited for me to walk by. Once I saw him hop out that truck, and bopped his sexual chocolate ass over to me. I just had to give him my cell number, one of the gifts Pop had given me, thinking he could reach me better "not." Even though Hershey and I had been hanging out pretty often, we still didn't have a sexual relationship.

I couldn't seem to take my mind off of Pop nor did I want to. Hopefully, he'd appreciate me more the next go round. *I would admit that I fell a little too hard too fast anyway,* I thought to myself as I slipped on a short black A-line skirt with a white T that read "girls just wanna have fun." It matched the black and white, and red and green heels that Hershey brought me.

He asked me to dress down sometimes so we could have some fun, saying I didn't have to always be in heels. I a sarcastically told him that those down the hill girls wore the freaky Rees. Not I.

"Going for a ride, Ma. I'll be back later."

I jumped in the truck, knowing Hershey, there was no telling where we were going. That was the reason why I liked him. He was tall, black, and cocky with a nice Adam's apple. He was spontaneous. He took charge, and he knew how to keep my mind off things I didn't want to worry about. Yea, he hustled, but I never saw it. We talked so much. Before I knew it, we were at the batting cage in Timonium. He picked me up again Saturday and drove us to the museum in DC. Sunday, we had brunch at this little cafe in Federal Hill. He always were full of surprises. Afterward, we went to the gallery. We both grabbed a few pieces from Banana Republic, but my cell phone was constantly going off. I got irritated and was ready to go. As soon as I got in the house, I called Pop back.

"What is your problem?"

"You! I need you to come down here. I have something for you."

"Okay, I'll come down tomorrow after school."

"It can't wait that long, Anaya!"

"What is it Pop? What's so important that it can't wait till Monday?"

"Just come and see."

Twenty minutes later, I stepped out the cab, but he didn't greet me with the normal hug and kiss.

"Come on so we could go upstairs and talk," he said.

I walked in the room. On his bed were a pair of black and pink trim Chanel snow boots and a fuchsia shearling coat with a hat to match. I felt like a kid at the candy store. He was right, this couldn't wait! All other matters went out the window. I threw my body across his bed and rolled around in the coat like it was a soft feather down comforter.

"That's not for you. I said we need to talk," he said, joking as he pulled me to my feet. "Look, I know you're seeing someone, Anaya, but like I told you months ago, I want you to be mine and only mine. I love you, and I know you love me."

It was crazy because the entire time he was talking, all I saw were dollar signs in his eyes and his dick.

"Okay baby, whatever you say," I sarcastically cut him off as I stuck my tongue so far down his throat, I swore it felt like I could feel his esophagus. I pushed everything from the bed to the floor and pulled his belt off like an animal as I watched him put his condom on. He flipped me over (he was harder than a bowing arrow) as he bit me on my neck nice and hard, just the way I liked it. We had the best sex on and off for almost two hours.

I was juggling two men at one time. I was on my way from Annapolis with Hershey. There was something about the way he was singing the lyrics to Slick Rick's "Teenage Love" that made me want to be all over him. I was softly planting wet kisses on his neck while he was driving, and that Versace cologne he always wore mixed with sweat was turning me on even more. I rubbed between his legs, and he was turned on just as much from the feel of things. We decided to stop at the hotel in Annapolis. I was glad he didn't see what I purchased from Victoria Secret because it was a secret he was about to get.

It seemed like weeks were going by faster than normal. Today was supposed to be the day my grandmother's shelf life expired as the doctors might as well put it since they talk like she was a piece of meat and they could determine her life span. I'd been staying here throughout the week just to prove to the doctors that she was not going anywhere. She promised she wouldn't leave me, and I believed her. As usual, I kissed my grandmother on her cheek.

"I'll see you when I get back from school."

"Okay," she said.

Like I said, she was not going anywhere. I had one more year of high school, then she'd be seeing me off to a school of fashion.

CHAPTER 24

Crack Kills

Jessica

"COME ON, BABY. I'll suck your dick. All I have is two dollars. You know my head's the best head."

"Go ahead Jessica with that bullshit! Somebody go find Stacey, and tell him to come get his sister."

"All the money I gave you over the months but you still can't do me a solid one. Here, shit, take my car for the day."

"No! Yo, your brother made it very clear not to deal with you and your shit! And I saw you going in and outta that crack house around the block. Better be careful fucking with them lil dirty niggas."

"Well that's where I'm going now if you don't give me some. Ain't nobody looking, and I ain't gonna tell. Come on," I said. I was damn near scratching the skin off what little arms I had left while anxiously pacing the pavement.

"Look, take this. Don't bring your ass back around here, and stay out that crack house before you fuck around and catch something you can't give back!"

"Thank you, man. I appreciate it you need anything at all let me know."

"Yeah, yeah. Go get outta here."

I jumped in the car and did a hundred miles per hour during my drive home. I hope to get there before it got late and Stacey decided to pop in. As I got in, I took one of my anxiety pills with a shot of Jack Daniels; then, I poured one more shot to take to my room.

"Jessica!"

Oh shit! Here we go. I swore I didn't feel like this shit today. "Yeah, Stacey."

"I was making sure you had your ass in this house. That drink right there is the last thing you need. Look at me. You gonna have to sweat this shit out. Yo I'll be making sure of that. Now, give me that glass. I wish I could chain you to a fucking bed post or something! I'm right out front rapping to this dude. I'll be right back. Go lay down and rest. You look tired."

I went in my room and locked my door, making sure this rubber band was nice and tight on my arm. I hurried and burnt the bottom of the spoon and slowly pulled back on the needle.

"Yes," I said as I stretched across the bed feeling no pain. It felt like heaven just a minute ago. I wondered if that was where I am. As I opened my eyes, all I saw were lights everywhere. I looked down and saw my body being worked on tubes, wires, and machines. A doctor pressed on my chest with a machine as if I were one of those crash dummies.

A strong force of wind hit me as I lied on the hospital bed. I coughed and opened up my eyes. Was I dreaming? Did I just have an out-of-the-body experience? What was wrong with me? Why was I here? I couldn't remember anything! What were these tubes? Was I dead? *Somebody please tell me something.*

I pulled at the tubes, knocking things over. They called more white coats in to restrain me while the doctor administered something in my IV. I was assuming it was drugs. If it wasn't, it damn sure felt like it. I was so relaxed, I fell asleep.

When I woke up, Stacey was talking on his cell phone while staring out the window. Who was he talking to like that, sounding like he was doing a job interview?

"Okay, thanks again. I'll have everything together and we'll see you soon," he said as he hung up.

"See who soon?" I asked.

"Do you know why you're in the hospital Jessica? Well let me tell you," he said. Before I got to answer, he continued, "You almost died. You had four different substances in your system. Coke, heron, prescription drugs, and alcohol. You had an overdose if I would have been just a minute later and wasn't there to hold you in a cold shower filling the tub with ice, you would be dead! Now I'm done with all this. Since I can't keep you tied up in the house all day, I'm sending you to a sixty-day rehab clinic. End of discussion! I already lost mommy. I won't lose you too, Jess. We all we've got," my brother said as he started crying. "I love you, Jess!"

"I love you too," I said as I started crying.

CHAPTER 25

Please Don't Leave Me

Anaya

TOWARD THE END of the school day, my cell constantly went off between Pop and Hershey. I couldn't focus on my studies, so I turned it off until I was able to call them back. Besides, I already knew Hershey wanted to know if I drove to school or if he could come pick me up.

Pop wanted me to come down. I really wasn't in the mood to talk to either one of them. Once the bell rang and school was over, I decided to walk home with the girls. Since the weather was slightly changing, I needed that fresh air. I felt like I was closed in and couldn't breathe. For some odd reason, something just didn't feel right. I felt like the universe was squeezing my chest tight and taking all my oxygen supply. I said bye to Tonya then stopped past my mother's who wasn't home. I was sure she's down grandma's.

I pulled a glass of water before I walked down. My uncle's car was outside, so I know he was in the house.

"Ma!" I yelled as I walked in but got no answer. Where was everybody? I walked upstairs and everyone was sitting around my grandmother's bed. Their eyes looked as if they had been crying, and they tried to get their selves together before I walked in.

"What's going on?" I asked as I made my way to my grandmother's bedside.

My uncle explained, "Today is the day, and we know she's trying to hold on until everyone gets here. Uncle Ron should be here any second."

Okay, was I hearing this right? Were they really putting my grandmother in her grave because the doctors wanted to play god? As I sit on my grandmother's bed, I lifted her to place her head on my lap. I rubbed what was now baby hair on her head.

"I love you so much, Grandma. Prove the doctors wrong. Show them you're a fighter." I began crying. "Please don't leave me!"

I heard my other uncle come in the front door and up the stairs.

"Hey, momma" he said.

As I looked at her, she looked at me as if there was something she really wanted to say, but didn't have the strength to get it out.

"Grandma! Grandma!" I screamed, but she was gone. Her lifeless head lied across my legs heavily. I stared into space as tears streamed down my face. It felt like it was all a dream, and I wanted so badly to wake up. Nothing seemed real. It had to be a nightmare, but once the ambulance came, lifted my grandmother off me, and placed her stiff body on the floor to try and resuscitate her, I knew it wasn't.

My uncle then told the medic, "We do not want her to have any more suffering."

He asked me to get on the floor, kiss my grandmother one last time, and make a promise to her that no matter what, I would make her proud. Staring at her lifeless body on the floor tore the most important piece from my heart, and I don't ever think I would get back.

Days had passed. I heard people coming in and out of the house. Some came upstairs and knocked on the door to give me their condolences, but I wouldn't unlock it. I felt sick to my stomach majority of the time and emotionally drained. I cried so much, I didn't think I had any tears left. I finally returned Pop's calls and told him why I hadn't called him in days. I could hear it in his voice that he felt some type of way. He knew there was nothing he could do or say that would take the knots in my stomach away, so he insisted on buying me something to wear for the funeral and I nonchalantly excepted his offer.

It had been three long days. I knew I had to get out of this bed and get myself together. My grandmother was a strong black woman, and I knew that she wouldn't accept nothing other than that from me. I got up, soaked in the tub, called Pop, and told him I'd be catching a cab down in two hours to pick the money up since today was Saturday and the funeral was tomorrow.

I rubbed my body down, pulled my hair up into a high pony, and slipped on some baggy sweats and some coach flip flops. Since Tonya said she wanted to go with me, I stopped pass her house. We walked to Harford to grab a cab. It was awkward that Tonya really didn't know what to say. It was crazy how all the three of us lost someone so close within months apart. The outside air did me some good. I didn't know what or how to feel, so I guess I just felt numb.

We pulled up to Pop's house. He and several others were sitting on the steps, talking smack as always. Pop's cat eyes got big and white as a golf ball. I guessed that meant he was happy to see me. He grabbed me by my hand and helped me out the cab. Before I could take a few more steps, he handed me a chunk of money. There was no need for me to count, he never half-stepped when money was involved, nor did I have to ask. I considered that as begging. He knew that was something I didn't like to do. Most guys would make you sit around and wait before they gave you what they said they would—but not Pop. If I didn't want to stay, he wouldn't hold on to the money just so I would have to.

I needed some conversation and a different scenery. I was tired of people coming past the house with cards, food, desserts, and flowers to remind me that she was gone.

As we were standing waiting for Pop to bring out the cushions so we wouldn't have to sit on the hard concrete steps, we were watching his brother and the rest of the crew shoot dice. I couldn't help but to notice a black Cadillac Deville with tinted windows. This was the third time it drove past us. Every time it got to where we were sitting, it drove slow.

"Here go your pillows, ladies. Do you need anything else?"

"No, but Pop, do you know who that is driving past here in a black Cadillac Deville with tinted windows?" I asked

"Yeah, that's the punk ass niggas from around Twenty-Fourth and Barclay."

"Well, the punk ass niggas drove past here three times already," I said

"You don't have to worry about anything, Anaya. Their punk asses ain't about nothing. Didn't I tell you that you're safe with me?"

"Yeah, I know you're here to protect me, and I thank you, but you can't protect you or I from a bullet baby. On that note, you can call us a cab, and I suggest you figure out the Deville's agenda. I don't want anything to happen to my baby, okay?"

"Damn, you just gonna leave me like that?"

Now, Pop you—"

"Naw, I'm joking Anaya. I understand how you feel baby," he said as he wrapped his arms around me and held me tight, whispering in my ear, "I love you so much, and I'm so sorry about your grandmother. I know how much she meant to you."

All the pain and emotions came back. It felt like my heart was being ripped out as I stood there, but I didn't want to cry so I kept my composure. I kissed him and said thank you. As the cab pulled up, we got in.

It was hard for me to fall asleep. Just one puff from a joint would really do me some good right now, but since I wasn't a regular smoker, I never had any with me. Just the thought of my momma—which was what we called her—being closed up inside a piece of metal had my teeth clenching. *Do I have to go? How, oh how am I going to get through this?* I thought as I drifted off to wake up to a day filled with sadness.

I woke up to which I had hoped had been a nightmare. Only to realize that it wasn't. As I went to the bathroom to try and get myself together, the aroma of home-cooked food went up my nostrils as if grandma was downstairs, preparing Sunday dinner as she always did, but I knew better. I knew it was only my mother and aunt preparing food for the funeral for which I didn't want to attend. Why did they invent such a thing? Funerals were nothing but torture, but there was no getting around it.

My uncle's wife did my hair last night after we came from the mall, so all I had to do was comb my wrap down. I put on a white long sleeve button-up shirt with a broach on the collar and a black leather hipster jacket with a matching skirt with shingles hanging from the arms. The family car arrived, and I really wish I could just disappear into the air where no one could see me. It took everything in me to get into that long black limousine, which makes it definite that your loved one has died and you're now going to the funeral.

We pulled up and was ordered to walk in to view the body and sit up front on the family side. I stood over her and froze. She looked the same. She was just really dark from the radiation treatments that burned her skin. I was standing there, having flashbacks. As I looked at her, all I saw was us, sitting on the front steps. She was doing her lotteries at the small kitchen table as I talked her head off about everything there possibly was to talk about.

I snapped out of that breath of fresh air as my mother came up, put her arms around me, and walked me to my seat. She said, "Don't torture yourself, baby. I know how much you loved your grandmother."

Others began to arrive. I didn't realize I stood there that long. I sat down and let some people shake my hand because I refused to stand to receive hugs. I'd always been mesmerized by my grandmother. The preacher did his preaching to the family, and many people sat and stood to pay their respects to her. All I did was stare in the casket. I couldn't hear or see anything but her, alive and well. I thought about our first bus ride when I was younger to Lexington market to get fresh lemons and peppermint sticks; how she snacked on her Mr. Good Bar she used to hide from my uncle for our Monday night 9:00 movies when he lived there; how she fell asleep in the yellow recliner while watching mash; and how as soon as I turn the station, she would wake and say, "Turn it back. I'm not sleep."

I daydreamed through the entire funeral. As long as I could see her face, I felt happy. But before I knew it, they were in the process of closing her up, taking her from me. I snapped out of the beautiful daydream I was having and began to scream and cry. I suddenly felt like someone stuck a knife in my gut and just kept turning. There was too much pain to bare.

Mona came over and took me to the rest room to get myself together while they carried the casket out. That was something I did not want to see. One of the ladies wearing white that walked up and down the aisles came and talked to me. She tried to explain that she was in a better place, but all I could think was why would he take her from me? He did not "think" that she was in a good place here on earth with me? What kind of god would take a grandmother away from her own family? She was getting old anyway. Why not let her die from old age?

My own child wouldn't have the joy of her presents as my faith was gone. I just couldn't understand. I just wanted this entire day to be over. How much torture must I endure?

All I wanted to do was sleep, but my girlfriends wouldn't let me. Tonya said I didn't need to be alone, so we all went and sat on her front. They had coolers and marijuana. I needed some numbness so I asked someone to roll me a joint in some top paper I always carried in my purse just for times like this. I went home once I knew all the company was gone. I climbed in my grandmother's bed, balled into a fetal position, and fell asleep like a baby.

CHAPTER 26

Always at the Right Time

Anaya

WAS IT REALLY a new morning? Waking up in my grandmother's room, I now knew this was reality. This wishful thinking of a dream could no longer happen. No school for me today. It was 11:00 a.m. It was too late to go in even if I wanted. My cousin didn't go either, but he decided to stay at his mother's. Everyone left but me. I was sure my mother came and checked on me again after she left while I was asleep. After sliding my slippers, I went downstairs and grabbed my cell off the table and went and sat on the front steps.

Hershey called me twice last night and once this morning, but surprisingly, there were no calls from Pop. I thought he would have called to check on me after the funeral. I knew his daughter was on her way down when I left Saturday. Maybe he was giving me time with my family, and friends I didn't call him either. He'd call eventually. I decided to call Hershey back.

"Damn shorty, what did I do to you? It's been almost a week since I heard from you? How are you on your phone in school?" he said.

"Well why would you call me when you know I'd be in school? Any way I'm home today. My grandmother passed away last week. Her funeral was yesterday. I don't feel like wrecking my brain with education today."

"I'm really sorry to hear that. I remember you telling me she was sick. I guess that's why I haven't heard from you lately. Are you okay? Is there anything I can do just to make things a little bit better?"

"No nothing I can think of, but thanks for the gesture."

"What are you doing now?" he asked.

"Nothing really. Just sitting out front of my grandmothers. talking to you."

"Have you eaten?"

"No. I don't have much of an appetite."

"Put some clothes on. I'm about to come scoop you."

"Naw, I don't think—"

"Anaya, I'm not asking you. I'm telling you to put some clothes on. No need to waste a day out of school, sitting around with the sad face."

"Where are we going Hershey? I don't feel like being around with a lot of people, smiling up in their faces."

"Just put some clothes on, please. I'll be there in an hour. I know you're slow and leave that hot box home so you won't get irritated and be ready to rush home like last time."

Wow, I didn't know he realized that. "Okay," I said.

I soaked in the tub as I thought about the last couple of months. There were so many thoughts racing through my head. *Where do I begin?* I thought as I washed my body from ear to toe. *Oh well, it is what it is. It couldn't get any worse at this point.* I thought as I stepped out the tub.

I headed to the room and just stared at the bags of new clothes trying to figure out which one I wanted to go in first. There's never a time I didn't want to get dressed up but shockingly, I wasn't feeling it today. I slid on some black yoga pants from Footlocker, a matching Nike T-shirt, and huaraches. I brushed my hair which I didn't wrap last night, applied my favorite Bobby Brown lip gloss, put my purse on the sofa, and sat outside. As I sat on the steps, the house phone rang. *Why didn't I bring it outside?* I thought.

"Hello, I'll be there in five minutes. I'm about to be coming around the corner."

Hershey pulled up. I hopped in.

"Where are you taking me, sir?"

"Don't worry about that. You're surprisingly dressed for the occasion."

I turned up KRS-One, laid my head back, closed my eyes, and enjoyed the ride. *I still couldn't believe Pop didn't call*, I thought. I'd just call him tomorrow.

I must've dosed of. When I opened my eyes, we were at the go carts in Glenburnie. I left it to Hershey to find something fun to do. Did I say that was why I like him? Oh, I did.

Driving the bumper cars, it actually took my mind of things for a while. I screamed, laughed, and smiled as Hershey rammed his car into mine. Afterward, we rode into Annapolis and ate at an outdoor seafood restaurant. We went and saw a movie. After that, I was tired, ready to go home. I wanted to check on my mother and aunt but since I didn't have my phone, I couldn't call them. I needed to make sure they were okay. She was too busy trying to be strong for me; but I was not thinking, they just lost a mother.

Hershey took me past my grandmother's to grab my phone and a few other things to take to my mother's. I really didn't want to stay there right now. It would just make me cry from constant thought.

"Hershey, thank you for a great day and for making me come out the house. I really did have fun," I said as I kissed him on his lips. I was sure he didn't want the day to end, but I did. I said bye as I jumped down from his truck.

My mother was lying on the sofa, watching TV while wrapped up in a blanket as the cool breeze came through the window. The fall weather was trying to creep in.

"Are you okay, Ma?"

"Yeah, where have you been?"

"Came down momma's looking for you. I'm sorry I should've called. Hershey made me come out to take things off my mind a bit. It took me go cart riding to eat, and we saw a movie."

"That was sweet of him. He seems nice."

"He is, but he's just a friend." I said, not wanting my mother to think he was a boyfriend since she might be meeting Pop sooner than later.

CHAPTER 27

Flat Lined

I T SEEMED LIKE the alarm went off earlier than it was supposed to. Or did I just need a little more sleep from being emotionally drained? I grabbed my cell from my night stand, surprised Pop still hadn't called me. *Maybe he was with the chick that had him arrested*, I thought. After all, niggas like crazy irrational bitches. All types of thoughts were floating through my mind. It just didn't seem like something Pop would do. I knew he had been pretty busy with his new connect. I was sure he'd call me later. As for now, I needed to get up and get ready for school. My grandmother always told me, "Learn as much as you can. Don't be afraid to experiment and try new things." Of course my mother was up, and my brothers were already off to school.

"You smell good, Anaya. What is that you wearing? You don't ever buy me any perfume," my mother said.

"It's Versace blonde, Ma. Just take what you want off my dresser," I said as I grabbed a piece of bacon from the stove and put butter and jelly on a piece of toast.

"Are you sure you're okay to go to school today, Anaya?"

"Yes, Ma. I'm all right." *Sitting around the house doing nothing not gonna help either*, I said to myself as I walked down the front steps.

I met Tonya in front of her house as she came out the front door.

"How are you feeling Tonya. Any news about Edward yet?"

"Nope, still nothing. Once I came to terms that everything was true . . . I finally broke down and told my mother since she refused to talk to the police about anything, but she said she wasn't surprised. Every time she looked him in his eyes, he didn't look like her son, especially with all the lying and the disappearing for days at a time. She said that I was the only one who didn't notice how much he had changed. It still hurt, but I'm adapting. What about you, how are you feeling? I'm surprised you decided to come back to school so soon. I'm still devastated about your grandmother. How are you holding it together so well?"

"I have no choice. I've already been out of school over a week, and while I'm home, I do nothing but make myself sick from crying and not having an appetite. I decided it was time for me to get out of depression mode, and the only way to do that was to get out the house. Hershey did come get me yesterday and made me come out, which I'm glad because it made me feel better, that's why I'm out today."

"Oh, what did you two do?" Tonya asked.

"Girl, he had us in Glenburnie and Annapolis riding bumper cars. Then we went and sat outside at a seafood restaurant with some wine then saw a movie."

"Well, looks like y'all getting along pretty good. Could it be that he's taking you from Pop? You haven't said anything about him yet this morning. His name is usually the first thing I hear. Wow! Go, Hershey."

"Whatever. You would be team Hershey, but honestly, I could spot a cheap wannabe player miles away. What Hershey and I do, that's something that he does with all the girls. He's probably doing it with somebody right now. I've already had people come to me and say, 'You know he used to mess with' so and so. You know his baby mother was full of drama, no, thank you. He's one of those hot boys he'll take you out. He'll buy you what he want you to have, but his splurging on things I like, is very limited. I haven't gotten in his truck and received a surprise yet. Not even a sympathy card or even flowers after my grandmother passed."

"Anaya, you really are picky and ungrateful sometimes. I mean, he came and took you out afterward. You told me yourself that you've been ignoring his calls, so as soon as you told him—which I'm sure it was yesterday—it sounded like he ran straight to you and made you come out the house to take your mind off things, and it seem like it helped."

"You're right, he did, and I appreciated that. I never said I didn't appreciate him and what he did for me. I just like a man that's more romantic and puts more thought into something and not do the same thing they're doing for everyone else they dealt with. I'm sure if you ask whoever else he dealt or deals with, they've all experienced Hershey's cocky ass the same way. We did make it to a hotel once. There was nothing really exciting. All I can say is he can eat a peach for hours, but I don't think that will be happening often. Besides, I think Pop learned his lesson. I just don't understand why I still haven't talked to him though."

"Yeah, but he's your night and shining armor that showers you with gifts. You don't think he hasn't done that for others before?"

"Whatever, Tonya."

"Yeah, that's what I thought. Have you heard from Jessica?" Tonya asked

"I called her aunt's house before my grandmother passed away. She had an overdose and was rushed to the hospital. She said if Stacey wasn't there, she would have died."

"Damn! She was getting high that bad?" Tonya said.

"Yup, Stacey paid to put her in a drug program even though they have insurance through their dad. He loves the shit out of his sister and now that's all he has."

"Yeah, they've always been really close. Anaya, you think Jessica told him about her and my brother?"

Oh, shit. I thought I knew where Tonya was trying to go with this. It was enough violence that had been happening lately, and even though no one deserved to take another person's life, all the things Edward's done to Jess and her Mom—that's enough for me to blow him away myself.)

"I doubt it very seriously, she knew he wouldn't have liked that." I played it off as we entered the school.

The school day was going by pretty fast. It was the last period already, and my cell haven't went off all day. *What the hell?* I thought as I grabbed my cell out of my purse. O wow, looked like my cell had been blowing up all day. When did I turn it to silent mode and take off its vibrate? Smiling from ear to ear, I was happy to see that Pop called me. I called him back as soon as my science teacher left the room.

"Hey, Pop. What's up?"

"Where have you been, Anaya?"

"Where have I been? You know where I've bee. Where have *you* been? Look, this is too much. I'll call you when I get home."

"Just come down, Anaya. I'll be here waiting."

"Pop—"

"Anaya," he said as he cut me off, "just come down please."

"Aight, Pop. I'm going home first then I'll be down." I couldn't wait for the bell to ring. It has been a minute since I had sex and all this built up stress. That was just what I need/

Waiting out front the school for Tonya, Stanley walked over, looking good enough to eat

"Well, hello Anaya."

"Hi, Stanley. How have you been?"

"Better now that I see you. Can I get a hug?"

"Sure."

"Damn girl, you always smell so good. What's that you're wearing?"

"You know it's my favorite Versace."

"I'm sorry to hear about your grandmother. I know how much she meant to you," he said as he pulled a card and a cute square box wrapped in a green—my favorite color—wrapper with a sparkly pink bow tied around as if it was professionally done.

I think my heart quickly skipped a beat. Why did I like bad boys so much? Stanley truly was a perfect gentleman. "Thank you, Stanley, but you didn't have to buy me anything."

"I know. I wanted to. Open it." he said

"Open it now?"

"Yeah, open it now. I want to make sure that you like it."

I proceeded to open the pretty wrapping that looked too cute to tear apart, only to see my favorite blue box of Versace blonde. I knew he remembered what I was wearing, but not enough to remember and purchase it after not seeing me in quite a while.

"Thank you, Stanley. You play too much. I knew you knew what I was wearing. You really didn't have to, but thank you again. I really appreciate it!"

"No problem, Anaya. You know I'll do anything for you."

All I could think of was how big his dick was and how I want Tonya to hurry up before I'd be going home with Stanley instead of going down Pop's, I thought with a smirk on my face. But just knowing how much he cared about me, I could never hurt him like that again. I gave Stanley a hug and said thank you again.

"Well, here comes Tonya. I'll catch up with you later, okay?"

"Oh, what's that?" Tonya asked.

"Stanley gave me a card and a gift, said he was sorry to hear about my grandmother."

"He's so romantic. Anaya, why—"

"Tonya, don't ask," I said as I cut her off because I already knew what she was going to say.

It was hot outside, but it was also nice and breezy. I went home and checked on my mom. She told me she would be moving in grandma's house eventually. I kind of knew that would happen since she was the only one of her children that wasn't a homeowner, but I didn't want to think about that right now. I took a shower, changed my clothes, sat on the steps, and waited for my cab.

Upon arriving at Pop's, I quickly applied my lip gloss, looked in my mirror, and pulled a couple strands of hair down from my high ponytail. Pop opened the cab door. There was no one else out front at the moment—only a pillow sitting on the steps, waiting for my arrival. I walked over and sat on the pillow.

"So what did you mean where have I been? You know the funeral was Sunday. I was surprised you didn't call, then Monday, and still no call, so—"

"I knew you were spending time with your family, and I was in New York. I thought I told you about my new connection."

"You did, but what does that have to do with picking up the phone?" I said.

"I'm sorry. I could've called you, but I really didn't want to call you from up there. I just got back this morning and hit you soon as I got in Baltimore, but I have something for you. Wait one minute."

He came back with a white bag over a hanger, a little tiny box, and a card. All I could think to myself was, *please don't let this be a proposal* because the answer is no. He took the bag off. It was a nice black Italian leather coat it had a big collar with fur no buttons but a belt to tie around the waist. The card was a sympathy card with the writing: "I love you. I always want to be there for you if you let me. I know how much your grandmother meant to you. I know I can't take her place, but I will try my best to fill your void."

Wow! *Who did he get to write this for him?* I thought as I laughed surprisingly, not knowing what to say, but scared to open the box. If he was proposing, he would present the ring instead of the box right?

"Okay. So what is in this box, Pop?"

"Just open it."

I opened it. It was a pretty gold ring. There were five diamonds with gold intertwining around them. It was sort of like a pretzel concept— very beautiful and different.

"That's a friendship ring," he said. "I want you to be my girl, Anaya."

I took a deep breath and thought for a minute. "I thought I was your girl, Pop, trying to slow things down from this extremely serious moment."

"I mean just me and nobody else. I'm your boyfriend, your my girlfriend. No more playing, no more bullshit."

I thought, *Okay, I care about him, and I do like being with him so—why not?*

I had to admit just when I thought things couldn't get any better, they did! Pop was making so much money, it wasn't even funny. It got to the point that we would be lying in bed, and his homeboys—which were also my homeboys because we were cool from school—would come in the room just to take my shoe orders. If I didn't feel like shopping, he had people to do it for me. We wanted as much intimate time as possible. Especially this particular day, I'd been so busy with school and helping my mother with my grandmother's house—kind of, since I did more watching then helping. This Saturday was my first time down in a couple days. We sent them to Kazins in Mondawmin mall for some pink pat and leather heels. Once they left, we fucked every way imaginable.

"Come here, Anaya lie on top so I can feel your breasts against me. I want to slow it down. Let me make love to your body." He wrapped his arms around me, nice and tight as he slowly went deep inside, asking me not to move and let him do all the work. It had to be my first time having an orgasm because I never felt anything like it before in my life.

After cumming twice earlier, he said he didn't need to cum right now. He just wanted me to relax and feel good, but for some reason, I got extra horny and wanted to try oral sex for the first time, so as I played beside him, I put my leg over his leg and slowly began kissing on his chest then his stomach. I kissed his legs, rubbing my face around in his pubic hair. I grabbed his dick and stroked it. As I kissed his inner thighs, his shit got rock hard with no problem. I rubbed his balls with one hand. I licked his head, flickering my tongue up and down his shaft. I knew it felt good because his dick was throbbing, and he was moaning. I formed my lips in an O-shape and placed it over his head, licking and sucking the tip at the same time. His moaning got louder. I then tried to suck it just a little deeper and faster, and there it was. I threw up all over him and his dick. I immediately stopped and ran to the bathroom before the rest got on the floor, not believing what just happened. *Oh how embarrassing.* Everything I studied worked until that part. *I couldn't understand how Vanessa Delrio managed to get the whole thing in her mouth,* I thought to myself while I was locked in the bathroom, too embarrassed to go back. Only I would give head for the first time and try to deep throat!

"Anaya," Pop called.

I didn't want to answer. I was too embarrassed.

"Girl, come out the bathroom" he said as I opened the door with a rag covering my mouth. He started laughing.

"It's not funny, Pop!"

"It's not, baby. It's cute. That was your first time, wasn't it?" He asked as he started laughing while holding me in his arms. It's okay. You did great for your first time—no teeth or nothing. You're a natural pro." He looked away with a smirk, as I gave him a sarcastic look. We decided to take a shower, put some clothes on, and go sit outside on the steps. The phone rang, and Pop answered.

"Baby, what size shoes did you say?"

"Six and half, and ask them to grab me a cheese and pepperoni Stromboli and a welches peach. Thank you." *Damn. Between the orgasm and throwing up my insides. I'm starving,* I thought as I sat down out front on the pillow.

"What's up, Anaya? Damn I didn't think y'all hot asses would ever come out the room."

"Be quiet," I said as I pushed his brother as he sat down beside me.

"All shit," he said.

"What?"

"Here she comes, looking all silly!"

"Who is she?" I asked as this light-skinned girl with short black hair, looking like she was ready to have a baby any day now. "Well, who is she?" I kept asking. Before he could say anything, she stopped and stood right beside the steps. He was right. She was looking all crazy. She was very quiet and shy. "Hello," I said.

"Hello, is Pop here?" she asked his brother.

"No. He's not here. Now go on back down the street somewhere!"

"Stop, he is here. Pop!" I yelled out for him to come to the door.

"Yeah," he answered as he came out front.

"Look, I'm not with this shit. Go on down the street with that bullshit. That's not my baby."

My heart started pounding. "What was going on right now?" I said. "More bullshit Pop? No more lies, right? Just me and you remember? When were you going to tell me about this? I told you, I don't want a man with kids! And now, another one?"

"That's not my baby Anaya!"

"How'd you know? Obviously you fucked this girl, or she wouldn't be standing right here, looking like she's about to buss! Obviously, she was pregnant before I came along. You had more than enough time to tell me. We just went through some bullshit!"

"There's nothing to tell you because it's not mine. I'm serious, Anaya."

"Are you sure, Pop?"

"Yes!"

"Okay then."

"Go ahead, and take your ass down the street," his brother said as she walked away and said nothing else at all.

Even though I wanted to believe him, something inside me again was saying, "Don't!" But I couldn't help it—I loved him. I felt all warm inside every time I was around him. He gave me all the love kisses and attention I was missing after my grandmother passed away. He was there for me and he still was. *So if he'd say it's not his, it was not his!* I thought as we enjoyed the rest of the day.

I sat between his legs as he planted soft kisses on my forehead cheeks and neck. He walked back and forth from the front steps to the phone booth across the street at the store. He never used his house phone to conduct business, and he didn't like cell phones. Shit it's like he lived at the store. That's where I would call when I needed to reach him. It was better than waiting for somebody to answer the house phone. My shoes arrived and so did my food. I spent the entire day with Pop. Every kiss and every hug made me fall deeper in love. I was looking forward to doing this more often.

It was Sunday morning. All I wanted to do was relax, watch the life of the rich and famous, and eat a huge bowl of captain crunch berries. I had no idea where my mother was; she was nowhere to be found when I woke up. Probably, she was down my grandmother's, getting everything in order since my uncles and aunt signed their shares of the house over to her. I grabbed my cell and called the missed call back. The number didn't look familiar. It must have been a phone booth down the hill from the looks of the first three digits: 2, 7, and 6.

"Yeah, who dis?"

"Somebody called, Anaya?"

"Yeah, hold up. Yo, DJ. Phone."

I wondered what DJ wanted on a Sunday.

"Hey, Anaya."

"Hey, what's up, DJ?"

"I got something to tell you, but you can't say anything, okay?"

"How are you gonna say I can't say anything? It depends on what it is and who it's about. Because if it's something about, Pop, best believe his ass gonna hear about it—"

"Girl, it doesn't have nothing to do with Pop," he said as he cut me off.

"Oh well, who is it about?"

"Promise you won't say anything."

"Boy, you know I don't gossip anyway. That's why you called me. Will you just spit it out already?"

"I heard Stacey killed Edward, and they found that the NY nigga body up there, kissing the bottom of the statue of liberty."

"Who told you that Dj? Is it like a lot of people talking or—"

"Naw. Naw, my man. You don't know him."

"You'll be surprised who I know, but naw, I definitely won't be saying nothing about that. Tonya would be devastated, knowing it's that close to home.

But shit, I was not surprised at all because on the real, that nigga Stacey ain't playing. If I knew all along the shit that was going on with his peeps . . . and Ed was that deep. I would've said something to y'all because I would have had to do the same thing. That was some real fucked up shit!

"Damn, DJ, I was a little mad at you because I knew you knew just by your comments. Every time we ran into you, you could've said something, we probably could've helped Jess before it got that far."

"Man, I ain't wanna get involved in that shit."

"But you're getting involved in this shit! Imma call Stacey and tell him what you said."

"What? Anaya!"

"Naw, I'm just joking," I said as I started laughing. "With your scared ass!"

"Bye, punk. Don't say nothing Anaya."

"Tonya already tried to put two and two together, but you don't have to worry about me saying anything," I said as I hung up the phone, thinking Tonya dug a hole she didn't want to be in.

Stacey was crazy, and he'd put her in one. When shit hit the fan Dj was right, I didn't want to be anywhere around.

I was thinking about my baby. He asked if he could come meet my mother and pay for her to have a house phone since it was cut off before she moved into my grandmother's. He said he would make sure I had more than enough money to help my mother with her bills. I called the number to the phone booth to see how my baby's day was going, but the phone just rang and rang, which was not normal. There was always someone lingering around—morning, noon, and night—around that phone booth.

I waited and called again twenty minutes later. There was still no answer. Maybe, he was in the house. It was a Sunday. Yea right, I didn't think he even cared about what the day was, so I called the house again.

"Hello?!"

"Hello," I said. All I heard was chaos in the background like somebody was fighting. Pop's mother screamed "hello" in my ear as if she knew it was me.

"Can I speak to Pop?"

"Pop just got shot!"

My heart flat-lined . . .

CPSIA information can be obtained
at www.ICGtesting.com
Printed in the USA
BVHW030728230123
656851BV00001B/90

9 781543 421392